A MILE OF RIVER

JUDITH ALLNATT

ISIS
LARGE PRINT
Oxford

First published in Great Britain 2008
by
Doubleday, an imprint of Transworld Publishers

Published in Large Print 2008 by ISIS Publishing Ltd.,
7 Centremead, Osney Mead, Oxford OX2 0ES
by arrangement with
Transworld Publishers, A Random House Group Company

British Library Cataloguing in Publication Data
Allnatt, Judith
    A mile of river. – Large print ed.
    1. Droughts – England – Fiction
    2. Motherless families – Fiction
    3. Teenage girls – Family relationships – Fiction
    4. Farm life – England – Fiction
    5. Large type books
    I. Title
    823.9'2 [F]

ISBN 978–0–7531–8152–2 (hb)
ISBN 978–0–7531–8153–9 (pb)

Printed and bound in Great Britain by
T. J. International Ltd., Padstow, Cornwall

For Spencer, James and Lottie,
with love

Acknowledgements

Heartfelt thanks are due to my mother, Isabel Gillard, for encouraging me to write from childhood onwards and for her invaluable advice, and to my father, Peter Gillard, for his support and for sharing with me his knowledge and love of the countryside.

I am indebted to Nora O'Keefe for her perceptive reading with a painter's eye. I am deeply grateful to Laura Longrigg, my agent, for her inspiration, and more help than I could possibly list here, and to my editor, Katie Espiner, for her creativity, generous enthusiasm and faith in the book. Many thanks also to Marianne Velmans and to the team at Transworld.

To my sister, Lou, and her family: thank you for the party; it meant a lot. To my husband Spencer: thank you for your steadfast belief in the whole project and for always reading my pages, no matter how late the hour.

CHAPTER
ONE

Jess

I stood in the middle of my father's bedroom, holding my breath. It was quiet, except for the creaks and groans of floorboards and old timbers expanding in the heat of an early-summer afternoon, as if the house was stretching out, straining to listen, too. The brass alarm clock next to the bed ticked fast and light. It was set for five thirty, to get Dad up for milking, and just the thought of the raucous noise of the bell brought me out in a sweat. I'd lied about having a headache today, so that I could stay at home to do this, and the lie had sat heavily on me the whole time, like a thick coat on a sunny day.

From up in Deeper's field came the stutter of the tractor. I crossed to the window, set low in the eaves of the house, and stooped to look out. The yard was deserted except for some hedge sparrows fluttering in the dust, and a pigeon turning circles for its mate. Small white clouds moved steadily across the sky's acres, taking with them any promise of rain. Their shadows passed slowly across the barley beyond the track, and the stems bent and stirred as the breeze combed through them. Distant on the hill, the tractor

1

moved across the field, a Matchbox toy. It swung round tight on the turn; Dad always aimed to get every last load of beets from a field, and he was making sure he top-dressed every one.

My shoulders dropped. Now I could start looking. I tried the dressing-table drawers; both were locked. I sorted quickly through the clutter of brushes and pencil stubs on top. No key. My eyes passed quickly over the bedside table with the clock and a brown bottle of aspirin, over the sagging bed with its pilled nylon cover in duck-egg blue, and rested on the wardrobe. I would have to go through his pockets.

I opened the door carefully, although there was no one to hear me. My father's jackets hung in a row like mute guardsmen, wide-shouldered, with a masculine smell of tweed and corduroy. The floor of the wardrobe was a jumble of overalls and pyjamas. I almost began to fold them. I slipped my hand into the pocket of the first jacket, lifting the hairy material of the pocket flaps with my fingertips, and felt in the depths of the silky lining. I moved methodically along the row of clothes. Nothing. Only a few old receipts and auction tickets.

Frustrated, I turned back to the dressing table, and caught sight of myself in the mirror, ghostly in my long pale dressing gown like the shade of my mother; slight and small-boned, with the same dark hair. It curled where it was moist against my skin, and my face, usually pale, was flushed and intent, a trespasser's face.

The dressing table was old but not elegant — just an oak chest of drawers with a separate mirror standing on the top — but Dad was always proud of the length of time it had been in the family. The mirror was tilted, the bottom edge pulled forward. I tilted it further to look behind it. There it was, the box covered all over with seashells, tucked away between the mirror and the wall.

Auntie Linda sent the box to Mum because they both longed for the sea, and Mum said she felt landlocked in the Midlands with hundreds of miles of solid ground in all directions, although at least here there was the river to watch. Then Auntie Linda went to live in Brisbane, so she got all the sea she needed.

I used to think the box was beautiful when I was little. Its thick coat of varnish made the shells look wet; there were cockle-shells at each corner, long blue-grey razor shells, and tiny white snail cases, like seed pearls. I used to ask to lift it down off the shelf.

"Why is it empty, Mum?" I'd ask.

"It isn't empty, it's full of sea air," she'd say. "Just take a little peep, or it'll all float away."

I used to open it expecting to find a sift of fine sand, or a lick of sea salt in the corners. When Mum left, I asked Dad if I could have the box. By then I was old enough to know that it was a cheap thing, a tacky souvenir from some grey seaside town, but he wouldn't part with it.

For a long time I thought, if I could just have the box, touching it would somehow be like touching her, that opening it would bring back her voice saying "Smell that sea air!" I thought that it could replay her like a musical box.

The tractor stopped and I listened. It was temperamental, prone to fuel-feed trouble; Dad might have to come back for tools. It started, then stopped again, then started and continued the long climb along the ridge. The noise of the engine ebbed and flowed, a long slow wave of sound that faded into the far corner of the field's length, and then built again from the turn. The tractor noise reminded me of ploughing with my father, and how the past hides in the earth just below the surface; a medieval coin, a flint spearhead, a clay pipe, to be turned up by the ploughshare, as it unravels time like knitting, row by row.

Deeper's field was the highest on the slope, and the biggest one — huge once Dad had taken out the hedgerows that used to divide it into three. I remember that day, although I can't have been more than five or six years old. I was sitting up high and proud on the hard tractor seat, and Dad was explaining how we were going to clear the field. Mum came running to the gate, waving her arms, all upset because of the greenfinches that were nesting in the hedges. Dad jumped down from the tractor and went and put his arm round her. I could see them talking and Dad shaking his head. Then Mum pulled away and walked back to the house.

The hawthorn bushes were going to be stubborn. Dad rigged the tractor up with great chains, hooking them to the hitch point below the axle so that the tractor couldn't tip. I had to stand well back up the field while he hauled the bushes out. When he was done I ran forward to see them laid out flat with their roots in the air. In the earth underneath was a muddle of rocks and scattered bones. We stood together at the side of the trench; it was too late to stop me seeing. Dad told me that it must be an old Anglo-Saxon grave site; the rocks were placed on the bodies' chests to stop the spirits of the dead from walking. He told me not to tell anyone, we would keep it secret between us.

"I don't want a load of academics with their teaspoons and their little brushes traipsing all over my land," Dad said, and back-filled the holes the same day.

Looking back on it, I suppose a burial site sat badly in the middle of a productive field. Now the only mark to show where those people lie is the darker green of the crop following the old hedge line. You would only be able to see it at all from a plane. But one day, despite the rocks, those bones will work their way to the surface to be turned up by the plough.

The fields at the front of the house were divided by the half-mile track down to the road, and were mainly pasture. They fell away towards the woods and the river, featureless but for the random scatter of cows, which resolved themselves into patterns of knots whenever rain threatened. Although these fields were grass-covered, even here hummocks gave away the touch of medieval hands, which worked their allotted strip until the contours of the earth itself were changed to mounds and dips. Perhaps it was Garton land even then.

The woods were always Mum's favourite place. We used to walk along the river every day and, in the summer, take a picnic. When she was pregnant with

Tom, she used to lie at the edge of the shallow stretch, with her legs right in the water.

"Look, I'm a mermaid," she'd call out. "Build me a pool."

I would work away at the mossy stones, shifting them to build dams for her to inspect, while she sunned herself, her face tipped back, her hair fanned out on the grass, like a blackbird spreading its feathers in the heat.

I picked up the box and weighed it in my hand. Such a small thing to ask.

I opened it and there, along with postage stamps and paper clips, was the key I was looking for, a crude, leaden object. I fitted it into the lock of the bottom drawer and turned it with a click. I pulled at the drawer; it was heavy and it stuck, I had to rock it this way and that. Inside, nothing but papers, files of farm accounts, bank statements and bills. I rifled through them. The yearning I had for Mum's belongings, for scarves and bracelets and powder compacts, for things that would feel like her, smell like her, bring her back to me, was so overwhelming that I stared stupidly at all these files with their scrawled labels. "Equipment leases 1969-72", "Profit & Loss Accounts '70-'75", and a new file for the current year, "Loan agreement 1976". I read the titles again and again, and wondered for a moment why Dad was taking out a new loan; then I fumbled at the lock of the other drawer.

It was full to the top with more files, along with back issues of *Farmers Weekly*. What had he done with Mum's things? I couldn't understand it. I pulled the magazines out, handfuls of them, and chucked them down. Each new pile skated across the slippery surface of the last until the floor was covered with them, and I was panting and out of breath. The air filled with dust motes and the smell of yellowed pages. I yanked out the whole drawer and dropped it with a muffled thud on to the pile, then sat down hard on the floor myself.

He must have got rid of Mum's things. I knew she didn't take everything. In the early days I used to give Tom something Mum had worn to help him go to sleep. Mrs Jones would come in to look after him while I was at school, and find him in his cot sucking his thumb, with his face against the lace of Mum's slip. Now, the only things left were the seashell box and the rose-sprigged lining paper in the drawers.

Slowly I got to my feet and lifted the drawer back into place. It wouldn't shut. I pushed harder; something was wedged at the back of the chest. I pulled the drawer out again and, feeling around, touched something hard and flat.

There was a distant rumble as the tractor turned out on to the track, heading for home, and I pulled back so sharply that I bumped my head. I pushed the drawer out of the way so that I could get closer and reached inside again. This time I managed to get hold of a corner and work the thing free. Out came a small hardback notebook. I flipped open the marbled cover. The pages were full of dates and jottings; neat and tiny, Mum's handwriting filled every line.

The tractor noise was nearer. I let my fingers rest for a moment on the pages, then put the book down. I shoved the drawer back and piled the magazines inside, stuffing them in anyhow, then set the mirror straight. The tractor clattered across the cattle grid and came to a faltering halt in the yard outside, and I grabbed the book and started for the door as my father was calling up the dogs. As the back door slammed I remembered the key, and ran back to put it in the box and replace it behind the mirror.

He was in the kitchen right beneath me; I could see him through the gaps in the old floorboards as a shadow moving to and fro. I froze, afraid to make the boards creak. I heard his boots hitting the quarry tiles as he pulled them off and the sharp sound of metal on metal as he dropped the tractor keys into the tobacco tin on the shelf. He came to the bottom of the stairs.

"Jess!" he shouted.

I stuffed the book into my pocket and pulled the other side of my dressing gown over it. There was nothing for it now; I couldn't get back to my room without passing the stairhead.

"Jess!" he bellowed.

I heard his tread on the stairs and up and down the landing as he looked for me. He opened the door and came in, ducking his head under the beams, and then stopped short.

"Why didn't you answer me? What're you doing in here?" he said.

"I felt worse," I said lamely. "I was . . ." I groped for an explanation. "I was looking for the headache tablets." I crossed to the bedside table and picked up the bottle. "Here they are."

"Well, go and take some quick," he said. "I've got the calves to see to with you laid up, and a Farmers' Union meeting at seven, so we need tea early, all right?"

He held the door back to let me pass. His eyes moved quickly over the room. "You'd better get on with it: Tom's going to be in from school any minute and want feeding." I slid past him. "The world doesn't stop, you know, just because you've got a sore head. Too much reading, in my opinion," he said.

"I'll do the calves, Dad," I said, "straight after I've sorted Tom out, honest."

"Too much time studying," he called after me as I walked away.

"Some chance," I said under my breath, but at the moment studying was the last thing on my mind. The corners of the book dug into me as I clutched it hard against my stomach. It was mine now, and no one was going to take it away from me.

I shut my bedroom door behind me and sat with my back against it. The spine of the book was bound in fabric, the covers cool and smooth, shades of green and blue marbling running into each other like a painting left out in the rain. The paper inside was stiff and creamy. At the top of the flyleaf was my mother's name, "Sylvie Garton", written in dark-blue ink. I traced the letters with my finger and then pressed the book to my face. There was only the faint vinegar smell of glue from the binding.

The entries started on the flyleaf, as though she was determined to use every available space, as if unsure when she would get another book. Each entry started with a date, but some were only a few words long, while others ran to paragraphs.

The first read simply: *7th April 1958. Willow warblers in the copse. Two or three singing well.* The next was: *10th April 1958. Cuckoo in the high field they call Deeper's field.* Mum must have started the book when she first came here, more than a year before I was born. It gave me a strange feeling to be reading words written in her life before I existed, as if I were looking into a past I had no business in. I flicked forward through the book, scanning the pages until I came to a longer entry. *24th August 1965. Nightjar put up as we walked through birchwood. Flight very distinctive, clapping its wings together above its back. Gave out a loud "coo-lik" call. Hard to say who was more startled, Jess or the bird.*

This was an entry in which I had a part. I closed my eyes in an effort to remember. When I thought of the birchwoods I could see the slim trunks shining, scored with dark splits in the bark, and the dappled shade of the small leaves as the light flickered through them. I saw my six-year-old self struggling through the bracken, which reached way above my head, releasing its pungent smell as I pushed the fronds aside. Vivid green and jungle thick, it sprang back behind me as if I had never passed. I caught the sound, an intermittent buzz of huge flies, which I flapped at when they landed near me; their gleaming heads seemed to be made only of eyes.

I tried for more, for my mother's figure in front of me, for the sudden clap of the nightjar's wings, but nothing would come. Did I cry out? Run to her for comfort? Or did we laugh at how it had made us jump? I turned the page, greedy for more, for a point of connection.

There was a loud toot outside: Mrs Jones sounding the horn at the yard gate to say that she was dropping Tom off. Quickly I hid the book among my textbooks and files, pushing it well in so that not even the spine showed. I pulled on a T-shirt, jeans and a pair of pumps and went down to see my brother and make him a sandwich.

Tom dumped his satchel and climbed up to sit on the table to eat. His skin was exactly the same colour as the pale brown of the bread crusts, and just seeing him made me smile.

"How did you get on at school today?" I asked.

"Mrs Jones says Mick Swift's tabby has had kittens, and I can have one if I want."

"You'll have to ask Dad," I pointed out.

He nodded. "It's going to be great mouser. It'll be a working cat."

"What, it's going to round up the mice, is it?" I chucked the tea towel at him and he hurled it back. We rushed round and round the table, and I almost caught him, but he ducked underneath and scrambled out the other side.

"Barleys! Barleys!" he called out from behind a chair, holding out his crossed fingers.

Dad came in and we fell silent.

"Too much noise," he said.

I straightened the chairs around the table and he frowned at the squeak that the feet made on the tiled floor.

"Pick your satchel up," he said to Tom.

He took a beer from the fridge and sat at the table. I felt his eyes on my back as I stood at the drainer, cutting up onions to go with minced beef and gravy, and the acid smell stole through the room like an ill-kept secret.

"Tom wants a kitten, Dad," I finally blurted out.

"Hasn't he got his own tongue in his head?" he said.

Tom looked up from unbuckling his satchel. "Mick Swift has got one for free," he said: "a good mouser."

"Aaah, for free, you say?"

Tom nodded.

"And would you clean up after it if it peed on the floor?" Dad said.

"I would . . . I could do that, couldn't I, Jess?"

I nodded, although I knew I'd end up doing it.

"And what about paying for its jabs and its vet bills? Would you do that too?"

"I don't think it's poorly," Tom said. "I don't know how much it would cost."

"He doesn't know how much it would cost," Dad mimicked. "See, he hasn't thought it through."

I glanced at Tom. He was beginning to look mutinous.

"Here," I said, thrusting the dogs' enamel bowls at him. "Go and feed the dogs — the tins are in the scullery."

"I really wanted —" he started.

"Go now, Tom," I said, my hand at his back.

"Mick Swift," Dad was muttering. He got up as the door closed behind Tom. "Do you hear me!" he shouted after him. "I don't want anything of his in this house!"

He knocked the table as he pushed back his chair, and the beer bottle toppled and rolled a little way, spreading a trickle of brown foam. He walked out without picking it up.

I left it where it was and went through to the scullery, where Tom was mashing great dollops of dog food and biscuits around in a bowl. He was crying silently, not even bothering to wipe his face. I put my arm around his bony shoulders.

"Don't cry," I said. "Please don't cry."

"Why did you have to go and ask him about it?" he said, pulling away.

"I'm sorry, Tom," I said. "I thought it would be better coming from me."

"You don't understand . . . The kitten, I've already got it, I've got it in a box." His voice rose to a sob. "He'll take it away. I hate him!"

"We'll sort it out," I said, moving towards him.

"Leave me alone!" he shouted, his face reddening. He thumped the dogs' bowls down, slopping the contents on to the floor, and took off running, out of the house, across the yard, and disappeared behind the cowshed.

It was no good following him: he could have been in any one of his hidy-holes, in the barn, or the feed store, or the loft above the dairy. I called up the dogs and let them eat the mess off the floor. They shunted the tin dishes around, their soft collie sides pushing against my knees. Kelpie pushed her wet nose into my hand, and I fussed her head.

"No, it's no good," I said. "C'mon, back outside again. Better stick to the rules."

CHAPTER
TWO

Sylvie

7th April 1958. Willow warblers in the copse. Two or three singing well.

Sylvie lay on her stomach in the field at the top of the ridge, writing in her notebook. The sound of the birds came again from the copse of hazel and elder behind her, "sooeet-sooeetoo", a soft and rippling note. It was a warm spring day, the air still had its softness and the sky its freshness, and summer hadn't yet dried and tired the world. She rolled on to her back and looked up at the faultless blue through the waving seed heads of grasses.

I'm happy, she thought, and at the same time realized that this was one of those rare moments when she both felt joy and was aware that she felt it. Happiness had so often before been a relative quality, a realization when things had gone wrong that, "Ah yes, I was happy before this," that it had seemed something only ever enjoyed in retrospect and, therefore, bittersweet. She put her hands behind her head and gazed upwards. I'm happy *right now*, she thought, and nothing can take this moment away.

She watched a buzzard circling against the thin blue of the sky, its wings outstretched and all but motionless. She let herself be drawn upwards in its spiralling flight and saw the landscape through its searching eyes. The farm buildings lay in the green valley like a collection of tumbled toy bricks, the cylindrical silage tower and the loaf-shaped barn mixed higgledy-piggledy with the angular shapes of house and outhouses. The colours, too, reminded her of children's well-worn bricks: grey slate roofs, walls of yellow stone, the dark green of the silo and the corrugated iron barn weathered to dull rust. Already she knew every inch of the buildings and, like the buzzard, looked on them as her own. From her vantage point the river valley spread out as far as she could see, and all of it was Garton land. From the road half a mile away on the far side of the river, the river itself now partly hidden by the half-clothed trees, to the sweep of the land below her, plotted and pieced into small ploughed fields and pasture, it was all her territory. She thought of the cramped children's home in the Birmingham suburb where she and her sister Linda had been brought up; the airless rooms, the locked windows, the smell of too many people sharing.

She spread her arms out wide and kicked off her shoes as she stretched out. The grass prickled her bare arms and legs.

Two fields away, the bird hovered for a few seconds, extending its wing-tip feathers like fingers feeling the air. She sat up to watch it plummet, dropping like a hailstone. A moment later it soared up, with a field-mouse in its grasp, and swooped away towards the wood. She made a little noise of surprise, and shook her head as if in disbelief, struck by the beauty and power of the bird. She watched carefully to see where it would land, but lost it in among the trees.

She drew up her knees, put her arms around them, and looked down at the farm like a child surveying the Christmas presents at the end of the bed. Somewhere out there was Henry. She remembered that he'd planned to start building new calf housing today. He would be up a ladder round behind the cowshed, his hair bleaching even paler in the sun. He would be working at his usual breakneck pace, overall sleeves rolled up, hammering new slatted timbers into place, his pockets weighed down with bags of nails as big as his ideas for the farm. He would keep going until his legs ached from bracing himself against the ladder, and then some more.

Tonight she would rub his tired shoulders and run him a deep bath. She would call him her golden boy and he would tell her she was beautiful, a beautiful wicked thing sent to tempt him away from his work. And all the time he would watch her with that hungry look, the look she'd seen in his eyes when they first met.

It amused her to think how she'd turned up in Henry's life quite by chance. A year out of the Home had seen her sharing a bed-sit with a girl called Janice; they worked together, waiting on tables at the Top Dog cabaret club. She made enough money to scrape by and felt that at least she wasn't in some boring typing pool. On a weekend off she'd joined Janice and a couple of boys Janice knew, Keith and Roger, on a trip down to London to do the rounds of the jazz clubs. Duke Ellington . . . Miles Davies . . . Janice had all the records. They played them loudly in their room on their nights off and hummed them at work on their way back and forth between the tables and the bar.

The boys had persuaded them that there was plenty of time to stop at a pub called The Green Man on the way down, and they'd stayed too long, so that it was beginning to get dark as they set off again in the car. A mile or so out of the village they'd broken down. Half drunk and with no torch, they'd decided to call it a night, pushed the Morris Oxford off the road and into a field and got what sleep they could on its hard leather seats.

Sylvie had woken first with a splitting headache and a dry mouth. The boys in the front were dead to the world and Janice was slumped against her, with her cardigan over her shoulders. Sylvie felt around for her shoes, but they'd slipped right under the seat in front. She lowered Janice's head down gently and got out of the car in stockinged feet; the cold dew soaked instantly through to her skin. The sun was already bright and every blade of grass shone. The road behind them was deserted, and on the far side of the field nothing stirred except the leaves of alder and aspen as a small breeze moved through a wood, ruffling the leaves over and back, green and silver by turns.

Sylvie took out a handkerchief from the pocket of her sundress and bent to wet it on the grass. She heard the noise of a vehicle approaching through the wood; she straightened up and wiped her face and neck with the damp hanky, then screwed it up and put it back in her pocket. She began to walk towards the track: they would need water, and directions to the telephone; she would flag the vehicle down. A Land-Rover emerged from the trees, grinding along in a low gear, but it immediately speeded up as it approached the field, rocking as it bumped into the ruts in the track. She stopped, uncertain what to do. It pulled up sharply at the field gate, its tyres spraying dust and pebbles. She heard the driver get out on the other side and slam the door.

"Bloody Gyppos!" she heard a man's voice cursing. He came round towards the field and she was surprised how young he was. Tall, well-built, wearing a checked shirt open at the neck, jeans and boots, he strode to the gate, staring all the time at the Morris, with a look of determination on his face. Then he saw her.

"Hello," she said. "Our car broke down."

His hand remained on the chain that fastened the five-bar gate. She walked over to him as though it were the most natural thing in the world to meet in a field, and held out her hand.

"I'm Sylvie," she said.

He wiped his hand on his jeans, and they shook hands over the gate. He blinked as though it was he who had just woken up, pulled the chain up over the gatepost and let it drop.

"You've got no shoes on," he said.

"No," she said.

"Your feet will get cold," he said.

"I don't care." She smoothed her dress down and loosened and retied her hair. He watched every movement of her hands. She smiled at him. "There, now do I look more respectable?"

"You look . . ." he stumbled, "you looked fine before."

She laughed. "The thing is, we've broken down, you see. And we don't have any water, and we need to phone a garage, so I was wondering . . .?"

"You'd better come up to the house," he said quickly, pushing the gate open.

"Don't you think I ought to wake the others first?" she teased.

"Of course, yes, go ahead." At last he smiled.

They walked together to the car and the others stumbled out sleepily. She saw him frown as the boys got out, stretching.

"These are Janice's friends, Keith and Roger," she said firmly.

He nodded. "Henry Garton," he said, regaining his poise. "Welcome to Home Farm. Can I have a look at the motor for you?"

The men crowded round the engine and quickly decided that a new fan belt was needed.

"Breakfast first, though," Henry said, "if you don't mind roughing it in the Land-Rover."

Sylvie retrieved her shoes and handbag and was ushered into the front seat by Henry; the rest of them clambered into the back to sit along the ledges over the wheel arches. Henry drove carefully back up the track, answering her questions about the farm: it was a mixed farm; he had some beef cattle and eighty dairy cows, mainly Friesians. She learnt that he had taken over the farm from his father when he began to suffer badly from arthritis, and that Henry wanted to expand and modernize. Sylvie was conscious all the time they were talking of his hand shifting from the steering wheel to the gears, where it almost brushed against her leg. His hands were brown and square: capable hands, she thought.

As they drove deeper into the wood, the track was bordered by bracken growing so abundantly that fronds brushed and clattered against the sides of the Land-Rover. The sound of rushing water grew louder and louder. They approached a stone-walled bridge, the river running fast and deep below. Sylvie craned round to see more of it as they passed over the bridge. The water ran in a torrent through the steep-sided culvert where the channel was cut deep and narrow to pass under the bridge. It emerged brown and frothing, then slowed to a calmer pace as the river bed widened further downstream.

"Hold on tight," Henry said as he swung into a tight turn on the other side of the bridge.

Sylvie held on to the handle above the door, ignoring the others laughing in the back as they fell against one another.

"Isn't it beautiful," she said. "You're so lucky to have all this."

He shrugged. "We've always lived here," he said, but he looked pleased.

Aspen and willow gave way to beech and birch, then they were out in open country and Henry accelerated up the track to the farm buildings. He stopped before the cattle grid to let the others out so that they wouldn't get bounced about, then drove slowly over it and parked in the front yard. He handed her down from her seat.

"This is it," he said and led them all inside.

They ate eggs and bacon, washed down by mugs of tea. Keith telephoned to arrange to have the fan belt fitted and Henry towed the car down to the garage. By the end of the morning they were ready to go, and Henry had taken Sylvie's address.

Two weeks later she visited him again on her Sunday off, putting up at The Green Man overnight, at Henry's expense, and then every time she could get away. They lunched together in the dim brown pub, heads close in conversation, knees touching under the table. If someone came in whom Henry knew — another farmer, the feed merchant, an old school-mate — he would just lift his head for a moment and nod, then return to their conversation.

Sometimes they would take a picnic and drive out to Oxfordshire to sit on a hillside. Sylvie always felt that, although Henry admired the view, it soon became his own farm that he saw laid out beneath him as he explained his plans to her. He wanted to farm the land more intensively, to invest in a modern milking parlour, and buy the newest type of baler. He asked her few questions about herself. He seemed to view her arrival on the farm as a gift from the gods, as if she had been delivered into his hands for safekeeping and now belonged in his world.

One day he announced that they were invited to his parents' house for tea. They lived in a new house on the edge of the village, which Henry told her was his mother's pride and joy as it had "all mod cons" and was easy to keep clean after years of coping with the dust of the old farmhouse.

Sure enough, as they walked up the garden path between neatly edged lawns and borders full of geraniums and snow-in-summer, the picture windows gleamed.

Henry's father opened the door, followed by a fat and rather smelly terrier.

"Your mum's in the kitchen," he said to Henry, then turned to Sylvie, "so you'll have to bear with me." He winked at her. "I'm a bit slow."

He shambled back along the hall, and then leant for a moment on the hallstand.

"Are your knees bad, Dad?" asked Henry.

"Fair to middling," he replied, pausing to gesture to the doors on either side of him. "Lounge or snug?" he asked Sylvie.

"I don't mind," she said.

"The lounge has been dusted," he said, watching her over his glasses, "so the dog can't go in there." He picked the terrier up. "You won't stay still to be dusted, will you?" he said into the dog's face.

"Snug," she said.

He nodded. "It's Sylvie, isn't it?" he said. "You can call me Pa Garton. In here."

They entered a small room with an armchair, draped in antimacassars, drawn up to a two-bar electric fire. Pa Garton settled himself into it, stretched his legs towards the heat and gave a moaning sigh. The dog jumped up on to his lap and he began to scratch its ears. Henry moved some newspapers on to a table and pulled round two fireside chairs.

"You're looking well, Henry," said his father. "Courting must suit you." He turned to Sylvie. "Perhaps you can talk some sense into him about this hare-brained scheme he has to refit the milking parlour. Have you seen it?"

Sylvie shook her head.

"He's got a perfectly good pipeline cowshed," he said. "Perfectly adequate. But no, he wants one bigger and better, a herringbone parlour so he can milk more cows more quickly. It'll cost a mint and put him out of business."

"It won't put me out of business, Dad," said Henry, looking bullish. "I'll be able to expand the herd and make more money in the long run."

"Aah, but will you have enough forage for all these extra cows, eh? Have you thought of that? And where's all the capital coming from?"

"I'm going to borrow it from the bank, Dad," Henry said wearily. "I told you before."

"*Neither a borrower nor a lender be*, that's what we brought you up on." He leaned forward in his chair. "Over my dead body will you put the farm in hock."

Sylvie looked uncomfortably from one to the other. Henry was scowling. She shifted in her seat.

Pa Garton glanced at her. "Oh well," he said, settling back in his chair, "it probably will be over my dead body," and he waved his hand as if swatting the problem away. "I dare say you think I'm an old codger who's stuck in the past. Fathers and sons, fathers and sons, 'twas ever thus."

"Can you two not behave yourselves when we've got a guest?" came a voice from the door. "Henry, show your father some respect."

Henry's mother was dressed in a navy skirt and a neat cotton blouse. She was a large woman with an upright figure. She had Henry's angular face, but none of the softness Sylvie felt she saw in his eyes. She wore no jewellery save her wedding ring, and her grey hair was stiffly lacquered. She gave Sylvie's yellow shift dress and bare legs an appraising glance.

"Would you all like to come through?" she asked. "Tea is on the table."

Over boiled bacon and garden vegetables, she quizzed Sylvie about her background.

"But who are your family?" she insisted when Sylvie explained that she had only one sister, married and living abroad.

"Yes, but where were your parents from?"

Sylvie coloured. "They weren't 'from' anywhere," she said, "in the sense that you mean. My father was a lorry driver — he was never there. My mother got ill and couldn't cope. We were taken into care. We lived in Birmingham. That's it."

There was a silence.

"I see," Henry's mother said.

"Wonderful museum in Birmingham," Pa Garton said. "Fossils. Natural history. I took Henry when he was little. Do you remember, Henry?"

Henry shook his head.

"Used to get about more then. You should go, you know," he said to Sylvie. "Get Henry to come with you."

"I'd like that," she said.

"I can't leave the farm, Dad," said Henry.

"You should get a relief milker in for a few days, take a holiday, take your lass out and about a bit," he said.

"You know fine I can't do that if I'm planning on this new parlour."

"I'll make more tea," said Mrs Garton heavily. "Henry, bring the plates through, please."

They left the room. Sylvie toyed with her spoon, unsure whether to offer help.

"He's a bit single-minded, my lad," said Pa Garton. "He wants to run before he can walk, if you know what I mean. He needs someone to steady him up a bit."

Sylvie smiled. "He's just ambitious — that's not a bad thing, is it?"

"No-o," he said slowly. "As long as he doesn't get pig-headed with it."

Sylvie, anxious not to take sides, excused herself to find the bathroom. As she passed the half-open kitchen door, she heard Mrs Garton talking urgently to Henry.

". . . She'll be no good to you, a town girl like that, she's just a slip of a thing."

"She likes the farm; she'll learn, she'll want to learn," said Henry.

"You don't know anything about her," said his mother. "Honestly, Henry, she could be a proper flibbertigibbet, for all you know. She works in a bar, for goodness' sake, and she hasn't had a mother's hand . . ." She paused, as if to let what she was implying sink in.

Sylvie held her breath.

"You don't understand . . ." Henry started.

There was a noise of water being run fast into the sink and a clatter as if crockery were being stirred round in it.

"No, Henry," came his mother's voice again. "Frankly, I don't."

Her eyes filling with tears, Sylvie stumbled upstairs and locked the bathroom door behind her. She sat down on the side of the bath and waited to feel calmer. Towels arranged in order of size hung neatly over a wooden rail, and a smell of Chemico lingered. Beneath her she could hear the continuing exchange of voices. The kettle whistled in the background, ignored until the noise became a piercing scream, then lifted off the gas and banged down. She didn't feel calmer, but she had reached a decision. She regarded herself in Pa Garton's shaving mirror: her eyes looked shiny; she practised a smile. She reached into her handbag for a comb and backcombed her hair a little, then pulled out some kiss curls at her neck and cheeks. Carefully she applied some lipstick in a deeper shade of pink, and dabbed on some perfume.

She breezed into the kitchen, where Mrs Garton was setting a tray with teacups.

"I was wondering if you needed any help clearing up?" she said, smiling at Henry.

"Clearing up?" said Mrs Garton.

"Before we go," said Sylvie. "You haven't forgotten, have you, Henry, that we said we'd meet Janice and Roger?"

Henry looked blank.

"For a drink this evening?" she went on.

"Oh yes, so we did. Um, sorry, Mum. We'd better just say goodbye to Dad."

He sidled past his mother and out of the kitchen. Mrs Garton put the tray down and made as if to go after him.

"Thank you so much for having us," Sylvie said primly, and followed Henry.

Pa Garton came to the front door with them.

"Here," he said, "this is for you." He put a stone into her hand; on it was the imprint of a shelled creature, a perfect outline preserved in rock. "From another old fossil," he said, giving her hand a squeeze. "A little piece of Garton farm for you."

"Thank you," she said. "I'll treasure it."

They said their goodbyes, Henry's mother looking tight-lipped. Sylvie took Henry's hand as they walked away, and swung it a little as they turned to wave at the corner of the street, then they were out of sight.

"You are *wicked*!" he said, making a grab for her. He pulled her into the bus shelter and kissed her hard, pressing her against the rough wood as she responded, arching her back to let him pass his hands behind her.

He broke off to kiss her hair, her face, her throat. She stroked his head.

"Shall we go back to the farm?" she said.

He kissed her again.

"Marry me," he said.

CHAPTER
THREE

Jess

The day after I took the book, I went back to school. I had cause to think about rules again, and how some people saw them as only there to be broken. One person in particular, Martin Stamford. I was sitting in the chemistry lab, trying to do some revision, when I sensed someone at the door. He still had his plimsolls on after sport and had made no sound. His shirt was half pulled out and he was carrying his gym bag slung over his shoulder, the way he always did. His hair, cut so short that it hardly showed when it was dry, was dark now, wet from the shower. I found I was staring.

He came in, shutting the door behind him, then walked over to the window, opened it and lit a cigarette.

"Do you think that's a good idea in here?" I asked.

He turned towards me, leaned back against the windowsill and took a long drag.

"Seems like a good idea to me," he said. "Want one?"

I shook my head. "I was just thinking of all the gas and everything in here . . ."

He raised his eyebrows.

". . . And the smell. What if someone comes?"

He came over to me and put the cigarette into my hand.

"No one ever comes," he said.

I wasn't sure whether he was laughing at me.

I drew on the cigarette and handed it back to him. He reached across in front of me, stubbed it out on the varnished surface of the bench between us and then flicked it into the sink. He straightened up but stayed close to me, almost touching. He smelled of grass mixed with the tang of saltpetre.

The door banged open behind us and ricocheted off the doorstop. Martin's friends erupted into the room, jostling and pushing each other, and one gave a long whistle.

"Sod off, Skinner," Martin said, moving away.

I piled up my books, my face burning.

"You been down the fair yet?" Skinner asked Martin. "It'll be good — lots of totty."

I'd seen the lorries that morning, on the waste ground at the edge of the town, as Mrs Jones had driven Tom and me to school. Over breakfast Dad had been going on about the litter and the noise the fair would cause; he'd called it an "imposition". Mrs Jones had pointed it out, though, and asked us if we were going. "A bit of fun," she'd called it.

"Might go tomorrow night," Martin said, and I felt my throat tighten. "I've got to work down the petrol station tonight."

"We've got a double free period," said Skinner. "Are you coming down the caff?"

Martin looked at me enquiringly. "I'm not coming back after," he said and picked up his bag.

"I've got chemistry," I said helplessly.

"The fair, then," he said, and disappeared without waiting for an answer.

The room was left quiet. I sat up at one of the high benches and tried to convince myself that it was the smell of bleach and rubber Bunsen burner tubes that was making my stomach churn. I felt odd. The polished surfaces of weights and balance pans glinted at me, and the thin trickle of water from a faulty tap sounded too loud. I wished I was on my own at home, where I could think straight. I thought of my mother's book waiting for me in my room, and wanted to touch it and look at her neat writing, her sure hand. Something had happened, something as sudden and startling as the nightjar flying up out of the bracken, and I needed someone who would understand and could tell me what it meant.

The rest of the class trooped in and Mr Bailey fussed about with the lab assistant, setting up clamps and retorts. Nicola sat down beside me and said something that I didn't take in. How on earth could I get to go to the fair? Dad would never let me. Just think how many of his edicts it would break — don't go off the farm, don't go off on your own, don't stay out after dark, don't mix with that set. It wasn't even worth asking. Nicola nudged me to open my book. Mr Bailey started the lesson, asking questions around the class until one girl got stuck.

"What law explains the rate at which gases expand?" he repeated, but everyone looked blank. "Is there a doctor in the house?" he said, his running-gag reference to my aspirations to go to medical school. He gave me a big smile that said "Come on, star pupil". I stared at the atomic table on the wall. The symbols seemed to spell out words which lingered just beyond my comprehension. I shook my head and looked down at my book. Science was all about rules; suddenly I was sick of them.

Caught in traffic on the way home from school I stared at the poster on the edge of the waste ground, memorizing the opening times of the fair. Mrs Jones wound down the window to let in some air, but there was hardly a breeze, just a smell of hot tarmac and exhaust fumes. Across the expanse of clinker-covered ground beside us, a huddle of caravans stood dwarfed by the half-erected framework of a Ferris wheel, their pastel colours indistinct against the ferocious red of its spokes and seats.

No work seemed to be going on; even the men had been forced to take cover from the heat under the awnings of the stalls. A few children sat on the roof of one of the vans, eating something out of paper, as if living in the shadow of the wheel had made them immune to considerations of height and danger. A woman walked towards the children from the shops, carrying a bottle of Tizer. She raised an arm to wave at them. Unaccountably irritated, I turned away.

Between Tom and me on the back seat, Mrs Jones's baby, Ralphy, stirred in his carrycot and gave a fitful cry. His slick of fine baby hair was plastered to his head and his face was flushed. I put my palm on his tummy to settle him.

"How was your day?" Mrs Jones asked.

"All right, thank you," I said automatically.

Tom said nothing.

Mrs Jones changed gear noisily and glanced in the mirror. "You're very quiet, Tom," she said. "Is anything the matter?"

Tom shook his head. "Just hot. Can we go a bit quicker?"

"Tom . . ." I said in a warning tone.

"It's all right, don't worry. He just wants to get home and get a drink, I expect."

I had a shrewd idea that it was the kitten he was thinking of, and hoped he hadn't left it shut up without water.

"How's your dad coping with this dry spell?" Mrs Jones tried again.

"OK, I think," I said, uncertain what she was getting at.

"It's set to last a long time, they reckon on the long-range forecast. Up at Grange Farm they're thinking of getting irrigation equipment in."

I thought about the drawers full of bills and papers hidden away in Dad's dressing table.

"It's too early to harvest," I thought aloud.

We drove on out of the town, past the cinema, then gloomy Edwardian villas, and into the suburbs of dormered bungalows with sprinklers greening their open lawns. Out on the "A" road I looked at the hawthorn hedges bursting on either side of the road, and the verges full of cow parsley. Were they already, in early June, beginning to have a tired look? Dust and exhaust fumes had taken the gloss off the leaves, the creaminess from the flowers.

"Isn't it very expensive to irrigate?" I asked.

"Not as expensive as losing all your sugar beet. Well, that's what they were saying in The Green Man at the weekend, according to my Ray."

I thought of the fields we'd put to beet last year, Dad's pleasure at a good crop. This year we'd planted more, and doubt passed through me like a dry whisper.

"It'll be all right," I said; "there's the whole summer yet for it to rain in."

"Let's hope so." Mrs Jones lifted her honey-blonde hair and rubbed the back of her neck as if to wipe away the sticky feeling of her collar.

"Are you taking Ralphy to the fair?"

"No . . . Way past his bedtime," she said. "We get him fed and tucked up and Ray and I aren't far behind him." She smiled at me in the mirror. "You should go, though — now's the age."

"If you're going, I'm coming," Tom said, suddenly alert.

"Dad'll never let us," I said flatly, "and that's that."

We drove in silence up the farm track and into the wood, the car instantly cooler and the glare gone as soon as we were under the trees. They leaned across the road, almost meeting, a green tunnel breaking into light and sound momentarily as we crossed the river and slowed for the sharp bend on the other side. The rush of water under the bridge, brown and peaty, made my worries about water seem ridiculous; here gnats danced in the damp shade, and alder drank greedily and shot towards the light, strong as sugar beet. We would always be all right: the water level never dropped more than a foot or so; we could always pump river water, even if the tackle was expensive.

The car climbed the slope, slowed over the cattle grid and swung round in the yard to stop beside the door. Tom leapt out and hared off towards the hayloft.

"Ask your dad if you can go with a friend," Mrs Jones said. "Get your friend Nicola to invite you round to hers for tea." She turned round, laying her elbow on the back of the seat. "'Bout time you young ones were revising, I'd say, what with the exams looming," she said in a mock serious tone.

"That'll only make him angry," I said. "He thinks I spend too much time on that already."

Mrs Jones sighed. "It's a tough old row to hoe sometimes, isn't it — for you and your dad."

She reached over and put her hand across mine. I felt I wanted to tell her everything, to let it spill out like a lid coming off a boiling pan, releasing the pressure, but my throat felt full and nothing would come.

Ralphy, disturbed by the cessation of the car's movement and vibration, suddenly woke up. He squeezed up his face as if making a fist and let out a pained cry.

Mrs Jones patted my hand. "It's a tough life," she said. "See, even babies know it," and we smiled at each other. "See you on Monday, then, kid," she said.

I climbed out, hoisted my bag on to my shoulder and raised a hand as she disappeared down the track.

Dad was sleeping in an armchair in the front room when I got in, something he never did. The curtains were half drawn and the room smelt stuffily of polish and old books. A shushing noise came from the record player, rising and falling in a repeated pattern of sound. I lifted the needle from the middle of the LP where it had stuck, covered with fluff, and replaced the arm on its cradle. The record slowed and *La Vie en Rose* became discernible from the looping italic script across the label. One of Mum's favourites surely? I touched the edge with my finger and brought it to a wavering halt.

I looked at Dad curiously. His head was thrown back against the red velour upholstery and one arm dangled at the side of the chair; a farming magazine lay on the floor, as if he'd been ambushed by sleep and the paper had slipped from his grasp. I saw how Dad's sandy hair was thinning, and his face, which I once thought so powerful and strong, looked old, with lines of discontent either side of his mouth and deep frown notches between his pale eyebrows. It occurred to me that this was his indoor face, that as soon as he was outside and working, his brow cleared and lost its creased and troubled look.

I picked up the magazine and looked at the rings Dad had drawn around some items in the "For Sale" columns. Sure enough it was irrigation tackle that he'd circled, all secondhand, but still pricey. I scanned the "Items Wanted" list and could see why: everyone was buying it.

A spatter of soot fell into the empty fireplace, through the grate to the ashpan below, and Dad woke up.

"Hello there," he said, his voice softened by sleep. "Must've had a bit of a nap." He rubbed his face, reminding me of when I was a little girl, tiny enough to still get away with climbing in between Mum and Dad in the early hours, when they were warm and bleary and just moved over to make room for me.

"Do you want a cup of tea, Dad?" I asked.

"Yes. Yes, that'd be nice. I've got to go and milk in a few minutes . . ." He seemed distracted.

I turned back. "Is everything all right, Dad? I mean with the bank?"

He looked at me blankly. Then, "The bank wants its pound of flesh," he said, as if talking to himself, "but to afford a pound of flesh you have to be fat. And fat we are not — not until harvest anyway."

"Mrs Jones says they're saying in The Green Man that there's going to be a drought . . ." I started.

"You shouldn't listen to gossip," he snapped. "What do they know, old men playing with dominoes!" He held his hand out for the magazine, kept it there while I hesitated. "Don't interfere in things you don't understand," he said shortly, and flicked the magazine open with a snap.

I decided to stick my neck out. "Why don't you talk to Grandad, if you won't talk to me? He might be able to help."

He looked up from the magazine with exaggerated slowness. "Are you going to stand there all day talking through your arse, or are you going to make that tea?" he said.

I walked out muttering "Make it yourself" under my breath, and went straight to my room. I couldn't help feeling a perverse satisfaction that my suggestion about Grandad had got him on the raw. Serve him right if he did have to suffer some parental disapproval, I thought spitefully, and see how he likes it.

I sat on the floor and looked out of the window, picking at the fringe of the rug. After a while I heard him running a tap in the kitchen, then saw him cross the yard to the milking parlour. I watched the cows as they obediently made their way across the field, udders stretched and heavy with milk, and stood flicking their tails, their patient eyes huge and unblinking, waiting for the gate to be opened; they were too hot even to low. The thought of the laborious monotony of their days, grazing punctuated only by trailing to and from milking, made me want to scream.

The open window only seemed to let in the heat; the room was close and seemed overstuffed with fabric: the prickly Turkish rug, the pink candlewick bedspread folded back on the end of the bed, thick denims thrown across the back of the plush-covered chair at my dressing table. The top shelf above the dressing table was full of my old teddies, a velvet monkey and assorted furry animals crammed together, their colours fading under a coating of dust.

I took Mum's book down, slipped off my school tie and pulled my shirt out of my waistband. I lay on the bed on my stomach and rested the book on the cross-stitch cushion Mum and I had made the year before she went away. It was worked in orange wool on a brown background, a stylized star, clumsily sewn by my nine-year-old hands, then in the centre my name embroidered in Mum's small neat stitches. I remembered her sewing, her hair falling forwards over the work, her long fingers moving pale against the dark cloth, the way she lifted the whole thing to bite the thread then held it up to show me, smiling.

"*Finito*," she'd said. "That's Italian for a job well done," and she'd smoothed it over her knees, my missed stitches and the knots and tangles dotting the wrong side included in her satisfaction.

I rested my face against the cool cover of the book as if invisible prints of her hands could transfer themselves to my skin. *Where are you?* I thought, and before I could help myself, *How could you go? What did I do?* filled my mind with its old painful refrain.

I opened the book and flicked over the many short entries that gave details only of place, date and type of bird — flocks of fieldfares and redwings out in the fields in the winter months, young blackbirds and thrushes seen in the garden in spring. Eventually I came to an entry that caught my eye. In the margin was a tiny ink drawing of a kingfisher perched on a branch, and the date, *1st August 1962*. She started lyrically:

Today I saw the most beautiful thing — a living jewel, a kingfisher. I told Jess she must keep as still as a statue, and we squashed up close behind the fallen willow down by the deep pool. Its movements were quick, so fast that if it hadn't been so brightly coloured we soon would have lost it among the leaves. It flitted across from the other bank, quite close to us, and even Jess kept still, amazed by its stunning blue. Its colour shimmered, like petrol in a puddle. It looked beadily at the water and I thought it might take a fish but it suddenly flitted downstream towards the bridge. Jess wanted to follow it, but that fast water's too dangerous, I'm not letting her near it. We were going to go upstream to paddle, but I remembered the calves' feed needed mixing, and Henry too would want his lunch. Everything always needs feeding here. We'll come again tomorrow.

I closed my eyes and I was three years old again. We were crouching in the crook of the fallen tree, and I was afraid the pebbles under my feet would shift; I knew I had to be very still. I could hear Mum's fast heartbeat through her blouse and her hair tickled the side of my face. I couldn't see what she was looking at on the other bank, then suddenly there was a fluttering noise and just a little way from us a bright bird landed, barely bending the willow twig. Mum gripped me tighter and

41

we both held our breath for what seemed like ages before it darted away.

It felt like yesterday, the sun on the water, the green willow bark, the softness of her thigh and breast against me. I remembered her grabbing me as I made to climb over the tree, and, before I could protest, swinging me round and round, so that the leaves and sun and water merged into one glittering arc. I knew the exact spot she meant, though it was years since I'd been down there, and I felt I must go now, this minute, and see if it was still there, the tree we hid behind. I so wanted it to be just the same, I couldn't even wait to change into proper shoes or shorts, but clattered down the stairs the way I was, in my smart school sandals and with my shirt hanging loose.

I ran across the yard and down the track, scattering the sparrows that were taking a dust bath in the tractor ruts, ducked under the barbed-wire fence and slowed, sweating, to a walk through the tussocky field with its dried cow-pats and thistles. As I skirted along the edge of the wood I saw Tom sitting with his back to an old trailer so that he was out of sight of the house. He was holding out a long piece of feathery grass and waving it from side to side. There was a dart of grey and I realized he was playing with his kitten, no doubt training her up to be an ace mouse hunter. I gave him a wave and he held the kitten up towards me.

"I'm calling her Lolly," he shouted, pointing at the white patch and streak that covered one eye and ran down her cheek.

"Good name." I gave him the thumbs-up.

Under the wire again and I was into the dappled shade of birches, their small green leaves hardly stirring.

I pushed deeper into the shade of beech and horse chestnut, the sound of the river growing louder all the time and the air freshening as I got nearer to the water. The bank sloped gradually down to a bed of sandy soil and grey pebbles; I picked my way over the long suckers of brambles that pushed up between them from the damp earth beneath. Memories flowed on the sound of the water, the pleasurable shock of the chill when we paddled, searching for fool's gold and stirring up minnow fry with a stick, Mum's hand around mine as she taught me to skim a stone and clip the water, sending it clear to the other side.

I found the tree. Except it wasn't how I remembered it at all. It had shrunk and fallen into itself. The massive bulk, which had seemed a wall to hide behind, was now something that I could easily step over. Of course I had grown, I tried to comfort myself, but its smallness seemed to affect my memories too: they receded and shrank as though suddenly telescoping down to nothing at all.

No leaf remained. The trunk was half hollowed out, imploded, and black beetles moved busily in and out of the loose, lichen-covered bark. What I touched was a past beyond recall, irretrievable. Dead. I sat down nearer the water with my back to the tree and rested my head on my knees, my eyes shut tight. Memory couldn't be trusted; it was as elusive as water in your hands, something that shimmered for a moment like the kingfisher's wing and was gone. And what help was it anyway? I needed Mum here now, to talk to, to help me decide what to do, about Dad, the farm, medical school, everything. How was I supposed to decide it all for myself?

Behind my closed eyelids pressed against my eyes, I watched lights flower in red and purple. My mind returned to Martin and the confusion of feelings that being close to him produced. I both longed to touch him and felt afraid that he would touch me. I couldn't wait to see him again and yet the feeling in the pit of my stomach when I thought of it was dread. I imagined what he would be doing now, working down at the petrol station — I'd seen him there before, when Dad filled up the Land-Rover, Martin centre-stage as usual in the group he hung around with. The charts were blasting out at top volume and he was leaning back in his chair, letting the lads linger over buying their fags, the girls taking ages to decide over Cream Soda or Vimto. He'd come out to tend the pumps and seemed surprised to see me, almost embarrassed that I'd witnessed a polite "Petrol, sir?" to Dad. And I'd felt stupid sitting up high in the front seat like Lady Muck; separate from everybody else, hoping no one would notice me. Then when he'd brought Dad's change out from the kiosk he'd walked down my side of the Land-Rover and given me a wink, and I'd smiled back from my metal box, frozen, unable to do the most natural thing and wind down the window to say "All right?" or crack a joke the way Nicola would — anything to get a conversation going. "You've got to give lads some encouragement," Nicola was always saying to me. "They're not telepathic, you know: you've got to show them you're interested."

I'd watched with fascination as we drove away, the other girls doing just that, Lisa Baker leaning back against the counter, just close enough to be in Martin's way as he went back to the till, a blonde girl passing a bottle to one of the boys to open for her, making sheep's eyes at him. Oh yes, I knew what Nicola meant; I just hadn't tried doing it.

My stomach churned as I thought about the fair the next night. Suppose Martin looked for me and I wasn't there? Suppose he paired up with someone else? It was Saturday, Dad's night for The Green Man, which meant I could maybe get out and back by closing time. But it also meant I would have to leave Tom by himself. That didn't feel good. He's a big boy now, though, I reasoned; he hasn't been up in the night with bad dreams or worries for ages now, a year even. If I left it until he was properly asleep, he wouldn't even know I'd gone. I could lock everything up so he'd be safe; he was nine, for goodness' sake. The part of me that remonstrated, that said I was responsible for Tom, must act as Mum would have done, I shoved aside. She isn't here, I thought; that's not my fault and why should I pay for it? *She went*, I thought almost spitefully, she left Tom and me behind. *She chose to go.*

I sat up and opened my eyes; explosions of yellow dots moved across them as the pressure was released, and I blinked and got up stiffly. The river gurgled lazily and I picked my way alongside it, letting its sound fill me up like water rushing into a hollow, blanking out my thoughts.

It was as I came to the place where the stony bank widened still further that I noticed something odd. The whole area ahead seemed unusually flat, as if the larger stones that usually littered the pebbles had been cleared away. Sure enough as I got closer I saw a pile of rocks — some of them big, too big for Tom to have lifted — a cairn at the foot of an aspen tree. Beside the cairn, a patch of ground the size of a room had been cleared and, I now realized, laid out in a design, a spiral like a gigantic snail shell, marked in dark and light pebbles. Each dark-grey stone had been carefully picked and pieced with others to stand out against the pale grey of the background. I walked slowly round it. It was beautiful, symmetrical yet free, its swirling shape generous and bold. It must have taken hours. I glanced around. Everything but the river was still, hot and silent.

I stepped on to the band of dark pebbles at its broad beginning and followed it round and round as it narrowed until I had to put one foot directly in front of the other, concentrating like a child on staying off the pale stones. At the centre was one large flat stone like a full stop. I stood balancing on it and looked around again. Nothing. I looked up through the overhanging branches of the tree and caught, high up, the glint of small shiny objects. I parted the leaves above me and saw that someone had hung pieces of silvery metal, shaped into spirals, from the ends of the slender twigs.

For a moment I indulged the fantasy that this was a message — imagined Mum back, living somewhere nearby, watching over Tom and me secretly. She would be afraid to come home, afraid of what Dad would say. She would watch for her chance to see me, try to let me know she was around . . . Such hopes were treacherous, almost too painful to bear.

Nonetheless, the thing was beautiful, and mysterious. The bright shapes turned in the slight breeze, glittering, drawing my eye up and up through the green, to glimpse the open sky.

CHAPTER
FOUR

The fair was a different animal at night. Nicola and I walked with the rest of the crowd, across the clinker car park towards the lights, already brighter than the dusky summer evening. Light bulbs strung out along the metal structures outlined circles and spokes, poles and awnings, a crazy three-dimensional version of a child's dot-to-dot picture. Music pounded out to meet us, at first indistinguishable beyond the under beat of bass line drums, then dividing itself into familiar songs of past and present as we got closer. "Babylove" from the waltzers competed with "The Monster Mash" from the ghost train, and the wistful strains of 10CC singing "I'm not in Love" to the queue for the Ferris wheel. Over the mixture of competing tunes, men's voices boomed out intermittently, distorted by bad PA systems so that the words were lost and only their pushy tone was left.

We paused at the waltzers and a stuffy draught blew across my face as the garish orange and yellow cars spun past.

"Is that fast enough for you?" a man in the booth was shouting into a microphone, grinning at a pair of girls clutching at each other and screaming. A lad leapt between the cars, giving theirs an extra push.

"Isn't it great!" Nicola yelled into my ear.

I nodded and smiled.

Everything had gone according to plan; I could afford to smile. Dad had gone off early to The Green Man and would by this time be well into a second round of both drinks and darts. Tom had been worn out after a whole day chasing around with his kitten. He still moaned all the way to bed of course, but had then fallen asleep within minutes of my drawing the curtains. I'd wavered over whether to leave his window open to let in some air, but in the end closed it for safety. I felt better knowing the house was secure while I was away.

I'd had time to spare for the long walk down the track and half a mile down the main road to the bus stop in the village, and every step made me feel lighter, my hair flopping soft against my back, bare in my new white halter-neck top, and nothing to carry except my shoulder bag, its fringe swinging as I walked. Nicola let out a low whistle when she met me at the stop in town.

"You look fantastic," she said. "Bit dressy for the pictures, though." She stepped in front of me as she waved at her mum's departing car. She ran her fingers through her brown feathered hair and put on some hoop earrings that she took from her jeans pocket. It had never occurred to me that Nicola too would have to fib to get away, and I said so.

"Got into a bit of trouble last week for getting in too late. Mum's got it into her head that I'm in with the wrong crowd," she said with a rueful look. "You're my alibi. Mum's heard what your dad's like, so she reckons if he let you come out it must be all right."

The mention of Dad made me feel uncomfortable and I found myself looking anxiously after the car as it queued to turn right at the lights.

Nicola nudged me. "Don't be a worry-guts," she said. "As long as we're back in time for the end of the pictures it'll be fine."

The waltzer music came to an end and we watched, mesmerized, as the mad whirling resolved itself into a slow and orderly dance in which it became apparent that a collision had never been a possibility. Like clockwork, I thought, it's all planned to go like clockwork. The girls who had been screaming climbed down, laughing now, and we moved back to let them stumble past, still not quite recovering their sea legs.

"Watch out," said Nicola, pulling me aside from a spread of sawdust on the grass. "Mind what you put your feet in."

I moved away quickly. "What about the dodgems?" I said.

"Good idea," Nicola said. "Best place to find the talent."

I didn't mention that there was only one face I was interested in finding.

We took separate cars at the dodgems. I would've been happy to let her drive but she laughed at me, saying I was a baby. She fitted snugly into the tight hollow of a car, looking neat and in control as she always did, tapping the wheel, impatient to get going. I wriggled uncomfortably, my legs jammed against the wheel, all knees and elbows. The other cars were filling up fast, mainly with teenagers, and a few fathers with kids, trying not to look as if they wanted a go but with hands sneaking towards the wheel. Mothers hovered at the edge, their smiles tinged with anxiety. Normal families. I scanned the queue waiting to get a place, and quickly looked away again; a crowd from school were there: Lisa, Carol and Angie, along with Martin and his mates. I hoped he hadn't seen me, though I knew he'd be bound to. I felt like a creature on a microscope slide, pinned down under the bright lights of the canopy.

A man approached to collect the money. He wore a baseball cap, and a leather pouch full of change was slung around his hips. I could feel Martin's eyes on me, but part of me was calm, detached, still working out that the little group consisted of three girls, three boys, neatly matched. The man was broad and tanned, and I noticed he had dirt or oil under his fingernails as he held out his hand to ask me for the money. I don't know why I did it but I found myself smiling at him.

"How do you make this thing go?" I said.

"First time?" he asked, and I nodded, looking helpless. He chewed on his gum for a moment, and then moved it to the side of his mouth. "Shove up," he said, and jumped into the car, swinging on the pole and sliding easily behind the wheel.

I was taken by surprise; I'd only meant to get him to talk, lean over me to show me the controls, appear to take an interest. Martin was at the front of the queue now. He said something to Lisa, who was hanging on to his arm and seemed determined not to be left behind. They got into a car with Skinner in the one behind them, busy catcalling at Nicola. An older man with a great beer-gut came out from the kiosk to collect the money; he frowned in our direction and lumbered back, shaking his head.

I was jammed in close against the fairground lad, our thighs touching and his body heating mine. With a high-pitched noise the cars began to move, the note climbing a rising scale. He put one arm behind me, the other hand on the wheel, to reverse out into the centre and free himself from the other cars. His smell was musky, warm like his tanned skin. The cars moved sedately at first, all going clockwise, with the odd bump when someone didn't keep up. I glimpsed Martin and Lisa over on the opposite side; her colour was high, with two bright spots on her cheekbones. She waved to Angie and Carol, her other hand resting on Martin's knee as she turned.

A father with his hand over his son's hand on the wheel caught us a glancing blow, jarring us to the side so that I fell against my driver. I made sure Martin saw me laughing. Things were moving faster now. Sparks flashed from the metal grid of the ceiling as the hooked ends of the poles moved across it. Someone ahead got caught against the barrier and was hit side on, then we, and all the other cars, piled up behind it. The fair lad threw the wheel left and got us clear again. Now it was a free-for-all, everyone laughing and squealing, cars jerked in all directions, the faces of onlookers blurred to white blobs as we twisted and turned to avoid getting mashed up. Suddenly Martin was alongside us, moving fast. Lisa was gripping on to the metal edge of the car and I could see her mouth moving. "Don't!" she was saying again and again. Martin looked across at me with his mouth set, then turned the wheel sharply to barge us into the side. The crash chattered my teeth and the pole above us juddered and jumped, showering us with sparks as we careered into the barrier.

"The little shit," said the fairground lad, jamming the car into reverse, ready to go after him.

I laid a hand on his arm as Martin spun away to the other side. I knew what I needed to know now.

"It's all right — forget it," I said.

Around us the cars were slowing, the machinery making a long downward note as they came to a standstill.

"Er, thanks very much," I said, unfolding myself and climbing out.

He put both hands on the sides of the car, lifted himself and swung his legs out in one easy practised movement.

"Any time," he said, "catch ya later," and swaggered off jingling his change, to collect the next lot of money.

Nicola had joined the group, where Skinner was fooling about, putting his arm in front of his eyes in a theatrical impression of Lisa on the dodgems. I sat down beside Nic on the steps.

"What got into you?" she whispered.

I shrugged. It was true, something had got into me; I felt as though electricity crackled all around me, so that if someone touched me I might throw sparks.

Martin came across to the group with his hands in his pockets, affecting boredom, leaving Lisa moaning at his back.

"What did you do that for?" she was saying. "Why didn't you stop when I said stop?" She turned to Angie for some sympathy. Her hair was half out of the bone comb that held it in a twist at the back of her head, and she had a smudge of something black under one eye, oil or mascara. I was glad.

What's happening to me? I thought. This is Lisa who you've known since primary, who you've swapped sandwiches with, had giggling fits with in the middle of the school play, comforted when she broke her wrist playing netball. None of it made any difference. I was glad.

"I'm going to find a loo," I said to Nicola, and walked off without looking at Martin. I walked straight down a wide alleyway of stalls, where there weren't too many people and I wouldn't be swallowed up in a crowd. I strode past the ghost train with its rickety door painted with skeletons in green fluorescent paint, and the rifle range where men let off a volley of shots that cracked the air. I slowed as the stalls thinned out and were replaced by trailers, and the smell of hot-dog onions and vanilla gave way to the smell of old beer cans and grass. There was the sound of running feet behind me and Martin caught my arm and swung me round.

"You bastard," I said into his face. Then I was shouting: "You could've hurt me, you know, you do know that! You're hurting me now!"

54

He dropped my arm, and I held it out to him, turning my palm upwards to show the marks of his fingers on my inner arm.

"Look, I'm sorry, but you shouldn't —"

I strode off deeper into the shadows between the shuttered trailers and the lorry cabs, knowing he would follow me.

"Jess," he called. "Jess, wait."

Then his arms were around me and his mouth was on mine, hot and salty. We stumbled back against the huge tyre of a lorry; it was warm, as though the engine had recently run, and there was a smell of hot diesel. We kissed harder, my hands pressing his back, feeling the coarse cotton of his loose shirt, bunching it against the skin beneath. He lifted my hair away from my neck, fumbled hopelessly at the knot of my top, then moved his hands down to encircle my waist, his palms hot against the bare skin between my top and my jeans.

The engine behind us made a series of ticking sounds as it cooled, which made me jump and push him away.

"Not here," I said: "someone might come."

He took my hands and held them down by my sides. "Oh God, Jess, don't do this to me."

I saw the outline of his face, and the glint of his eyes, bright as he turned his face and leant against me, resting his head on my shoulder.

A dog barked in the distance and the rest of the world rushed back: voices from a radio playing somewhere, a tinny thud nearby like a bag of rubbish being dumped. Martin was breathing hard. I stroked his short hair, soft on the downstroke but prickly the other way. My fingers rested on the smooth hollow at the back of his neck.

"I'm sorry," I whispered. I hadn't understood before, hadn't realized what feelings I was playing with. "I'm sorry, I didn't know."

He pulled himself upright and passed a hand over his face. I straightened my top, suddenly embarrassed. He was looking at me strangely, appraisingly.

"Well," he said, "Jess Garton. Sweet seventeen and never been kissed," and he attempted a laugh. He fished a squashed packet of cigarettes out of his pocket and shook two out on to his palm. "Here." He passed one to me and lit a match, which flared blue, then yellow.

As I bent forward to take a light my hand was shaking.

I perched on the step of the lorry and shifted over so he could sit beside me. He inhaled deeply, then let the smoke out in a long slow breath; it hung blue-grey in the still air and faded gradually against the darker blue of the shadows.

"Look," I said. "Bats!"

Flickering against the glow of the fair lights, bats sliced the air in search of insects. Their grey streamlined forms appeared momentarily against the sky, vanished as they swooped lower and were lost against the dark bulk of the lorries, then reappeared against pale clouds of midges that danced in swarms. We watched for a while in silence.

56

"You're not afraid of them, then?" he said. "Like the other girls?"

"I'm not like the other girls," I said. "Come on, I'd better find Nicola or she's going to be really fed up."

I put out my cigarette on the metal of the step. We walked hand in hand back towards the movement and music. The Ferris wheel towering above it all was moving slowly round for people to get on.

"Do you want a go on it?" he asked.

I glanced at my watch. "We haven't got time. I've got to get the bus home."

"Tomorrow, then."

"I can't get out tomorrow."

He looked moody, as though he thought I was trying to give him the brush-off.

"It's difficult," I said. "My dad . . . well, he doesn't like me going out."

"Thinks you'll get into trouble?" he said with a cheeky sideways look.

"Something like that." I couldn't explain that it was much more than concern for my welfare. That it was all about control, the farm, his territory where his word was law and from which his subjects weren't allowed to stray.

"There's the end of year dance, then. *Everyone's* going to that."

"OK," I said, terrified he'd say "Forget it" if I didn't come up with something. "OK, fine."

He suggested that we get something to eat. As we ducked under the awning of a brightly lit food stall he stopped me.

"Hold it. You've got something in your hair." He bent forward, carefully picked something out and held it in closed hands.

"What is it?" I smoothed my hair back down.

He opened his hands to reveal a tiny silvery moth, its wings spread flat against his palm. Disturbed by my breath it folded its wings and began to move.

"It's walking along your life line," I said.

"My what?"

"Your life line — the one that shows how long you're going to live, and how many accidents you're going to have, and here's your heart line . . ." I put out a finger to point, and the moth took flight, blundering first into the fluorescent light, and then dropping below the awning and disappearing into the night.

I let out a sound of disappointment.

He looked at me curiously. "You really are a very strange girl, you know."

"Didn't you think it was beautiful?"

"Bat food," he said.

He ordered a hot dog for himself and a candyfloss for me. I watched the threads of sugar like spider silk being caught on the roughness of the stick as the drum spun round and round. I couldn't remember ever feeling so happy.

We wandered around, looking for the others. I pulled bits of candyfloss off, marvelling at the way the soft pink fluff turned to sticky orange sugar between my finger and thumb, eating it greedily like handfuls of childhood.

We found the others at the penny arcade. Nicola was watching Skinner getting grumpy with the shove-ha'penny machine as he fed it pennies which never quite tipped the teetering pile of coins over the brink and back into your pocket.

She looked up. "What have you done to your mouth?"

"What do you mean?" My hand went up to cover it.

"It's bright red, for God's sake. You look like Marilyn Monroe." She rooted in her bag for a mirror and a tissue.

It was true. My lips were stained candyfloss vermilion. I stuck my tongue out at her; it too was a vibrant red. I licked the tissue and rubbed away ineffectually at my mouth. My lips felt swollen. I touched them with my fingertips: yes, tender and swollen where we had kissed hard. I looked at them in wonder, as if they were a different person's lips.

"Oh hell! Look at the time!" said Nicola. "The pictures have finished. Mum'll be there. Come *on*, Jess." She snatched the mirror from me and pulled me away.

"'Bye!" I called out to Martin, but his head was already bent over the machine with Skinner, mesmerized by the slow nudging forward of the coins.

We ran back across the car park, stumbling on the loose surface in our wedge heels, towards the lighted windows of the bus.

"Slow down," said Nicola as we neared it. "We want to look as if we just sauntered round the corner, remember."

The driver was still reading the paper, waiting for his customary ten minutes to make sure all the cinema-goers got home. Nicola's mum had parked in a side street and I waved to her as I climbed the steps of the bus, impatient now to get home before the pubs turned out and Dad got back.

The bus driver gave me a knowing look over the top of his paper. I looked right back, as I fed the money into the plastic coin box, then walked to the middle of the bus and slid into a seat. Was it so obvious? I looked at myself in the darkened window. My mouth was dark; I looked like a child caught eating stolen raspberries.

Walking back from the village, I kept in close to the side of the road, hugging the hedges, dreading the sight of headlights in case they announced the rumbling approach of the Land-Rover. Then I was on to the track and glad I knew every step of the way in the depth of the country dark.

As I came out of the trees by the river I saw that the house was lit up like a beacon; every light in every window was on. What on earth was wrong? I ran, praying that Tom was all right. I couldn't see the Land-Rover in the yard but Dad might turn up at any minute. My heart thumping, I let myself in.

"Tom! Tom!" I shouted.

A hunched shape in a kitchen chair unfolded and Tom's tired face peeped out from under a blanket.

I knelt down to put my arms around him. "What happened?"

He turned his face away from me. "Where *were* you?" he said, his voice hoarse with trying not to cry.

"Never mind that — tell me what happened."

"I woke up and there were funny noises. And then, when I got up, there was no one here."

"I've told you before," guilt made me impatient, "it's only the beams and the boards cooling down. It's just the house settling down for the night." He pressed his face against my arm. I gave him a squeeze. "Here, you didn't ring Grandad did you?"

He shook his head. "He wouldn't have been able to come, would he? Not with that long walk in the dark?"

I nodded absently; I'd remembered that all the lights were still on.

"Listen, Tom," I said. "I'm really sorry I didn't tell you I had to go out, and I'll make it up to you, I promise I will, but if Dad finds us up like this he'll go mad. We need to switch all these lights off quick and then jump into bed. OK?"

Tom wiped his nose on the blanket, looking at me with an expression that dared me to tell him off about it.

"You do upstairs and I'll do down, right?"

He shook his head, now determined to milk the situation for all it was worth.

"All right, all right, we'll go round together, but we have to be quick." I gave his hand a tug.

He followed me round as I flicked off the lights downstairs, his blanket trailing behind him and a stagy woebegone look on his face. We were just going into the front room when we heard the Land-Rover come bouncing up the drive and stop in the yard in a spatter of grit. I stopped. Our best chance was to run upstairs quickly, and get away with a telling-off for leaving lights on and wasting money. As if in slow motion, I saw Tom's eyes widen in panic, then he moved in front of me and turned off the light.

"No chance of Dad thinking we're asleep now," I hissed, and pulled him out into the darkened hall, making for the stairs. "Quick, you get to bed."

As he groped towards the stairs he stumbled against the telephone table. It banged against the wall with a clatter and a faint ping from the phone. The light went on in the kitchen, and we stood like rabbits caught in combine headlights as Dad opened the door.

"What the hell's going on?" he said. "What are you doing out of bed at this hour?" He took in Tom clutching his blanket and then turned towards me. "What the . . ." He looked incredulously at my best outfit and apparently cherry-painted lips.

I opened them to speak but only a whisper came out. "Let Tom go to bed, Dad," I said. "This is my fault." I tried to edge in front of Tom.

"You stay right where you are," he said to Tom, pointing a finger at him.

"The fair was on," I said miserably, "and Nicola asked me to go." It was best to get this over quickly. "I . . . I really wanted to go; I've never been to one before . . ." I tailed off.

He reached out and took my shoulders. He smelt of beer and pub smoke. He turned me round and round in a mockery of a mannequin's twirl.

"You look like a tart," he said, "a common tart."

He was swaying slightly, moving forwards on to the balls of his feet and back on to his heels, like a boxer, I thought, and my stomach felt as though it was turning to water. I'd had plenty of smacks as a child — a slap on the back of the legs for disobedience or cheek — accepted with tears and quickly forgotten, but this was something different.

"I suppose that's it," he said, his eyes narrowing. "You were meeting some lad, some randy little yob, that's what would make you a liar to your father."

I felt my colour begin to rise, and my eyes filled. "Let go of me, Dad," I said.

He reached up and smudged his thumb across my face under my eye.

"That's right; wash it all off, get all the muck off your face." His voice had softened and taken on a wheedling, coaxing tone. "That is it, isn't it? There's a boy, isn't there? I'm right, aren't I . . ."

Suddenly Tom was pulling at Dad's sleeve and shouting at him.

"No, there isn't! There isn't a boy! It was me, I wanted to go! I went on at Jess until she took me."

Dad looked down at him as if he'd woken from a dream. Tom tugged again at his arm.

"It was me who wanted to go. Ask Mrs Jones. She knows — I told her in the car."

Dad looked from Tom to me, and then pushed me away. In silence he picked Tom's hand off his sleeve as though it was unclean.

"There'll be no more going off the farm," he said flatly. "This is where you belong, and this is where you'll stay, so content yourselves with it."

"You can't do that, Dad," I said. "You can't keep Tom off school, you'll have the Welfare up here."

As soon as the words were out of my mouth I could see I'd made a terrible mistake. A sly look crossed his face.

"No, not Tom," he said, "but then Tom's not the one concerned to get an education, is he?"

CHAPTER
FIVE

Sylvie

4th September 1964. House martins gathering. Thirty or more flying to and from the telephone wires.

Sylvie led Jess in to breakfast. Henry looked up from the paper.

"My word, you look smart," he said.

Sylvie neatened up Jess's brand-new school tie and stood back once again to boggle at her daughter's transformation. The bare brown skin of summer, with scratches and freckles she knew like a map, was gone. Jess was wrapped like a parcel in full-length white socks, gym-slip, white shirt and tie, a hand-knitted bottle-green sweater contributed by Henry's mum, Rose, and, like the bow on a gift as far as Jess was concerned, a pair of shiny Clark's T-bar shoes.

Jess did a twirl for her dad's benefit, then pulled at her hair, which was tied either side of her head with green ribbons.

"I don't like these bunches," she said.

"Come and let me see," said Henry.

Jess climbed on to his knee. He wound each one round a finger and then held them out from her head in shiny twists.

"See, now you know why they call them pigtails." He showed Jess her reflection in the curve of the stainless-steel teapot. He set her back on her feet and she sat up to have her breakfast.

"I bet those ribbons'll be out by break-time," he said to Sylvie.

"More than likely."

They smiled at each other.

Sylvie found that she couldn't eat. She moved restlessly around the kitchen, tidying up, while Jess tucked into scrambled eggs. Something about her daughter's back view, the straight white line of her parted hair, and the exposed paleness of her neck, made her want to cry. Tiny wisps of wavy dark hair were already coming loose, as though the very spring of her hair was trying to turn Jess back into herself. Good, Sylvie thought: I hope the ribbons do come out.

Henry downed the rest of his tea, patted Jess absent-mindedly on the head and picked up his keys.

"Where'll you be today?" Sylvie said.

"Fencing. Up the back. Don't forget that feed order, will you? They're very slow to deliver and we'll need it soon."

"OK." Sylvie glanced at the clock. "Come on, Jess, we don't want to be late." She laid Jess's dark-green coat over the back of the chair.

"Right." Henry left.

Jess was struggling into the straps of her satchel. "Can you carry my coat, Mum?" she said.

Sylvie couldn't help but smile; the satchel was so alarmingly huge and the leather was dyed such an unlikely colour, almost orange.

"I don't know what kind of cow this came off," she said, loosening the creaky straps for her.

"I'm a tortoise," Jess said, and was off out of the door.

"You mean you're a hare," Sylvie called as she followed after her. She caught up with her when Jess stopped to climb on a gate. "Hinge end, remember," she said automatically.

They paused to look at the fields. Mist filled the bottom of the river valley in the morning, like a bowl of milk. In the lower fields the trees stood up to their knees in it and cows appeared silently and faded again as they lumbered away. Higher up the slope, the sun was beginning to burn off the mist and the grass and weeds glittered. Jess found a stick and tapped the barbed wire as she went. Drops fell from the strands each time they pinged, like notes released from a staff.

They walked on, changing to single file when they reached the road, Jess in front.

As they came into the village, other children were making their way to school and a group of older ones were hanging around outside the corner shop, hoping Mrs Bartlett would open up early. There was some pushing and shoving to get nearer to the door and a squabble broke out. A boy had his cap knocked off and two others scuffled with it on the ground while onlookers shouted encouragement. Mrs Bartlett gave a sharp rap on the window. Jess moved close in to Sylvie's side.

Sylvie raised a hand to wave to Sandra, the postmaster's wife. Her little boy, Andrew, was holding tightly to the handle of the pram that she was pushing.

"There you are, Jess: look, there's Andrew — he'll be in your class," Sylvie said. Jess was dragging her feet and wouldn't look up. "Come on, love, it's time to go in now."

They reached the gate of the steep gabled Victorian building, and Jess grabbed on to her mother's hand. Sylvie kept up a stream of talk as she walked Jess to her classroom, telling her about the hopscotch and tag she would be able to play with the other children at break-time and pointing out the crate of dumpy milk bottles in the cloakroom sink, which they would drink mid-morning.

They entered the classroom, where some children were already sitting on bench seats at desks, boys at one side of the room and girls at the other. The infant teacher, Miss Turner, came towards them. She had very soft white hair, so fine it looked almost powdery, and thick glasses that magnified her watery grey eyes and the lines around them. Even to Sylvie she seemed incredibly old.

"This must be Jess," she said, bending down to child level.

Jess's grip tightened until her nails dug into the back of Sylvie's hand.

Miss Turner tried again. "You come with me now, and I'll show you which one is your desk."

Jess hid her face in Sylvie's coat and shook her head vigorously. The teacher gave Sylvie a look that clearly said "It's best if you go now."

Sylvie squatted down and spoke in as firm a voice as she could manage. "Mummy's got to go now, but I'll be back at quarter past three to bring you home." She tried to turn her to face the teacher, and caught sight of Jess's face crumpling, her chin trembling.

"Come along now," Miss Turner said more briskly, and laid a hand on Jess's shoulder.

"Be a good girl, Jess, and Mummy'll be back soon," Sylvie said, taking a step away.

There was an unseemly struggle as Jess began to bawl, "No-o, no-o," in great, choking sobs, and Sylvie had to uncurl Jess's white-nailed fingers one by one from her own hand. She turned and made for the door, feeling like a traitor.

The teacher spoke firmly. "That's enough now. None of the other children are crying," and Sylvie heard Jess making gulping noises as she tried to swallow down her feelings.

Sylvie walked through the stream of children coming in through the cloakroom and went quickly round the group of mums talking at the gate. She hurried away, her heart beating fast, thinking over and over, "I never gave her a kiss. I never said goodbye." She walked straight out of the village, forgetting her plan to pick up some shopping. Alone in the lane, she put her hands to her face. Six hours, she thought, six hours and ten minutes until she would know Jess was all right. She told herself not to be silly, that Jess was probably settled by now, and tried to imagine her joining in with counting or story time. Sylvie walked slowly home. She had no idea how she'd fill the day.

As she let herself back into the house the phone was ringing. She wiped her hands on her coat before picking up the receiver. It was Henry's mum.

"Yes, she went off fine," Sylvie lied, unable to stand the thought of Rose's advice on the transition to school, or what a perfect pupil Henry had made.

"Oh good, I am glad," Rose said. "And how about you, dear?"

Sylvie was so surprised by Rose's solicitous tone that for a moment she didn't say anything.

"I'm fine," she said. "Coping."

"Good, good," Rose said, without picking up on the implication of Sylvie's response, "because I was wondering if you could help me out with something, now that you've more free time . . ."

Sylvie said nothing. To admit to free time might be a bit like writing a blank cheque.

"Are you still there, dear?" Rose said sharply.

"Uh-huh," Sylvie said, holding out.

"I'm organizing a Mothers' Union meeting for tomorrow night. We've got Reverend Jamieson visiting with his slides of the Holy Land."

Oh no, thought Sylvie, she's not going to ask me to come. She could just imagine the glee of the Lastcote ladies as they sized up their new member; her youth, her unsuitable dress, her *inexperience* as a mother (which could be so very easily and enjoyably put right with a little timely advice).

"I wondered if you could make me a quick batch of your flapjacks and perhaps a Dundee cake. We're very welcoming to young wives, as you know, but it *is* expected that new members contribute — it's important to get off on the right foot."

Sylvie took a deep breath. "I'm very sorry, Mrs G," she said, affecting a familiarity she knew would be annoying, "but I'm much too busy with the farm."

"But you don't —" started Rose.

"I've got all Henry's paperwork to do, the tax returns, and the orders."

"I have a hair appointment," Rose let slip. "I don't think it's too much to ask, when I'm offering to introduce you to our circle."

Sylvie thought that if she faltered now she'd understand as clearly as a sheep on its back for shearing what the term "roped in" was all about.

"No," she said. "I'm sorry, but I can't."

Rose spluttered at the other end of the phone.

Sylvie finished with an argument she knew her mother-in-law would find incontrovertible. "I'm afraid I have to put supporting Henry first," she said sweetly.

Rose put the phone down.

Sylvie stood for a moment, winding the curly flex of the phone in her fingers. Its dial-tone hum went on and on like the ripple of repercussion. She replaced the receiver gently in its cradle.

Pricked by conscience, she now felt obliged to make her claims true by working on Henry's paperwork, at least until coffee time.

She sat down at the heavy oak bureau in Henry's study, a cubby-hole off the hall with room only for the desk, a modern swivel chair which Henry insisted was comfy, but which Sylvie found unyielding, and shelves full of grey box files. There was a small window high up, set back in the thickness of the stone wall, leaving a sloping windowsill on which no ornament could stand. The room had probably once been a larder; its walls were whitewashed and it had a smoky smell, like hanging bacon. Although it was pleasantly cool, Sylvie found it oppressive. Sitting on the hard seat, the window half obscured by the wisteria that covered the gable end of the house, the yellowish-green light made her feel submerged. The weight of the building seemed to press down on her, and her eyes kept returning to the small patch of visible sky.

She made herself open the bureau and started to sort through the bundles of papers piled inside — invoices waiting to be paid, gripped together with bulldog clips, receipts waiting to be filed, held by clothes pegs. It struck her that the wadges of crackly sheets in the bulldog clips were by far the thicker of the two. She placed the file of feed orders to one side. Henry kept the bank statements in a locked drawer, one of a series of small drawers between the pigeonholes in the bureau. Early in their marriage Sylvie had realized that the long-term financing and future of the farm were considered "his business" in both senses of the phrase.

Sylvie didn't bother trying the drawer but fished out the chequebook, where Henry kept a running total of his spending. She ran her eye down the columns of figures expertly and calculated the balance in the account; they were well into the red again. She flicked through the bills, picking out any red reminders and invoices with a credit period about to expire, and worked steadily for an hour writing cheques and envelopes, which she left open so that Henry could sign them and write the amounts up into the accounts.

He's so stubborn, she thought; did he think he was saving her worry by not telling her what was going on? He was so proud of his pet project, the new milking parlour with its up-to-date cooling system and its complicated arrangement of pipes and ducts; said he had a vision of how the farm would be, successful, thriving. It would have been easy just to let herself be carried along by his lovable enthusiasm, but not safe. The truth was, the loan was almost bankrupting them. Henry hadn't been able to raise enough cash to expand his dairy herd as fast as he'd have liked, so they were left with a gleaming parlour that was only half full. The irony was that milk prices were good.

Sylvie leant her chin on her hand. Henry carried on regardless, as if everything was hunky-dory. He made no comment about all the little things she did to make the housekeeping money stretch: deep hems on Jess's clothes, cottage pie and half-pay pudding. He wouldn't talk to her, or anyone else; his dad had been so frustrated when Henry signed for the loan on the parlour that he'd called Henry "pig-headed".

"The trouble with Henry," he'd confided, when Sylvie had tried to get them back on to speaking terms again, "is that he'd rather pick up a ladder on his own and smash a window than ask anyone else to catch hold of the other end."

Well, she supposed that all she could do was to keep trying to pick up the other end of the ladder without him noticing. She began to write out the feed order, and thought about what Henry had told her they would need. The grass had had its last cut for silage, and both the calves born this year and the steers from the year before needed concentrates to supplement their diet over the winter. She glanced at the charts pinned to the cork board. The summer had been kind to them, providing good forage, but it would still be months until the beef cattle were up to weight and ready for slaughter, a long time to wait for the cash. She typed out the order and put it in an envelope, then stood it up against the wall on top of the bureau where she would see it. She would post it when she went to get Jess from school.

The thought of Jess among strangers made her stomach lurch with renewed anxiety. She turned off the lamp, returning the room to its murky green shade, and went to make sandwiches and coffee. She would take lunch to Henry; perhaps they could eat together and she could get him in the mood to talk. Walking up to Top field would in any case keep her busy.

Henry was fencing some pasture on the hill at the back of the house, on the boundary line between his land

and Home Farm. A line of spruce stakes was already in position, running from the corner of the field to halfway along the hedge line.

"What d'you think?" he called as she pulled the chain over the gate behind her. "Nice and straight?"

She made a show of standing behind the last post in the row and eyeing in the line.

"Looks good to me," she said. "Why do we need a fence when there's already a hedge, though?"

"I never got around to hedge-laying this year." Henry grimaced at the hedge's leggy growth and gappy roots. "It's hardly what you'd call stock-proof." He blew out a long breath. "Not enough hours in the day," he said.

"I brought us some lunch," Sylvie said quickly, sensing Henry's defensiveness.

"It's a bit early yet." Henry's face was red, and the armpits and back of his overalls were stained with sweat. "I'm going to try to get a few more of these in before I stop."

Sylvie put the packets of sandwiches and the flask down on top of one of the big reels of barbed wire in the back of the Land-Rover. She stood and watched as Henry measured five paces from the last post, lined up the stake with the others and pushed its pointed end into the ground. He hefted the drive-all on to the top of the post, gripped the two handles and beat the stake two feet into the ground with a series of mighty thuds. He lifted the drive-all off, pushed against the wood to see that it was firm and glanced at her as if to check that she was watching.

She nodded her encouragement. "It seems funny without Jess," she said as he paused.

"She'll be all right," he said. "Stop fretting."

Sometimes it seemed to Sylvie that Henry was being deliberately obtuse.

"I mean it seems too . . . too quiet here. To me," she added.

Henry looked at her as if he were humouring a small child. "Look, why don't I do a few more and then we'll stop and have a drink?"

"Or an early lunch?" Sylvie said, thinking that they could sit in the Land-Rover and talk. "I can help." She glanced around for the pile of stakes, hauled one off the top and began to drag its cumbersome length back towards him, bumping it over the tussocky ground. As he took it from her it ran through her hands.

"Aah!" she cried out and cradled her right hand in her left.

"What? What is it?" Henry laid down the post and caught hold of her hand. A splinter half an inch long had lodged in the flesh of her palm, and a bead of blood oozed to the surface at the point of entry.

"Oh God, Sylv, I'm so sorry. I shouldn't have let you do that."

"I'm not a complete incompetent," she said.

She raised her hand towards her mouth.

"No, don't suck it! These spruce things have been treated. Let me look." He took off his heavy gloves and tried to get hold of the frayed end of the splinter between his finger and thumbnail.

Sylvie involuntarily jerked her hand away. "I'll do it."

76

Henry pulled a face. "You'll have to go down to the house and have a go with some tweezers. Put lots of antiseptic on it afterwards — it could be nasty." He put his arm around her and gave her a squeeze. "I think you'd better call it a day on the farm labouring front, eh?"

Sylvie found it hard to muster a smile. She trailed home back down the hill, teased out the splinter, washed the inflamed welt, then covered it with sticking plaster. By the time she had climbed the hill again Henry was sitting on the tail of the Land-Rover, finishing off his sandwiches.

"Thanks for the lunch," he said, screwing the lid back on the flask. "That hit the spot."

He pulled on his gloves, walked over to the pile of stakes and picked up an armful as easily as if they were broom handles.

Sylvie gave up. She wasn't going to try to talk to his back. She picked up her packet of sandwiches and set off.

"Where're you going now?" Henry called after her.

"For a walk."

"Yes, but where? I like to know where you are."

"Oh, I don't know, anywhere. I'm no earthly use here, am I?"

She looked back to see Henry with a look of bewilderment on his face. She half hoped he'd follow her, but as she reached the gate she heard the thump of the drive-all begin again.

Sylvie turned left and walked fast across a field scattered with straw bales, glad of her Wellingtons in the prickly stubble, then into pasture spread with great swathes of thistles, their flowers turned to seed-heads now, the colour of an old man's beard. Her steps disturbed crane flies, which rose from the grass in front of her feet and mingled with the thistle-down heads as they floated randomly, like hundreds of tiny hot-air balloons released into the air.

The next field was ploughed and the heavy soil slowed her down, sticking in clods to her feet. She tramped doggedly around the edge to the other side and then wiped the worst of the clogging earth off on the grass and nettles at the foot of the stile. She climbed up on to it and sat on the crossbar of damp green wood.

The field stretched in front of her, its furrowed surface like a rich corduroy, the sun lending the sheen of velvet to the slabs of soil. For a moment she saw the land about her as a cloak spread out around the farmhouse, its folds the undulating slopes and dips, its pattern the piecework of fields seamed with hedges. She scanned the textures and colours in the scene before her, the pale gold of stubble fields against the green of pasture, and the tinge of yellow and rust softening the line of the woods in the valley. It was beautiful: she could see why Henry loved it so.

She remembered how, at the beginning, she'd hoped to share it with him, be part of the planning and shaping of it, not just admiring his handiwork from the fringes. But like a royal cloak it seemed it could only have one wearer. It was his pride, his mark of status, but it also wrapped him up, protecting him from the outside world, and, she thought sadly, hiding him away from her.

The regular beat of Henry's fencing reached her on the breeze; a distant thudding, a break, then it resumed again. He would carry on now until he'd finished or it was milking time, whichever came first. Then fall asleep over his tea.

She suddenly saw that what she feared about the farm's problems wasn't just that they could lose their livelihood, but that if they didn't fight for it together, she might lose Henry.

She balled up the sandwich paper tightly and put it in her pocket. She needed a plan, something that was really helpful, that she could present to Henry like a gift. She reached a decision and jumped down from the stile. She was going to see Pa Garton, whether Henry liked it or not. She knew just where he'd be on a fine afternoon — "keeping out of Rose's hair", as he put it.

The smell of wood smoke hung over the allotments on the edge of the village, and a thin blue column rose into the still air from a pile of smouldering leaves gathered in the corner of the site. Sylvie saw Pa Garton's back view: he was digging over a strip of ground, wearing the old stockman's coat he still kept for gardening, and his checked flat cap. He leant on his fork for a few moments between each levering action, as if bracing himself for the next lift and push, then set to again, a muttered swear-word punctuating his efforts every now and then.

Sylvie swung her leg over the twine that marked off Pa Garton's plot and called out to him. He came towards her, smiling and wiping his hands on his pockets.

"Hello, hello, hello," he said, sticking the fork into the earth. "I have a visitor no less. Thank God for that — my knees are nearly shot away."

"Should you be doing that? With your arthritis, I mean?" Sylvie said.

"I don't suppose so. I just reckon I've got to try and keep moving, otherwise they'll seize up altogether, like bits of rusty machinery."

"You look as though you've had enough now, though. Why don't you let me finish it off?"

Pa Garton's face brightened. "Give it a good going-over then, so the frost can get in and kill off all the weeds. I'll get the Primus on."

He disappeared into his shed and Sylvie dug along the rest of the row, enjoying the ease with which she could drive in the tines of the fork and the way that the soil crumbled and broke. By the time she reached the fruit bushes at the end of the plot she'd worked up a sweat under her oilskin jacket, but it made her feel better to look back over the ground she'd covered and see the dark line against the drier, untouched soil.

She joined Pa Garton in his hut, where he sat in a fold-out garden chair. She kicked off her boots at the door and found a place to perch on a pile of sacks of compost and grit covered with some folded fruit netting. He handed her a mug of tea.

"Want a top-up from the flask?" he asked.

"I thought you just made this fresh?"

Pa Garton smiled and produced a hip flask from his pocket, which he tipped generously into his own mug. "Mine's the only kind of flask tea that doesn't taste terrible," he said.

"Oh, go on, then," said Sylvie: "a drop of Scotch'll cheer me up."

She took a slug of the fortified tarry brown tea and felt the warmth start in her stomach and spread out through her limbs.

"So," he said, looking at her over the top of his mug, "what's troubling you enough to drag you away from your tax returns to visit an old codger who doesn't like making cakes either?"

"Oh Lord, is she still cross?"

"Spitting nails." He laughed. He twisted round to the shelf at his side and fished a roll of tobacco out of a flowerpot to fill his pipe.

Sylvie told him the latest about the farm's cash-flow problems, and how hard Henry was pushing himself. He listened carefully until she'd finished, then tamped his pipe tobacco down and lit it, the yellow flame bobbing in and out of the pipe bowl as he sucked and pondered.

"He's over-extended the business," he said after a while. "He'll be very vulnerable if anything out of the ordinary happens — a crop failure, or illness, or a sharp rise in interest rates, come to that."

"Do you think we can manage once the steers go for slaughter?"

"Well, that'll keep you going for a while. But if, as you say, there's more money going out than coming in, the problem's going to come up again, isn't it?" He sipped his tea. "What worries me most is that there's no margin for error. You could do with a bit of a cash injection, a bit tucked away just in case." He fell silent.

"Did this ever happen in your day?"

"Oh, yes, we had our lean times. I always thought that if things got really bad, we'd sell off Turner's."

Sylvie looked blank.

"You know: the thin slice of land, village end, where it narrows down between the road and the river — the bit where the derelict cottage is."

"Ah yes."

She knew the plot he meant: about four acres of land that Henry used as pasture, partly because it was dotted about with small shelters, triangular structures made of wood and corrugated iron that looked like tents scattered randomly over the grass. She'd explored the cottage and outbuildings when she'd first come to live at the farm. The house was a redbrick two-up two-down, still watertight but very basic with an old stained sink and an outside toilet, and there was a barn divided inside into small pens. The whole place had a sad deserted air; the click of the gate had sounded loud in the heavy silence as she'd closed it on the brambly garden and walked away.

"What happened there?" she asked.

"The Turners used to live there when I was a little boy. I used to play with Betty, the daughter — pretty girl, had the blondest hair you ever saw. Anyway, they kept pigs . . ."

"Is that what all those wigwam things are for?"

"That's right. Well, Fred Turner went west in the war and Ada couldn't manage on her own. The heart had gone out of her. She sold up to my father but he had no real interest in pigs. He was always a dairyman really . . ." He tailed off, his face assuming a dreamy look as he wandered into his past.

"What happened to the Turners, Ada and Betty?" Sylvie asked.

"Ada got sick and Betty looked after her for a long while. Sad, really, because by the time her mother died Betty had missed the boat as far as getting married was concerned. Mind you, she always says she's got a bigger family than anyone else in the village, all thirty of 'em."

"Miss Turner?" said Sylvie. "Jess's teacher?" She pictured the wispy-haired woman with her liver-spotted hands, her blonde hair faded now to white.

Pa Garton nodded. "I offered the cottage to the cowman we had in my day, but his wife was like Rose, wanted all mod cons, so it got left empty."

"So things never got bad enough to sell it?" Sylvie said, sloshing the last of her tea round in the mug.

"No. It was a kind of insurance policy that I never called in."

"Could Henry sell it, do you think?"

"No reason why not if he can find a buyer — and you can persuade him to part with it."

Sylvie's mind raced ahead. If they could raise some cash they could maybe pay off part of the loan and things would ease up. Or, more likely, Henry would want to buy more cows, but at least that would pay off in milk production.

Pa Garton was sorting through a box of lumpy-looking brown-paper bags, picking out a selection and spreading them on the shelf beside him. He paused with a bag in mid air.

"Mick Swift might be interested," he said. "He's been looking for a place with outbuildings."

"The chap in the village who's always on his drive, tinkering with a motorbike?"

"Motorbikes, gear boxes, lawn mowers — you name it, he fixes it. If he had more room he could take on more work. Worth looking into anyway."

Sylvie almost clapped her hands with excitement. "Yes, yes, I'll talk to Henry about it tonight."

Pa Garton frowned.

"Y'know, Henry'll see it as a backward move. He's always said he wants to pass the farm on as something bigger and better than when he took it over. Take it a step at a time is my advice." He pulled out an empty paper bag from the bottom of the box and passed it to her. "Here, hold this open."

Sylvie rolled down the edges as Pa Garton produced handfuls of bulbs and piled them in, small waxy white ones and larger ones like shallots, which rustled as they shed part of their pale papery skins.

"There," he said, topping it up with several big round ones with whiskery white roots: "crocuses, narcissi and hyacinths — a proper spring garden for you. Keep you busy for an hour or two. It always cheers you up to start something growing."

Sylvie leant over and gave him a hug, her face pressed against his cheek, dry as glass-paper.

"Hence the allotment," she said. "Old farmers never die, eh?"

He turned a little pink and squeezed her hand. "Don't forget to save a few for Jess to do," he said.

"Oh Lord," said Sylvie, "what's the time?" She glanced at her watch and saw it was after three. "I've got to dash," she said, pulling on her jacket and shuffling into her boots. "What a sight I look! All the mothers'll be there in their good coats." She laughed and tucked her curly hair behind her ears in a half-hearted attempt to tidy it up.

"Go on with you," he said, "you look a proper picture. Tell Jess I want to hear all about who's naughty at school so she'll have to come and see me soon."

"I will," she picked up the bag of bulbs, "and thanks — for everything."

By early evening Sylvie felt as if she'd been piloting a boat through the rocky course of the day. She stood at the sink, washing up the supper things, watching the last of the sun tinge the edges of clouds with brightness and draw the fences and the bars of the cattle grid in shining lines. Jess had been quiet when she came out of school, tired out by the excitement of the day, but had told them a little after supper; that she'd played hopscotch with some girls, that she'd written lots of letter S's, which Miss Turner said were nice, smooth, snaky ones, and that a boy got told off for scratching something inside his desk lid. Sylvie smiled; it sounded as though Jess was settling in all right. She'd gone to sleep with her satchel at the foot of the bed, ready for the morning.

From the front room came the sound of a record: Ella Fitzgerald singing in her rich, full voice. Sylvie dried her hands, opened a bottle of beer and poured a glassful for Henry and a shandy for herself, and took them through. If the day had been rocky, the strait she was embarking on now was going to need all her piloting skill.

Henry was stretched out with his feet on the sofa and his arms behind his head, his eyes closed, losing himself in the music. Sylvie settled in an armchair and sipped her shandy, contenting herself with a browse through Pa Garton's books. Dickens, Wodehouse, gardening and history were mixed in with weighty texts on cattle diseases and pest control, all left here because of lack of room in his parents' house. She began to read a fat nineteenth-century novel. There was no point hurrying Henry: he enjoyed what he called a "companionable silence"; it helped him wind down after the day.

At length she passed his beer over to the low table at his side and he roused himself and took a drink. He lay back again but couldn't seem to find a comfortable position.

"My shoulders are killing me," he said, "and tomorrow I'll have to get the wire up."

"Won't that be easier?" Sylvie said.

"Nope. It takes a fair bit of elbow grease to get a good tension in it. It uses all the same muscles really."

"Do you want me to give your shoulders a rub?" she said.

He swung his legs down and sat up. She stood behind the sofa and began to knead his shoulders through his shirt, pushing her thumbs up towards his collar. He moved his head slowly in a circle, releasing the tension in his neck, and letting out a big sigh.

"I paid a lot of bills today," she started tentatively. "I couldn't help noticing . . . we seem to have quite a few piling up." She felt Henry's back stiffen, but kept on with the rhythmic movement of her hands, squeezing down on to his shoulders, pushing up towards his neck, smoothing down and starting again. "I was wondering if there was anything I could do to help."

He sat up straight, pulling away from her. "Your hand must be hurting doing that."

Sylvie touched the patch of plaster on her palm. "I know I wasn't much use as a fencer," she said, "but I can use my head. We could talk about the money side of things; I might be able to come up with some ideas."

Henry made a snorting noise.

Sylvie come round and sat at the other end of the sofa. He took a long pull at his drink, avoiding turning to look at her. She waited.

"Look, love, we both know that what's coming in each week just isn't enough," she said.

Henry set his glass down with a thump. "Do you think I should take on more beasts, then, without any more men to handle them? Do you think I'm not working hard enough?"

"No, no, that's not what I'm saying at all. What I think is . . ." she paused, forcing herself to slow down, "that we should try to raise some capital, just to tide us over until things get easier, or to pay off a bit of the loan."

He looked at her as though she were witless. "You just don't understand at all, do you? The farm has been in this family for generations, and every Garton who's ever farmed it has added to it, in extra acreage, or buildings, or stock. You can't seriously expect me to be the first to *sell some land off.*"

Sylvie coloured, stung by his tone. "Why not? It's not as if you can put Turner's fields to much use anyway, you're so busy you'll never get round to clearing them. And if you did, you can't get the combine down the track." She got up and stood with her back to the fireplace. "And who's going to criticize you if you sell them? You talk as though your ancestors are watching you, sitting in judgement. It's just something in your head; yet another thing you've made for yourself to live up to."

Henry spoke with exaggerated slowness. "I a-m n-o-t going to have anyone think my farm is on the skids."

"Is that what this is all about, then: your reputation in The Green Man?"

Henry remained stubbornly silent.

"I think it must be, because your dad certainly wouldn't disapprove."

Sylvie busied herself putting the record back into its sleeve and finding the tray to collect up the glasses, hoping Henry wouldn't notice her slip.

"What do you mean Dad wouldn't disapprove? Have you been discussing it with him? He's put you up to this, hasn't he? He's never been off my back since I got that bloody loan."

Sylvie bit her lip. She stood holding the tray and made no move to take it to the kitchen.

"Yes," she said quietly, "I did talk to your dad because I was worried. He happened to mention that Mick Swift was looking for a bigger place and we kind of put the two things together. You could at least consider it; it'd solve a lot of problems."

"I tell you what: I don't consider having Mick Swift and his odd-job-man clutter on my land as solving any problems whatsoever."

Henry stood up, took the tray from her and marched into the kitchen with it. Sylvie, left standing like a dismissed attendant, felt her patience wear out. She followed him and planted herself in the doorway.

"Now listen, Henry, this isn't going to go away and it's no good us sticking our heads in the sand. If you won't even consider doing anything about it, I'll have to do something myself."

"Such as?"

"I'll get a job."

"You can't," said Henry, shaking his head in disbelief. "I'd be a laughing stock; people would say I can't keep my own wife. I won't have it."

He dumped the glasses and the tray on to the draining board and went to lock up. He shot the top bolt with a force that rattled the door.

Sylvie found that she was trembling. "I will do it, Henry", she said.

Later they lay back to back in bed, both holding themselves stiffly away from the dip in the middle of the mattress, where they usually slept as close as spoons in a drawer. Sylvie thought how painful his shoulders would be in the morning if he kept this up all night.

"We could always just rent that bit of land out", she said into the room. "That wouldn't be so final".

He reached out of bed and made a great fuss of checking that the alarm was set for milking. "Did you post that feed order?" he said.

"No. I forgot. I'm sorry".

"Fine job you'd get; can't even be trusted to post a letter".

He pulled the blankets taut. Sylvie felt a coldness slip between them, as icy as the air on her bare skin.

CHAPTER
SIX

Jess

The phone rang as I was coming downstairs and I grabbed it before it could ring again and bring Dad out from the front room.

"Hello?" I said.

"It's me," said Nicola. "Are you all right? You've been off all week. I was beginning to get worried."

"Dad's not letting me come to school," I said flatly.

"What?"

"I got into trouble about the fair and now I'm not allowed out at all. He's got it into his head that people at school are a bad influence."

"I'll get Mum to bring me over to see you," Nicola said.

"Uh-uh. You're public enemy number one, I'm afraid."

"Oh." There was a pause. "I see. God, I'm sorry, Jess. I shouldn't have persuaded you to come."

"Don't worry," I said, my voice catching, "I would've gone anyway."

In the background I could hear the faint sound of piano scales being played and a sudden burst of laughter.

"Martin asked where you were," Nicola said tentatively. "He wanted to know if we were going to the end-of-year dance. It's two weeks on Saturday."

"I can't see it happening," I said miserably. "Dad says he's not even sure whether I should do my exams."

"You're joking!"

"He says there's no point, because I'm only going to be helping here anyway."

"But what about you wanting to do medicine?"

"He doesn't think it's for the likes of us." I sat down in a huddle on the bottom step of the stairs.

"Hang on a minute, that's not right, he should be proud of you! Crikey, my mum and dad'll be pleased if I just scrape in for sociology."

I couldn't answer her. I'd been doing all right at home all week, keeping busy, seeing to the calves, and the house, and trying to make things up to Tom by cooking him all his favourite dinners. I'd even bitten my tongue when Dad had made heavy comments about how nice it was to have a bit of support and how a home needed a woman's touch. I'd been all right as long as I didn't start thinking about what I couldn't have.

"Jess — are you still there?"

"I'm still here," I said with a gulp.

"Now listen to me, you're not to give up that easily. This is your life we're talking about. We're on study leave from now on anyway, so you're no worse off than anyone else, so you're going to get your books out and start revising."

"I've only got half of them, though. All my chemistry books are still in my locker and I've missed all the revision notes."

"Don't worry about that. I'll sort that out," she said.

I blew my nose. "Well, I shouldn't bother posting them. If he thinks I'm getting anything from the outside world he'll probably confiscate it."

Nic laughed.

"You think I'm joking. I tell you, he's getting seriously weird. The bank rang up today and he told me to tell them he was away and he wouldn't be back until next Tuesday. I felt such a fool. The manager said, 'Just tell him to ring me,' in this flat, fed-up voice."

The sound of a chair being pushed back in the front room brought me up short.

"I'd better go," I said.

"OK. Chin up. Or, rather, head down over your favourite biology book, eh? And don't worry: I'll get you your notes somehow. Speak to you soon."

There was a click as Nic hung up. I put the receiver down softly and went quietly to retrieve my school bag from the scullery, where it had lain since the Friday night before the fair. The dogs came to meet me, whimpering and squirming with excitement as I bent to stroke them. "Shh," I said, taking their collars and leading them back to their bedding. I dusted the dog hair off my bag and hefted it on to my shoulder.

Dad had been strangely formal since what I thought of as "the Big Row". He wasn't likely to even call out goodnight these days, never mind put his head round the door the way he did when I was a child; I could work in peace in my room for as long as I could stay awake.

The next morning I struggled through breakfast, yawning over the fried bread and sausages I'd cooked. I ran out to the car as Mrs Jones was about to pull away, to give Tom his spelling book, which he'd left on the table. Mrs Jones wound the window down and I passed the exercise book in.

"Are you feeling any better, Jess?" she asked.

"I'm fine," I answered, momentarily puzzled.

"Your dad said last week you'd had a bug. I must say you do look drained."

"No — really, just a bit tired, that's all. School's finished now anyway. How's Ralphy?"

"A bit fretful at night. It's the heat, I think. We got my grandma's old zinc bath out of the garage yesterday and had it out on the lawn. He loved it in the water; he was kicking his little legs like mad." She leant out of the window. "Well, to be honest, I got in too, I was so frazzled. I suppose I'm going to have to stop doing it, though, now they're bringing in these water spies."

"Water spies?"

"Didn't you see it in the paper? The Water Board is sending people round to check if anyone's wasting any — you know, hose-pipes and suchlike." She nodded as if to convince me of the truth of what she was saying. "Apparently you're liable to get a knock on your door if your lawn's too green. I said to old man Wilmore next door, he'd better get some camouflage on his marrows, but he just laughed. Turns out the crafty old trout's been piping his bath water on to the garden! Not a bad idea, though, come to think of it."

"Still no forecast of rain, then?" I asked.

"Not a drop. Water Board's saying they warned after last year's dry spell that a drought was on the way and the reservoirs were getting low but no one took any notice. So now we've got to have shallow baths and put stones in the loo cistern."

Over in the fields behind the car I could see the flash of our new spray-lines as they rotated over a field of sugar beet, sprinkling the field with water pumped from the river. Mrs Jones followed my gaze.

"You'll be all right," she said. "Farming's got top priority, hasn't it? And the river runs over your land."

"We still have to have a licence, though; we're only supposed to take so much out, and if the reservoir's getting low already . . ."

We both watched the glittering mist being thrown out on to the crop.

"Je-ess," Tom moaned. He was fiddling in the back seat, flicking the tiny ashtray drawer open and shut. "I'm going to be late and then I'll have to do book duty."

"I'd better be off, then," Mrs Jones said. She peered at me once more. "I'm going to bring you some iron tonic tonight," she said: "you've got half-moons under your eyes."

I watched the car move off, its tyres kicking up little spurts of dust as it bumped into the potholes in the track. I felt like something washed up on a beach from a ship that's steaming purposefully away.

Dad came into the yard, wiping the sweat off his forehead with the back of his hand. "Breakfast?" he said.

"On the table under a plate," I said. "I'm just going to clear up."

I followed him in, waiting behind him as he pulled off his boots in the scullery. I went over to the sink in the kitchen to start washing up and he made a small impatient sound. I lifted the bowl out of the sink and stood to one side to let him wash his hands. He scrubbed at them, leaving veins of dirt in the cracks of the dry sliver of soap, then rinsed them, then started again. Holding the bowl full of plates and pans was making my arms ache, but I didn't say anything. This was how it had been all week, treating each other with the kind of distant consideration that you might give to someone you'd just met. He dried his hands and sat down to his breakfast and I lowered the washing-up bowl back into the sink slowly so as not to make a splash.

"There's brown sauce there," I said.

"Thanks", he said, but carried on eating, staring at the calendar pinned to the beam.

The picture for the month of June was of a prize Hereford bull sporting a red rosette, with a stockman in a pristine white coat standing beside him, arms smugly folded. Dad was making slight nodding movements with his head as his eyes passed over the dates under the photo, counting down the days to the end of the month. When he got to the end he started again, as though unwilling to believe his own mental arithmetic.

"Dad?" I said.

He turned slowly towards me. His eyes regained their focus. "Sauce," he said. "Yes, I know." He put his knife and fork together, as if ordering his thoughts. "I'll need you to fill the bowser and take water to the cattle troughs," he said. "The pond at the corner of Five Acres is drying up."

"Right," I said, stacking dishes on the draining board. "Does it have to be today, though, if the pond's not empty yet?"

"With the water so low the cows'll walk into it to get cool and get away from the flies. It'll end up like a slurry pit if they stand around in it all day. I'm going to have to move them while I fence it off."

"It'll take ages to fill the bowser from the yard tap," I said. "The pressure's right down."

Dad tutted. "Don't be daft," he said. "Fill it from the river. The pump on the old tractor that's feeding the spray-lines: just switch it over to fill the bowser. Then you can take the tractor to haul it and fill the troughs."

"I don't know how . . ."

"Just switch them over," he said with exaggerated slowness.

I put the frying pan on the pile of draining dishes and it slipped sideways and clattered on the enamel surface.

Dad gave a heavy sigh. "Make sure you rig it all back up to the spray-lines, won't you. We can't afford to lose the beet. I'll come down and check the pump filters and the oil level on the tractor later; that John Deere's living on borrowed time."

"What time do you want lunch?" I asked.

"'Bout twelve."

He picked up his fork again and pushed a piece of bacon rind around on his plate.

"Is something on your mind, Dad?"

"I can't decide whether to cut the hay; what with all this water hauling and fencing I'm a bit short of time. But then, it's ideal for mowing now: what if I leave it and the weather breaks?" He tapped the side of the fork on the edge of the plate, thinking.

"What does the weatherman say?" I asked.

He pushed his plate away abruptly. "Dry," he said. "But what do they know? They said we'd have a wet winter and it was so dry the grass froze hard without a drop of frost." He snorted. "Trouble is, if I leave cutting it too long and the weather breaks while it's still drying, we could lose the lot. That's nigh on five hundred pounds' worth of hay."

He sat for a while with his elbows on the table, his chin resting on his balled fists.

I dried the plates and put them back in the rack one by one.

"We will be all right, won't we, Dad?" I paused with the last plate in my hand.

Dad fished the Land-Rover keys out of his pocket and slid them across the table towards me. "If everyone pulls their weight," he said.

I hitched up the empty bowser to take it down to the tractor to fill. Already the inside of the Land-Rover was unbearably hot and smelt of rubber tyre and dog. My bare legs stuck to the seat as soon as I sat down and I wound the windows right down, to try to get a bit of a breeze in. I'd been driving it for about a year now and was free to go where I liked within the boundaries of the farm — well, almost where I liked. Dad had finally given in and taught me, on condition that I didn't go further than the fields this side of the river. He said the bends down by the bridge were dangerous and I might meet the milk tanker or a delivery lorry coming the other way. Even when I could turn the damn thing on a pin he wouldn't change his mind. All he'd said was: "Your manoeuvring isn't bad, but you're still riding the clutch." After that he let me do a bit of fetching and carrying in it on my own. "Don't get big-headed," he said. "You need lots of practice before you'll be safe anywhere near another vehicle."

As I wove from side to side of the dirt track to avoid the worst of the ruts, anxiety niggled like a buzzing fly. The feeling stayed with me while I switched the pump over, making my fingers feel all thumbs. I pulled away slowly in the tractor, afraid that despite its fat moon-buggy wheels the heavy bowser would stick in a rut and the engine would stall. Diesel fumes filled the air and a bluish cloud of exhaust rose behind me, but finally I pulled safely away.

I stopped at the field entrance and jumped down to open the gate. It made me think of Tom, because this was usually his job. I wished I had him with me; he would soon shake me out of this anxious feeling. He enjoyed the bumps and jolts of driving over a field, making great play of bouncing up and down in his seat and shouting out, "Thunderbirds are go!" He at least was highly impressed with my driving ability and would make me laugh with the comic racing commentary he kept up as we went.

Sometimes he asked me why Dad never took him out with him to do jobs, and I had to say Dad was very busy or that he wouldn't have time to show him how to help today, or palm him off with some task that I needed him to do for me. We both knew Dad hadn't got any patience with him. He would blame Tom for fidgeting or not listening, for letting go of something, or for holding on too tight, for not being near enough to pass something to, or for "getting under my feet". Dad would never stop his headlong rush to get things done long enough to explain to Tom exactly what he wanted him to do.

I shut the gate after me, then drove slowly across the field, nosing my way through the groups of cows, which lumbered off a little way as I approached, then stood, gazing curiously, swishing their tails. When I stopped they began to move in a leisurely way towards me, the heat slowing their pace.

I backed the bowser up close to the feeder so that I didn't have far to lug the heavy hose. The ground around the feeder had been stripped of grass and churned up by the cows' feet to stand in dry ridges of orange earth that crumbled as I stood on them. The grass itself, still green on top, had an under-layer of feg, a dead fawn colour, like old hair left caught in the bristles of a hairbrush.

100

I hauled the plastic hose across to the water trough and then opened the tap. The hose twitched and water splashed on to the earth, darkening it to a rich mocha, and I straightened the hose out again. It gushed into the trough, making me feel parched. I could feel sweat spreading in a patch on the back of my shirt and my clothes felt itchy and uncomfortable. It had taken ages to pump the water and cart it up here; now I imagined it starting to evaporate into the clear blue sky. I banged against the side of the trough to hurry the cattle up, then clanged it again and again. "Oh, come on, for pity's sake!" I shouted at the beasts, then threw the hose in a loop on top of the bowser and climbed back up on to the tractor seat.

I rested my head on the steering wheel. I'd been trying to impress Dad with how hard I was working, hoping he'd relent and let me pick up the reins of my life again. Surely, I'd thought, if I show willing and help out, he'll let me go back to school and carry on. At least I would see Martin, even if it was difficult for us to be alone. And if I could just do my exams and get my grades, I would worry later on about persuading Dad to let me leave home for university.

Now it seemed that everything was far worse than I'd thought. If Dad was really banking on having me to help, this wasn't just him punishing me, setting one of his strange tests of family loyalty. This was a crisis. Dad really would have me throw away my one chance of a different life, for the sake of the farm. And it would fail anyway. Pictures flicked through my mind: the newspaper headlines about the drought — SAVE OUR

SUPPLIES, COUNTRYSIDE A TINDERBOX, STANDPIPES THREATENED — the letter in a brown envelope with the news of rising bank rates; the red reminder for the electricity bill, which Dad had shoved behind the clock. I shut my eyes tight. It was all hopeless. I would miss my exams and my chance for a future and it would all be for nothing. And if by some miracle we were to make it through this year, it would be proof to Dad that having me home made the farm viable, and he would never let me go. It was what Nicola called a "no-win situation".

I sat up and stared out at the dusty backs of the Friesians pressing around the water trough. Satisfied, one raised its head, water dripping from its black muzzle. It gazed levelly back at me, then, butted under its chin by another animal trying to get through, it stretched up, rolling its eyes, and turned to walk a few paces away.

Towards the back of the group was the cow Tom and I had nicknamed "Pirate", because it had been blind in one eye from birth. One eye was the dark liquid brown you would expect; the other was covered with a milky-blue film, as if the caul had stuck there, never to be removed. I watched her standing waiting for some space to clear at the trough side, making no effort to move to the front, accepting her place in the herd. She blinked, disturbing the flies around her head momentarily, but they immediately returned, settling around her ears and eyes. Only when the first crush had drunk, and the hot bodies had thinned out, did she step forward and bend her neck to drink, long and deep.

Maisie-May, the boss cow, stopped to scratch herself against the bonnet.

"Give over!" I said and gave her a push. Dust rose from her flank, smelling of cow-pat. "Give over, you great lummox."

She stepped lazily aside and looked at me with huge uncomprehending eyes.

The rest of the day passed in a series of tasks. I filled other troughs, then re-attached the spray-line to the pump and left the bowser down there for later, as that evening I'd need to go through the whole palaver again. I cooked lunch and sat and ate it with Dad in near silence as he pored over the paper, and then washed up all over again. I handed him nails while he fixed some loose shuttering on the cowshed and fed our three calves water from pop bottles fitted with teats, because the milk they were getting wasn't enough for them in the heat.

When Tom came home from school I made him a jam sandwich and sent him off out with it, so that I could iron his school shirts, a biology book propped up on the sideboard in front of me. By half past five the rhythmic strokes of the iron were coming slower and slower, every muscle ached and the words on the page blurred and shifted in front of my eyes. I shook my head like a dog coming out of water, then went to call Tom in to lend a hand and set the table.

The heat in the yard took my breath away. It radiated from every surface, striking up from the concrete hard-standing and bouncing back from the stone walls of the house and the barn. It was like being in an incubator. As I pulled the door shut behind me the metal handle felt almost too hot to touch. "Tom!" I called, but the heat seemed to deaden the sound and cut it short, holding it within the walls of the surrounding buildings.

The yard was deserted save for the house martins renovating their nests in the eaves, and suddenly another summer came back to me: my mother standing right where I was now, calling me to come and see the mud nests and the birds darting in and out, feeding their young. We'd stood together, watching them.

"They always come back to the same nest to patch it up," she'd said. "Mind you, they only really stop to nest. Imagine that! They can live and feed and sleep in the air, like a fish does in water." I'd leant against her loose overdress, my head against the swell of her belly, and she'd laughed and said, "That's right. I'm well and properly grounded."

Now here I was, standing in her place: *standing in*, yes, that was how I saw myself, a substitute holding the fort until she returned to take over. I was trying to keep everything going so that she could just walk back in one day and pick up where she had left off, the pans in the kitchen still hanging in the same order, Tom's bath nights still the same, Tuesdays still fish pie and Sundays a roast dinner. *Come back*, I thought closing my eyes, *come back while it's all still here!* I conjured her figure beside me, the upward tilt of her chin as she watched the birds, one hand shading her eyes, the other resting just below her breast as if to hold herself steady. But when I opened my eyes it was to the same dusty, empty scene. The birds twittered and dabbed at the nests above, undisturbed by my sudden march across the yard or my voice calling more and more stridently for Tom.

After half an hour of fruitless searching I began to feel worried. Tom knew we'd eat around six and was usually back in good time, bringing with him an adult-sized appetite. I climbed up into the hayloft. There was a stale, fusty smell and a den made out of the remains of last year's bales and some old sacks. It was empty; all that was there were a couple of saucers, one with a circular crust of old milk and the other with a few scraps of chicken. A jumper stuffed with hay made shift as a pillow, and a pile of *Beanos* and *Dandys* suggested that this was a regular hideout.

I was turning to climb down the ladder when it struck me that tom had asked me at breakfast if a kitten would miss its family. I'd been packing up his lunch at the time and had said I didn't know and asked him if he wanted cheese or Marmite. Swift's, I thought, that's where he'll be, and I laboured down the ladder with a sigh of annoyance.

I went back to the house and set out the salad and some ham in case Dad came in, so he'd just think we'd gone ahead and eaten without him. Then I set off down the track towards the river, more and more convinced that despite Dad's strictures Swift's was where Tom would be.

I reached the fields of Swift's smallholding, where goats were tethered to chew over the grass they could reach, while eyeing the grass being saved for another day. Bantams strutted and pecked among them, or roosted under the hen-house, where there was a scant patch of shade. Radio One played loudly from the barn-like building, the old farrowing shed.

I picked my way across the yard, where three motorbikes were parked at angles, among piles of car batteries, a lawn mower and a cement-mixer. I hesitated at the garden gate, unsure how to let them know I was there. The garden path was almost overgrown with lavender bushes, their flowers losing their vivid blue as they dried on the stalk. A washing line hung with sheets and overalls stretched across the path, supported in the middle by a long wooden clothes prop to allow passage to the house. The cottage itself had a shuttered look, with the curtains half drawn across, as if everyone might be asleep. I rested my hand on the gate.

Mrs Swift came round the corner, carrying a washing basket. She wore a long sleeveless smock dress covered with tiny mauve flowers, and a pair of yellow flip-flops. Around her neck was a daisy chain.

"Excuse me," I said, "but I wondered if my brother Tom was here."

She smiled and came towards me. "You're Jess, aren't you?" she said. "Tom's told us all about you." She opened the gate. "I've seen you in the village too, at the post office, remember?"

I remembered all too well my embarrassment at my father's curt nod when Mrs Swift had said hello as we stood waiting for Mrs Bartlett to serve us.

"Is Tom here?" I said. "Only, it's really his tea-time."

"Oh, don't disturb him yet," she said. "He's having such a lovely time. Come in, come in."

She put the washing basket down to open the gate still wider. I followed her up the path, amazed at her long plait of greying hair that hung almost to her waist. Her dress pulled on the lavender stems as she passed, dislodging drowsy bees and dusty seeds. The overalls strung across the path had dried as stiff as boards; we pushed through them, cardboard cutouts pegged up by the shoulders.

She led me into a dim kitchen. As my eyes grew accustomed to the pinkish light, the unfamiliar shapes in the room began to resolve themselves: a basket of eggs on the drainer waiting to be washed, still stuck all over with feathers, a kitchen table with plastic-topped stools, two easy chairs and a stove. A twin-tub washing machine in the corner stood with its hose still dripping into a plastic bucket full of sudsy water.

"I'm saving it for the garden," Mrs Swift said, following my glance. "It vexes me to see the flowers dying."

Along the window-sill a row of demijohns bubbled intermittently, filtering the light through the pale gold of elderflower and the rose pink of rhubarb wine, to make stained-glass-window patterns on the far white-washed wall.

"What can I get you?" Mrs Swift said, gesturing that I should sit down.

A stool grated on the lino floor and two kittens shot out and skittered across the shiny surface and out of the door. Tom's head emerged from underneath the table.

"Can I have some dandelion-and-burdock?" he said.

"Tom!" I said, embarrassed by his lack of manners, but Mrs Swift just smiled.

"You know where it is," she said. "I expect we'd all like some while you're there. Give Mick and Grandpa a shout, would you."

Tom ran off outside and Mrs Swift took some ginger biscuits from a tin marked "Flour", and put them on a plate. Tom returned, followed by Mick Swift, who had to duck his head as he came in. He wiped his hands on his overall front. His skin was tanned a deep brown and his longish dark hair and unshaven chin gave him a gypsy look. He was followed by a very old man whose bald head poked forward as he walked, his back misshapen by a hump. Mrs Swift plumped up a cushion in the armchair opposite me and the old man lowered himself slowly into it.

"How's your father coping with this weather?" he said, his posture and keen gaze giving me the impression of being questioned by an inquisitive tortoise.

"We're managing," I said. "We're pumping water from the river."

He sucked air in through his teeth. "The river level's dropping, y'know. They're taking water out for the reservoir. Not that it's doing much good. It'll be just like 'forty-four all over again," he finished, underscoring his point by tapping a bony finger on the arm of his chair.

"Here, Grandpa, have a ginger biscuit," Mrs Swift cut in, handing him a plate.

"You know I can't eat them without a drink, with my teeth," he said testily.

"Oh well then," said Mick, reaching a big hand towards the unwanted biscuits with a broad wink.

"Not with hands like that," said Mrs Swift. "WD40's no good for the digestion. Go and give them a good scrub."

Mick crouched down at the bucket of soapy water by the washing machine and rubbed his hands in the suds.

"That'll do my zinnias a whole lot of good," Mrs Swift said, but she was smiling.

"Where's my cup of tea?" said Grandpa.

"We haven't got tea, Grandpa — it's too hot."

She handed him a glass and he began to dunk his biscuit into the dark-brown liquid. He nibbled at the edge with a suspicious look.

"You all take the river for granted," he said, "because it's never dropped hardly at all in years. But back in 'forty-four it all but dried up; they had to get the army in", he said, peering round at everyone to make sure he had our attention.

Mick Swift was wearing the patient smile of one who's heard a story many times before and knows he's about to hear it again, but Grandpa's attention had returned to saving his soggy biscuit from dropping into his glass.

I took a sip of my drink. "Has the dry spell affected you very badly?" I asked Mick.

"Not really. Our livestock's pretty limited. It's not the same as having milking cows to keep watered." He pushed his sleeves up further, beyond his elbows.

"Makes for hot work, but we mustn't grumble. To be honest, the machine business was never better: everyone's getting out equipment they haven't used for years and finding it's in pretty bad nick." He grinned. "Not the kind of thing to say down The Green Man, though."

"Canvas ponds," Grandpa said.

We all looked back at him. I noticed that he and Tom had quietly finished off the biscuits between them.

"That's what they used in 'forty-four," he added, "the army. They set up canvas ponds in all the villages and you had to get your water in pots and pans." He gave a wheezy laugh. "You should've seen us all trying to carry it home without spilling it."

"Like an egg-and-spoon race," said Tom and they both started giggling.

"Any more biscuits?" said Mick. "Me and Grandpa had better get on."

Mrs Swift handed him the tin and Grandpa followed him slowly out to the shed.

"You see what I have to put up with?" Mrs Swift said good-naturedly. "Pour us some more drinks, Tom, would you?"

Tom picked up the earthenware bottle by the small round handle at its neck and poured a little too much into each glass so that it frothed over on to the tray.

"Mind, you're dripping," I said as he picked his glass up and took a long drink. He ran the hem of his Aertex shirt under the glass absentmindedly. I rolled my eyes in mock despair but Mrs Swift was unfazed. She picked up my glass, ran her finger underneath it and licked it before handing the drink to me. We looked at each other and started to laugh.

"He's a proper boy, isn't he, your Tom?" she said, putting her hand on his shoulder.

"I can see he's made himself at home," I said. "I hope he's not been any trouble."

She shook her head quickly. "No trouble — in fact, he's my head cook and bottle-washer, aren't you? He's a dab hand at egg-hunting too."

"I got all those today," Tom said nodding at the basket. "Can I go and find Lolly?"

"Don't be long," I said. "Dad'll wonder where we've got to."

"You can take some eggs home, Tom, you got so many." Mrs Swift gave his shoulder a squeeze, then made a shooing gesture as if giving him leave to go. She began to wrap the eggs individually in newspaper and place them carefully in a brown-paper bag. "You're doing a good job with that lad," she said over her shoulder.

"Thank you," I muttered, unsure whether to feel wary at her knowledge of our family affairs.

She settled in the chair opposite, still nursing the bag of eggs on her lap. She said nothing more, and seemed to be waiting for me to speak.

"It's funny sometimes, being a sister who has to be a mum," I blurted out all of a sudden.

She nodded, as if considering what I'd said carefully. Her eyes were brown, and around them were many tiny lines that crinkled and deepened when she was thinking.

"Twice the responsibility." She rolled the top of the paper bag, folding it over in neat creases. "Hard on you. I know your mum would be proud, you know, of both of you."

I looked up quickly. "Did you know Mum? I didn't think Mum was . . ."

"Allowed to mix with the interlopers?" She smiled. "I saw her around the place. She used to walk a lot, watch the birds, and sometimes she'd call in . . . at least, until Tom came along, then we sort of lost touch."

"You were friends then?" I asked eagerly.

"Yes, we were friends," she said quietly. "You don't stop being friends just because you don't see someone."

"Why? Why didn't you see each other any more? Was it to do with Tom?"

Mrs Swift sighed. "Partly," she said. "Mick and I never had kids — it just didn't happen for us — and your mum knew how much I wanted to." She looked down, twisting the corners of the bag into little peaks. "I think she stayed away to save me hurt. And I didn't go to her because I didn't want to make things difficult for her . . . with your dad."

"I'm sorry," I said, not really knowing how to respond to this confidence from an older woman. "That's really awful."

"Well, I suppose we both thought we were doing the right thing." Mrs Swift looked towards the window as if it could show her the past. "Although now I don't think I was a good enough friend to her, given the circumstances."

112

I concentrated on the bars of pink and gold light falling across the draining board and on to the kitchen floor. My voice came out very small.

"Why do you think she left?"

She shook her head. "She was sometimes very lonely, I think."

"But that doesn't make sense! She had us." My voice was trembling. "If you're lonely you don't run away from the people who love you."

She reached across and touched my hand. "I know. I know. It wasn't anything to do with you and Tom: she loved you both to distraction. It was the farm, the farming life; it just didn't give her what she needed."

I frowned. "It was Dad, wasn't it? That's what you're saying really. She didn't love Dad any more."

She said nothing.

I felt sick. "Or Dad didn't love her."

"Oh, no; your dad was distraught when she went. Wouldn't eat. Wouldn't leave the house. It was your grandad who went driving all over the countryside looking for her. It was him filed the missing person's report. Your dad was much too ill — he was good for nothing."

I sat in silence, remembering those awful days after Mum had gone: the drawn curtains, the grown-ups talking in hushed voices, taking Tom into bed with me when he cried and Gran couldn't comfort him. Days I'd tried hard to wipe from my mind.

"I'm sorry." Mrs Swift took my hand in hers. "I didn't mean to drag all this up for you. I only meant to be encouraging. I just wanted you to know how very much she loved you."

"But not enough to stay," I said.

"Do you talk to your dad about this?" she asked.

I said nothing.

"Look, sometimes people find themselves living a life that's slowly killing them and they just have to get out. It's sheer self-preservation. I know you're young, but can you understand?"

She looked into my eyes, searching. I blinked away tears, refused to hold her gaze. She got up, crossed to the ironing basket and brought me a creased handkerchief.

"Here," she said.

"She didn't ever write to you, did she?" I asked, my voice hoarse.

Mrs Swift shook her head. "You?"

"No. Never."

The word *never* sent a chill through me. I thought about the stones and the chimes down by the river. Letters weren't the only kind of message you could send, I told myself.

"I should be going." I looked around vaguely. "Thank you for looking after Tom. I hope he hasn't been a nuisance. I'm sorry . . . for what you said about not having a family," I said, feeling awkward.

"Oh, it's all right." She smiled, then moved the conversation back on to more conventional ground. "You're welcome to send Tom over any time; we're always pleased to see him. It's extra company for Philip too," she added. "He's at a bit of a loose end at the moment without a summer job."

I blew my nose. "Who's Philip?" I asked.

"He's my nephew, on loan from my sister for the rest of the holidays," she said with a wry smile. "Hardly a child any more, though." She glanced towards a large pair of biker's boots lying on their sides beside the chair. "He's nineteen now, and halfway through his degree." She righted the boots and stood them up in a pair against the chair leg. "I don't suppose your dad's looking for any help, is he?" she asked.

No way would Dad take on any relation of the Swifts'. "Not at the moment," I lied. "I'll ask him, though, if you like," I stumbled, feeling my colour rise.

She sighed, appearing not to notice. "He says he wants to earn his keep, you see. Not that that bothers us at all. Still, he's got his name down with Lasenby's, so by harvest he should get some contract work."

"Good idea," I said, making a move to get up. "I'm sorry, but I think we'd better get back."

She took my empty glass and put into my hands the bag of eggs, still warm from her lap. I went to the door and called for Tom. He was in the yard, crouching astride an ancient grey Harley Davidson with RAF stencilled on its tank. He was leaning forward, making racing noises, with Lolly draped over his shoulder. I called him again and he climbed down reluctantly.

"Don't forget," said Mrs Swift, "you're both welcome — come any time."

"Thanks for the eggs," I said.

"See you!" shouted Tom.

★　★　★

As we walked home across the fields Tom kept up a constant chatter about all the things he did at the Swifts', how Mick let him make things in the workshop and Mrs Swift had shown him how to make popcorn. I let him talk on, making encouraging noises from time to time while inside my head Mrs Swift's words went round and round. My mum had sometimes been desperately unhappy. And we had not been enough to console her. Conscious of Tom trotting beside me, earnestly telling me everything he'd taught Lolly to do, for a moment I felt the shadow of a different feeling, not my usual sadness and longing, but the stirring of anger. How could she, I thought, he was only a baby. On an impulse I took his hand and gave it a squeeze and he looked up at me, surprised.

"Don't go off without telling me again," I said gruffly.

When we reached the track I saw that there was a car parked in the yard. A blue Renault with a parking sticker on the windscreen, it seemed somehow familiar. I shoved the eggs at Tom.

"Put these in your den with Lolly, so Dad doesn't ask where they've come from," I said. "I'm going to find out who it is."

"It's not the Welfare, is it, Jess? Is it?"

"No, of course not. Don't be silly. You hide Lolly away and then come in just as normal. OK?"

Tom slipped away towards the hayloft.

As I came in through the scullery all was quiet. The kitchen too was empty; the table still set as I'd left it, the salad beginning to look tired, the lettuce limp. It looked as though the visitor must have been here for some time. I crept through to the hall. The door to the front room was a little ajar and I could hear two low voices. I sidled nearer.

"You say she's a promising student," my father was saying, "but, frankly, I don't see the point for a farmer's daughter."

"All I'm saying is that the potential is there and it seems a shame not to develop what God's given her."

It was Mr Bailey's voice. I froze, pressing my shoulders against the wall, the rough plaster chilly against my back.

"Let's not bring God into it," said my father in a deliberately pleasant tone that belied the snub. "Jess is needed at home. Farming's a family affair, you know, Mr Bailey."

No response came and I imagined Mr Bailey furrowing his brow as he listened with the intense concentration that he applied to anyone else's argument.

"Ah, yes. Family, that's important," he said at length. "How old is Jess now? Seventeen?" There was a creaking noise as though Dad was shifting in his chair. Mr Bailey pressed on. "So she's got perhaps three years, maybe five, before she meets someone and wants to settle down herself?"

"Exactly!" Dad said. "That's exactly why spending a lot of time and money on a course would be wasted." There was the muffled thump of a hand hitting the chair arm as he drove home his point.

Mr Bailey spoke in a carefully measured tone. "Or you could say that those few years are her only chance to grasp an opportunity that she can draw on in later life."

"Well, we have different points of view, I'm afraid," said Dad, not quite managing to match Mr Bailey's mildness.

"Ah, it's a hard job being a parent," said Mr Bailey. "I know it myself."

"We agree on that," said Dad.

"A big responsibility, children, running a home, paying a mortgage . . ."

"True enough," said Dad.

I heard the back door bang as Tom came in.

"Not something perhaps that we would wish upon our children before they've had a chance to stretch their wings, to see what they can do for themselves, so to speak."

There was a long pause.

"Jess! Je-ess!" Tom called from the scullery.

I edged back to the kitchen door to sign to him to be quiet, still straining to hear. It was no good: the low voices had sunk to a mutter. I scowled at Tom from the door, putting my finger to my lips.

"What's the matter? I'm starving," he said, reaching for a piece of bread, regardless of its curling corners.

There were noises now from the front room of leavetaking.

"Come on." I grabbed myself some bread and pulled Tom by the hand.

"Is it the visitor? Who is it?" he said.

118

"It's my teacher." The thought of being confronted by Mr Bailey and Dad together was too embarrassing to contemplate. I pulled Tom outside.

"Where're we going?" he said.

"I'm going for a walk; you can do what you want."

Tom shrugged and sauntered back off towards the hayloft, rolling the bread into dough balls. I walked as fast as I could back down the drive towards the river, hoping that anyone watching would think I looked purposeful, and not filled with an agony of curiosity.

I was just coming level with the gate into Five Acres when I heard the car behind me. I stopped and stepped into the gateway to let it pass. The Renault drew up on to the verge and Mr Bailey got out of the car and walked back to me.

"Hello, Jess," he said. "I've been having a word with your father about your exams." I thought my chest would burst with the breath that I seemed unable to let out. "I seem to have talked him round to letting you sit them," he said in the same level tone he used in class.

"That's good," I managed to say.

"It is. It is good, Jess." He came and leant his elbows on top of the gate, looking out over the fields towards where the river swung round in a great curve. "Now what you have to do is your very best. You won't let me down now, will you?"

I shook my head. "How did you convince him it wouldn't be a waste?" I ventured, then coloured as I realized I'd given away that I'd been listening.

His mouth curled slightly at the corners. "Well, I'm not sure. He really seemed quite adamant until I started talking about careers in the sciences."

"He's dead set against me being a doctor," I said.

Mr Bailey tapped his fingers in a light rhythm on the wooden bar. "I'm afraid I rather stressed the benefits of veterinary practice," he said.

"But I don't want to . . ."

He turned towards me, his face again wearing its serious, patient look. "I know; I know," he said, "but one step at a time, eh?"

My protest subsided.

He turned back to scan the view. "You have a beautiful place here," he said. "Don't forget that — if it doesn't all work out."

I gazed out over the fields shining in the low evening light. "I know this sounds silly," I said, "but I want to be able to miss it."

"I understand," he said.

Out of the west a skein of geese flew, following their leader in a purposeful arrow. The noise of their creaking wings grew louder as they came nearer, the sound like a wet finger rubbed on plastic. They passed almost overhead, their long black necks outstretched, disturbing the still air with their rushing flight.

"Canada geese," he said. "Did you see their white chin straps?"

I was still staring after them. "Mum would've loved that. She used to say Mother Goose must've been a Canada goose, you know, because they look as though

120

they've got a bonnet strap." My angry thoughts dissolved again in a rush of memory.

The geese flew lower and came to rest on the far side of the river with a honking and a clattering of wings. Perhaps it was a good omen.

"We don't usually get Canada geese on the river," I said.

"No," said Mr Bailey. "They've come because they've got no choice. They've come because the reservoir's about to run dry."

CHAPTER
SEVEN

Over the next couple of weeks I crammed for the exams. In the circle of my dressing-table light, I pored over diagrams of the molecular structure of isotopes, the central nervous system, and the linkages of human bones. In the daytime I worked on geometry and algebra, solving a different kind of puzzle, but with the same underlying elegance of pattern.

The curtains were drawn against the heat outside, which still seemed to penetrate the room through the pinpricks of brightness scattered randomly across the threadbare material. Muffled by cloth and glass came the sound of the contractor's baler, distant in the fields, moaning and clattering. Worried by the deteriorating quality of the grass and the rising number of hedgerow fires in the county, Dad had decided to get some hay cut. In the soporific stuffiness of those mid-afternoons, I imagined the machine labouring through the heat, a shimmering element re-forming again behind it like mercury.

On exam days Dad drove me to school and dropped me off. I sat with the others in long columns in the school hall, which smelt of Quink ink and sweat.

Afterwards he picked me up next to the ice-cream van outside the school gates. He always asked me the same thing, "Did you do all the questions?" and gave a nod to the driving mirror when I said yes. I didn't point out that quantity was no guarantee of quality, but nursed the hope that he was feeling the beginning of some kind of sneaking pride in me. On the last day we bought ice-cream wafers to take home for me and Tom. Although the man wrapped them in waxed paper they soon began to melt and dribbles ran on to my hands and down my wrists.

"You'd better eat them — I'm driving," he said, and smiled as I tried to lift to my mouth the slippery wafers sandwiching squishy ice cream. Things you don't have often, taste sweet.

I'd hoped I'd see Martin a lot while the exams were on, but in fact our subjects only coincided on one day, when he finished a morning exam as I was waiting to go in to set up for my Chemistry paper in the afternoon. He looked rumpled, his short hair sticking up where he'd been leaning his forehead on his hand as he wrote.

"Are you going to the dance next Saturday?" he asked, taking my arm and steering me away from Nicola and the others.

"Might do," I said, aware of his mates nudging each other.

Martin kept glancing back at them.

"Try," he said.

The hall doors were being unbolted and a teacher emerged to usher us in.

"See you there," he called over his shoulder, loud enough for his friends to hear.

I read the exam paper twice without taking anything in at all. Everyone else's head was bent over what they were writing. I made myself read the first question again, this time underlining the key points, and was able to get started. By the end of the two-hour paper I was writing furiously, but I still hadn't finished when the invigilator told us to put our pens down.

I nodded when Dad asked his usual question. I just hoped I'd done enough.

At the weekend we visited Gran and Grandad for our once-a-month Sunday lunch. Gran answered the door and gave us one of her cheek-pressing kisses that left the scent of face powder on your skin. She held her apron in one hand; even though it was only family, she always took it off to answer the door.

"Come right on in," she said as we followed her. "We're having salad today — it's far too hot for cooking."

Tom pulled a face; Gran's Yorkshire puddings were his main compensation for having to endure grown-up talk for hours.

The men and Tom sat around the dining-room table while Gran and I brought in plates of cold meat, a green salad and bowls of tomatoes, radishes and beetroot.

"It's important to make food look colourful, Jess," she said: "it makes it more appetizing."

I looked at the cut-work tablecloth, the polished crystal tumblers and the food displayed with roses in a bowl as a centrepiece. I thought of the quick meals I often served up: beans-on-toast, fry-ups, omelettes. Gran would be horrified to see us shovelling it down before evening milking, from plates set straight on to the bare boards of the kitchen table.

"It looks lovely, Gran," I said, slipping into my place.

The men looked hot in their long-sleeved Sunday shirts and Gran pulled the curtains partway across to shut out the glare of the sun on the table, so that the light in the room became muted and dim. Tom tried to move out of her way to give her more room.

"Sit still, Tom," Dad said. "Stop fidgeting — you're wobbling the table."

Grandad picked up a bread roll. "So," he said, starting to butter it, "how're things at Gartons?"

"Fine," Dad said quickly.

"Dad's going to sell the hay," I said without thinking.

Dad scowled at me.

Grandad looked up sharply. "Things aren't fine, then," he said. "What're you going to use for forage?"

"I'm not selling it all," Dad blustered. "It's just to tide us over . . ."

". . . With the bank." Grandad finished his sentence. "Didn't I say that loan would lead to problems? This is not a good idea, Henry."

"Well, it's the only option I've got unless you want to help us out," Dad said shortly.

Gran gave them both a warning look and reached out to serve some food. "What can I help you to, Tom? How about a nice slice of ham?" she said. She put some meat on to his plate. "Jess, could you take the salad round, please?" I got up and went round the table, carrying the big cut-glass bowl. Gran carried on determinedly. "You know Grandad and I won't be here for a while so we'll miss our next Sunday get-together, don't you?" she said to Tom.

"Where will you be?" Tom said, bemused by the sudden attention.

"In Spain!" she said. "Just think, we're going touring with Mr and Mrs Bevin in their motor-home. They're from the Rotary Club," she said to me.

"What's a motor-home?" Tom asked.

"It's like a truck that's got a bedroom and a kitchen in the back," I said. "When are you going?"

"The week after next," Gran said, relaxing back into her seat. "We're going to have a week in their villa first." She turned a little pink.

Grandad, who hadn't touched his meal, turned back to Dad. "Henry," he said, "I wish I could bail you out, but I can't. It's not because I'm being vindictive or trying to say 'I told you so', it's because it wouldn't be enough." Dad opened his mouth to speak but Grandad raised a hand to stop him. "It'd only be a sticking plaster. You're going to keep hitting the problem because of the burden of this loan; you haven't left yourself any slack."

"What do you suggest, then?" Dad said coldly.

Grandad sat back and looked at Dad as if weighing up how unpopular his advice was going to be. "Sell Turner's to Mick Swift, instead of renting it. You don't need the land and the sale would make enough to see you right and have some over."

Dad heaved an exaggerated sigh. "I've told you before, I'm not selling Garton land," he said, "and especially not to Swift."

Gran said, "Mick Swift's an incomer. His family isn't from these parts."

"He may be a little rough around the edges," Grandad said, "but he's honest and hard-working."

"His family were casual labour," Gran said. "He's little better than a gypsy."

"He's a good man," Grandad said. "Come on now, Henry, he doesn't make a bad neighbour, does he?"

"For God's sake, how many times do I have to say it — *I'm not selling!*" Dad banged the end of his knife handle down on the table, making me jump as the crockery rattled.

Grandad said, "Now, Henry . . ."

Tom was looking from one face to another, his expression full of anxiety.

Gran nodded towards him. "Little pitchers have big ears," she said to the adults.

We carried on eating in silence.

At length Grandad asked Gran to pass the jug of water. "How's school, then, Tom?" he asked while pouring himself a glassful. "Who's the naughtiest in your class?"

Tom looked at me from under his fringe as if to check whether it was all right to answer. "Richard Eastwood," he said. "He throws things on the floor — food and stuff."

"And what do Miss Turner and her staff do with Richard Eastwood, then? Make him eat double helpings of school dinners?"

Tom's expression lightened. "He had to stay in at breaktime," he said, "but then he did something worse: he drew moustaches on the pictures of all the teachers that had been put up in the hall."

Grandad began to laugh. "Did he indeed! Imagine Miss Turner with a moustache. Triple helpings of marrow-fat peas and double lumpy school custard for that!"

Dad put his knife and fork together with a click and pushed his plate away. "Very nice, Mum," he said.

Gran said, "Jess, your father's finished. You clear the plates and I'll bring in the dessert." I picked up Dad's plate and plonked it on top of mine. Gran said, "I've made pineapple upside-down cake."

"That's my favourite," said Tom.

"Come on round here," Grandad said to him, pulling a penny from his pocket, "and we'll toss for the biggest piece." He soon had Tom learning to flip the coin with his thumb and slap it down on the back of his hand. Between calls of heads and tails, Grandad said to me, "How did you get on with your exams, do you think?"

"It's hard to tell really. I think I did all right but Mr Bailey says I'll need top grades to get on to the course I want." I blushed and fell quiet.

128

Gran stopped, her hand poised above the dessert plates. "I wouldn't have thought in the circumstances . . ." She glanced at Dad.

"Have you got a grant yet for your studies?" Grandad interrupted.

"I've sent the application off but I don't know what I'll get or whether I'll even get anything."

Dad glanced over at us as if about to speak, but changed his mind. "Lovely cake," he said instead to Gran. "You should give Jess the recipe."

"It couldn't be simpler," Gran said.

I tried to look as though I was interested as Gran started to tell me that it had to be brown sugar in the bottom of the dish to get the right caramel flavour. We carried on talking about baking while the men moved on to sport and other neutral subjects.

When we were leaving, Grandad patted Dad's arm. "Selling the hay's not the answer, you know," I heard him say.

"It's all very well saying that when it's not your problem any more," Dad said. "Have a good holiday," he added pointedly.

"Will you bring me something back, Gran?" Tom said.

"'Course I will. We'll be touring, so we'll send you lots of postcards from different places too."

She bent and gave him a hug and Grandad gave him a handful of pennies, telling him his challenge was to be able to flip a coin as high as the ceiling by the time they came home.

★   ★   ★

On Monday morning I woke late. The house was quiet, and the only noise from outside was the faint phut-phut of spraylines turning. I pulled back the curtains and blinked in the brightness. The sun was high and there was no sign of activity; the tractor and baler stood abandoned in the field to the left of the track. It was half mown and dotted with bales in tumbled lines of six, as if a child had been suddenly called away from some counting game. The air was full of dust that hung thick over the mown section of the field and which was now dispersing with barely perceptible movement, drifting over the grassy remainder and earthwards. I opened the window to let in the smell of summer and freedom. Tom was at school, Dad out on the farm somewhere; no one would miss me.

I pulled a cheesecloth top over my head without bothering to undo the row of tiny buttons down the front, and wriggled into a pair of cut-off denims. I grabbed an apple and some bread from the kitchen and headed straight for the river.

As I approached through the trees I heard a noise, the sound of something heavy hitting the water. I stood still. I'd come further upstream than usual, thinking that I'd stretch out on what Mum used to call "the beach", a place where the river bank had crumbled on a curve, leaving a hollowed-out slope where you could walk straight down into the river on a stretch of sandy soil. Now I would have to give up my idea of sunbathing and paddling and go to find out what the noise was all about. *Plunk, plunk,* there it was again. Probably village boys, I thought, bunking off school to play in our river. I moved from tree to tree through the bracken until I could get a good view.

On the opposite bank a tall figure sat cross-legged, methodically throwing stones into the water from the pile amassed by his side. He was wearing a black T-shirt with something written across the front, frayed jeans and boots. He had a deep tan and dark-brown wavy hair, "over his collar", my dad would have said, although it would be hard to visualize this person in a collar and tie. He raised his arm again and a pebble arced towards a rock in midstream where a collection of other stones already lay. It skittered over the surface of the rock and fell over the edge into the water. Unperturbed, the stranger picked up the next stone.

"Hey!" I called out, "what do you think you're doing?"

His arm dropped back to his side, then he put the stone carefully back on to the pile.

"I wondered when you were going to come out," he said.

"Never mind that," I said, "don't you know you're trespassing?"

Irritated at having lost the advantage of surprise, I came further down the bank towards him, then stood still. I felt disorientated by passing from shade into dazzle, suddenly light-headed, as if the light and air were too much, after being indoors, the river too loud, the green too bright.

"You look hot," he said, stretching his legs out in front of him and leaning back to scrutinize me. "Why don't you cool off a bit?"

Stretched out, he was long-limbed and wiry, I could see — an easy six foot, a man really, but still with the slight gangliness of youth. Big clumsy feet, though, I thought uncharitably.

"No, thank you," I said, sounding unbearably prim, even to myself. "What're you doing here?"

"Well, I'm trying to get as many stones as I can on that rock," he said with mock innocence. He sat forward and fingered another pebble. "Want to join in? We could have a competition — see who could get the most on there."

This boy was impossible. I frowned in exasperation and he laughed.

"Or if you're really angry, you could see if you can knock mine off." He flipped the flat pebble between his fingers like a magician warming up for a card trick. Under and over his knuckles it passed, appearing and disappearing. Expertly he flicked his wrist and the stone flew across the water and landed neatly with the others.

The ease with which he'd done it was infuriating. Unable either to make him leave or to go away myself without appearing to back down, and deprived of my afternoon of lazing and paddling, I felt a childish anger getting the better of me. I picked out the biggest stone I could see, intending to pitch it as hard as I could at his little island, reckoning that, even if I missed, the splash would make a satisfying protest. The sun was hot

132

on the crown of my head as I bent to unearth the stone, and as I stood up I felt dizzy. There was a rushing sound in my ears and my legs felt weak and began to buckle under me. I sat down quickly in an inelegant heap.

"Are you all right?" He was standing at the edge of the water, unlacing his boots.

My head was swimming. I nodded half-heartedly.

"Put your head between your knees," he called out.

I stared stupidly as he pulled his boots off, tied the laces together and hung them round his neck.

"Oh, no, don't . . ."

I waved my hand ineffectually but he was already in the river, his faded jeans turning a deep indigo as the water travelled up his legs. Midstream here the water was waist high and the current slowed him down. He slipped and stumbled a little on the stony bed as he reached the shallows and emerged, dripping, beside me.

"You look ridiculous," I said, "like some kind of commando." My mouth felt strangely numb, as if my tongue had grown too big for it.

He crouched beside me, chucking his boots down, and, putting one wet hand on my forehead and the other on my back, he bent my head down on to my knees.

"You've had too much heat," he said matter-of-factly. "Stay like that."

He pulled out a hanky from his pocket, now soaking wet, and gave it to me to hold against my face. I closed my eyes into the blessed cool. I heard him sit down opposite me.

"Better?" he said after a little while.

I straightened up and handed the hanky back to him. It was splodged with blue dye from his jeans.

"Have I got a blue face?" I said.

He shook his head. "No, but you did go a nasty putty colour for a minute." He was looking at me with puckered brows, weighing up what to do next. "Do you feel up to putting your hands and feet in the water?"

He put out a hand to help me up and I leant on his arm to stand; then, feeling steadier, I let go and walked carefully down to the water. I stood in it, sandals and all, then crouched to let it run over my wrists and forearms, felt the slowing of my pulse and the cooled blood spreading through me like sap through a tree.

He was lacing his boots back on to bare feet. *Those boots.*

"I know who you are." I stood up with a jerk. "You're the Swift boy — Philip."

He paused with the lace held delicately between finger and thumb. "There you are, you see: not a marauder from the wild North, just a neighbour," he looked me in the eye, "who's going to see you safely home."

I splashed back on to the bank.

"No . . . That's worse, you can't do that, you don't understand . . ."

He tied his boots tight and stood up. "I do," he said, "but, believe me, it won't be a problem." He started up the bank, then turned to hold out a hand to help me up. "Come on," he said. "You need a drink — you might wobble over again."

Helplessly I followed him. "My dad'll really go spare," I said. "He hates people coming on his land. Don't you think being a hero once in a day is enough?"

He made a noise that could have been a snort of derision or could have been suppressed laughter.

"Well," I said, "if you've really got a death-wish."

He strode on through the wood, making a direct line for the farm, avoiding all the dead ends and rabbit paths. I caught up with him.

"You know, your boots are squelching every time you take a step," I said to his back.

He turned round with a mischievous look. "You know, you've got blue on your nose."

I tutted and wiped at it, which only made him smile more broadly. I gave his arm a push.

We reached the bottom of the track.

"You can leave me here, I'll be fine," I said, scanning the fields and the yard.

"It's all right," he said. "I'll take you to your door."

"I don't want to be rude or anything," I said, "but I really don't think this is a good idea."

However infuriating this Swift boy was, I didn't want to see him humiliated and ordered off the premises by Dad. Nor did I want the inquisition that would inevitably follow.

He clomped on in his big boots, and actually started to whistle.

As we reached the yard, Dad came out of the tractor shed, carrying a toolbox. Without thinking, I took a step or two away, widening the distance between Philip and myself.

Philip gestured towards the toolbox. "Need a hand, Mr Garton?" he said.

"When I can't hit a nail in straight, I'll ask for you," he said. "You just get on with what I'm paying you for."

"Right, sir," he said. "Baling it is." He sneaked a glance in my direction, his lips pressed together as if to stop himself from laughing. "Could I just get myself a drink before I start again?" He made a move towards the kitchen.

Dad glanced at me. "Tea break will be at four," he said. "Meanwhile, help yourself from the tap." He pointed to the tap in the yard and, switching the heavy toolbox to his other hand, set off in the direction of the barn.

Philip raised his eyebrows at me and turned the corners of his mouth down as if to say "hoity-toity". I was speechless for a moment as the penny dropped.

"You're working for the contractors," I said flatly.

He stuck his hands in his pockets with his elbows sticking out, striking a comic pose. "Ye-e-s, ma'am," he said. "I'm just a little old balin' boy come to help out your daddy."

"Ha ha, very funny," I said. "You let me worry . . ." I stopped.

"Oh come on, where's your sense of humour?"

"I lost it in the river. Same place you appear to have lost your brain. If Dad finds out you've pulled the wool over his eyes he'll be livid."

"He's not all that bad surely?"

"And if he finds out that I knew, then I'll really cop it."

His shoulders slumped and his smile faded. "Look, I'm sorry, OK?" he said. "Seriously."

"Well, it was a stupid thing to do." I sighed. "You'd better go and get on with your work now if you don't want him on your tail."

I went inside and drew off a long glass of water, downed the lot, then filled it again. Over at the yard tap Philip squatted down to get his mouth low enough to take a drink. He ducked his head quickly under the running stream of water, then stood up and shook it like a dog. I remembered the way he walked into the river without hesitation, as if it was his element. Instinctive, that was the word for him. I thought how, when I'd told him what trouble he might have caused, his face had fallen as if he'd suddenly understood everything. He turned to walk back to the field and I moved back into the room.

I spent the afternoon catching up with the jobs that had remained undone over my study break. I cleared out the fridge and cleaned the kitchen and washed and pegged out clothes.

The garden, at the side of the house, was something of a rebuke to me. In the spring it was lovely; it filled every year with crocuses and daffodils, which came up like a blessing in untended borders and forgotten corners. White narcissi grew around the apple tree and spread in drifts across the grass like constellations. Now, in late June, with the weather gone mad, the garden was afflicted with insects. Ant hills patterned the lawn with bare patches of earth, making it impossible to sit anywhere to sunbathe. The apple tree had strange blobs of furry white stuff on its bark, its leaves curled crisp and brown at the edges, and tiny hard apples no bigger than cherries strewed the ground, nipped off spitefully by the heat.

Our few straggly roses, which Mum had planted, were crawling with aphids and the air was thick with them. No sooner did I peg a sheet or a shirt on the line than it was dotted with greenfly. A hoverfly hung in the air in front of my face and I flicked at it; others crawled on the washing and landed on the peg bag. I gave the whirligig clothesline a spin and the creatures settled again in seconds. There was nothing I could do: the weather had gone daft and the usual order of things had gone astray; not even the cycle of flowering and fruit was predictable any more. I fetched the rinse water and tipped it on to the roses. The apple tree would have to dig deep and fend for itself.

I heard Mrs Jones draw up and gave her a wave over the wall. When I went indoors, used mugs and scattered biscuit crumbs told me that the men had taken their tea break already. There was a note from Dad to say that the bank had insisted that he go in, so would I please start the milking in case he wasn't back in time. I felt a stab of guilt that I hadn't been there to field the phone call and then a rush of anxiety about the news Dad was likely to hear from the bank now they'd caught up with him. I reflected that I hadn't milked without Dad before, and felt even more hot and bothered. Well, Tom would just have to be my second man, that was all.

"Tom," I yelled upstairs, "put your scruffs on! I've got a job for you."

Once we had let the cows into the collection yard, I realized I was going to have to keep Tom busy the whole time. After a day in school he was like a cork let out of a bottle; he was climbing up and down on the gate into the parlour and asking me questions every two seconds.

"Now listen, Tom," I said. "I'm going to give you a very important job to do."

He stopped climbing and sat scratching the ears of the boss cow at the front. "What've I got to do?" he said sulkily.

"Well, you can be in charge of opening the gate and they'll let themselves in. They know their order, so that won't be difficult."

Tom lifted his chin in the mannish nod he'd seen Dad exchange with the tanker driver.

"The hard part is this," I went on: "when they're in and I'm ready to start them off, I want you to pull the feed handle so that each one gets the right amount of concentrate, OK?"

"Yep." He clambered down and stood almost to attention at the gate.

"But what you *mustn't* do is pull the handle before I'm ready, because the clatter of the food in the tray makes them let down their milk. All right?"

I scrambled down into the pit in the centre of the parlour, so that I could work at udder height.

"Right. Let the first lot in, then."

The boss cow, Maisie-May, and a group of the high-yielders clattered in over the paved floor and filled the cool parlour with the sweet smell of dung and chewed grass. I worked slowly and methodically, moving along the pit, swabbing the teats with mild antiseptic and drying them off, then drawing off the foremilk as Dad had taught me, to check for signs of mastitis. Tom was at Maisie-May's head with his hand on the feed lever.

"Hang on, Tom," I said, quickly putting the units on the cow's teats and reading the number freeze-branded on the top of the cow's leg. I checked Dad's list. "Right, then," I said, "give her three lots."

The cereal clattered into the tin pan and we were milking. Soon the *slush-pop* of the milk pumping along the glass pipes established its hypnotic sound. We worked alongside each other in a concentrated, companionable rhythm broken only by the pauses when I let one group out into the holding yard and Tom let the next lot in.

After a while my mind began to wander to Dad and the meeting at the bank. The manager, Mr Dixon, was a portly, self-satisfied sort who liked to think of himself as a leading light in every kind of club that the area had to offer — golf, Rotary, and, some said, Freemasons. Dad referred to him as a "bean-counter". I pictured Mr Dixon ordering and reordering his set of brass golf-ball paperweights while Dad explained about milk quotas and feed prices and pulled at his best shirt collar.

"You know how it's sometimes really hot at night and I can't sleep?" Tom said suddenly, all in a rush.

140

"Mmmm."

"Well, can I sleep outside one night?" he said.

I gave Brindle a push to make her move over, so that I could get the unit on her.

"How do you mean?"

"Like camping. Like in that book when they go to an island in a boat."

"One small problem," I said, peering round Brindle's broad behind: "we haven't got a tent."

Tom squatted down so that he could see me better.

"You don't actually need a tent," he said authoritatively; "you can make a den with bales."

"Hmm. Well, maybe. Not on your own, though — we'd both have to do it." Brindle moved back over into her original position, blocking my view. "In the holidays, perhaps, when you don't have to get up for school and we can plan it properly."

There was a silence. "Not tonight, then?"

I'd moved on and was trying to get a newly calved cow, unused to the parlour, to settle and let me untangle the vacuum tube that had got twisted.

"Tom," I said, "could you hold her still?"

Tom slipped past Brindle and started talking to the new cow.

"Is this the one that was bellowing in the night?" he asked.

I grunted. "Missing her calf," I said. "Which reminds me; they need feeding after."

We were nearing the end when we began to run out of feed and I asked Tom to let some more down into the trap. There was a squeaking noise this time as he pulled the lever.

"What's the matter?" I said.

"It's stuck."

"Give it a good pull," I said. "Use your weight."

There was a grating noise and a rushing sound as the food came down. Then quiet.

"What's up?" I called.

After a pause Tom said, "It's come off." He appeared at the head of the pit, holding the handle, looking as guilty as a burglar caught with a jemmy.

"Blood hell," I said, pushing my sweaty hair out of my eyes with the back of my wrist. "Let's have a look."

Tom opened up his other hand to show that the mechanism was bent. I took the handle from him and saw the mark where a bolt had sheared away. I couldn't think of any way to fix it. Tom looked defiant.

"You said pull," he said.

I sighed. "I know." I put the pieces on the floor in the pit. "Let's finish up here and then I'll see if I can mend it."

The last lot of cows passed through the system and out into the holding yard, and Tom went off to let them back out to pasture. I went through to the dairy, where it was quiet except for the hum of the refrigerated tank and the muffled slap of the paddles cooling the milk and splitting the cream. Carefully I turned the valve to the left as Dad had shown me, to let in the cold water to rinse the pipes, and it rushed through, frothing away the milky residue, paling white to blue.

I heard Tom shout a greeting and assumed Dad was back again. I grabbed the handle and tried to fit it back into its socket. I wanted him to see we'd made a good job of it, then I would praise Tom's part in the proceedings to try to get him a little appreciation. I was still on my knees, trying to see how the spring-loaded mechanism connected with the offending bolt, when Tom returned with Philip in tow. I scrambled to my feet, dusting off my knees, and looked daggers at Tom, aware that I must smell like a midden.

"Philip says they'll be able to fix it at his house," Tom said.

"The bolt's sheared off," I said, "and it needs to be working for tomorrow's milking."

Philip took it from me. "Uncle Mick'll drill that out and fit a new one for you," he said. "Come over now and you can wait and take it back with you."

The Swifts' old farrowing shed showed little sign of its former purpose; the pens had been stripped out to lay bare a wide area of concrete floor. A tractor was parked over a pit that had been dug out to allow vehicles to be inspected from underneath, and workbenches and equipment were ranged along the walls. The huge metal doors were open to let in some air and natural light. A black-and-white cat, perhaps the mother of Lolly, wandered in and settled down to sleep under one of the benches in a patch of shade.

"It's too hot even for the cats," Mick said, putting down his spot welder and pushing his visor up on to the top of his head. "What have we got here, then?"

I passed the bag of bits over and explained what had happened. He nodded quickly a couple of times.

"No problem," he said. "I'll have it done in no time." He turned to Philip. "Show Jess around while she's waiting."

I glanced at the coils of flexes, hoses and drills hanging up on hooks on the walls and the lathes and vices set up on the workbenches.

Mick looked amused. "No, not my bits and pieces. Go on, lad, show Jess your creations."

Philip hesitated but Mick turned the radio on and started picking through a box of drill bits.

"You might not like them," Philip said, leading me round behind the tractor to the back of the workshop. "They're not everybody's cup of tea."

Shapes shrouded in sacking stood around haphazardly, like pieces in a giant game of chess. Philip switched on a spotlight over a table where sheets of metal lay next to an acetylene torch. He started to lift one of the sheets to show me, but I was past him in a moment to stand and gawp at the one object that stood uncovered on a workbench. It was the figure of a man, about two feet tall, carved in wood on a plain square wooden plinth. He was standing upright with his hands by his sides, as straight and as thin as a pole, naked except for a loincloth carved to sit low on his bony hips. Yet despite its slenderness the sculpture had solidity and strength. The head was thrown back and the mouth was open, as if uttering a great shout. Something about the figure reminded me of a tree — a fir or a Scots pine — far out on a mountainside; it had the stubborn presence of something holding on, way above the snow-line.

I touched the hollow above the collar-bone; you could almost imagine that a sound would issue from it. I glanced back at Philip.

"It's called *The Song*," he said. "I got the idea from some photographs one of the lecturers took in India last year."

"You're studying art, then."

"Art and history of art. I'm doing an exchange with an art college in Germany from September, so perhaps I'll get some new ideas from travelling myself."

I ran my fingers over the polished smoothness of the shoulder, admiring its pale nutty colour, then the ripple of the ribs, each one in relief as if the singer had just taken a huge breath.

"He seems to be just about to start," I said.

Philip smiled. "Good. That's what I was after, the feeling of expectation."

"Can you speak German, then? I gave it up; I'm more a science person than a languages person."

"I can speak it but that's only because we lived there when I was little. Dad's in the army, you see. They're moving again at the moment — Gibraltar this time."

The noise of drilling interrupted us and I stood back a little, then walked around the figure, noticing the details, the grooves suggesting the texture of the hair falling back from the face, the curve of toes and the delicacy of the wrist bones. The drilling stopped and the radio's chatter took over again.

"It's great," I said. "You're really talented."

He flushed. "I'm not much good at the written stuff, though. Look, let me show you the one Tom likes."

He took a piece of old sack away carefully from a figure on the floor, revealing a life-size model of a deer, apparently made out of woven sticks.

"How on earth did you do that?" I said. The form was so lifelike, its head turned slightly back over its shoulder, its back legs tensed as if for flight.

"Chicken-wire mainly," he said. "You build up the basic structure with wood and wire and then you use the chicken-wire as a base to weave the twigs through. Tom helped with that; he's a dab hand at cutting twigs to length."

Yet another thing Tom had been quietly up to when I'd thought he was out on the farm. I had been so tied up in my own affairs that I was unaware of a great chunk of Tom's life. The pang I felt wasn't exactly guilt; it was a kind of loss. Perhaps he wanted it that way, I suddenly thought; he's growing up and perhaps he needs to have some secrets.

Philip was looking at his work appraisingly.

"It's for Alice and Mick, for the garden." His voice dropped down low. "It's a kind of joke really, because they've had a long-running battle to keep things out that eat the flowers — rabbits mainly, but once or twice a goat's got in and eaten the lot."

"Have they seen this?"

He grinned. "No, they don't know anything about it. I thought I'd just put it on the lawn early on the morning when I go, and wait for them to notice it over breakfast."

146

"What kind of wood is it?" I asked, wondering how he'd managed to achieve such fluid lines.

"This one's birch, but willow is good. Nice and bendy, and the willow sculptures can last for ever, whereas the birch ones need painting with preservative if you're going to have them outside."

"How do you mean, last for ever?" I said, crouching to look more closely at the matted pattern of twigs.

"Well, you just stick them in the ground, basically, and as long as they're healthy withies, willow being willow, the next year it starts to sprout."

"I suppose, strictly speaking, your sculpture doesn't last for ever, then. I mean, nature must take over, unless you keep clipping it."

"Like a hedge."

We both laughed.

He laid his hand on the back of the deer. "I quite like the idea of just leaving them. You might come back year after year and find that they'd changed into something different every time." He wrapped it up carefully in the coarse cloth.

"Are you going to do this for a living," I asked, "when you've finished your course?"

He shrugged. "Dunno. There's probably not much of a market for it. I might teach. Anything that lets me keep on doing it, basically."

I felt shy in the face of his determination. "Have you always . . . made things?" I said.

"Apparently. We had bean canes in our garden when I was about four, and I used to crawl inside. You know, I thought it was like a little house."

"A kind of tepee?"

"Yeah. Anyway, we had builders at the house — they were putting on a new porch — and I took some of the bricks and slates and piled them up to make a table and chairs inside my green house."

"What happened?"

"Well, the builder ran out before he'd finished the job and he blamed his lad for not bringing enough, and then my dad blamed the builders, and I could hear all this going on outside." He paused and frowned. "The strange thing was, I just sat on one of the chairs, looking at my table with all the leaves and red bean-flowers I'd laid out on it, and I just thought that what I'd made was so brilliant that everyone would say how clever I was."

"But they didn't."

"No. They took them all back. I got sent to bed and cried for ages." He pulled a comic sad face. "I'd forgotten all about that," he said, and scratched the side of his nose. He paused and then said, "Anyway, how about you? What're you going to do now you've finished your exams?"

"I want to do medicine," I said. "At least, that's what I'm hoping."

He whistled through his teeth. "Nothing like aiming high, I suppose."

I frowned. Yet another person who thought it would be wasted on me.

"I mean, it's very expensive, isn't it?" he said more gently. "I've shared with a medical student and you have to buy all your own kit, anatomy books, stethoscope, everything."

"I don't mind hard graft," I said, only partly mollified. "I can do chambermaid work or something."

Philip looked at me curiously, as though weighing me up. He seemed about to add something but then changed his mind and went over to the table where the sheets of metal lay.

"This is my latest thing," he said in a neutral tone. He lifted up a huge disc of silvery metal, a perfect circle, which let out a hollow boom as it flexed in his hands.

"It's steel," he said. "I got it off the bottom of a water butt that was no good any more because the rivets had rusted through. It polished up pretty well, I thought."

There was a hole punched near the edge at either side, just above his hands. The surface of the disc was marked here and there with darker circles, which were dull like pewter, giving them a smudgy look.

"What about those marks?" I said.

"I made those with the torch, then smoothed them off. Can't you see what it is?" He moved his hands to cover the punched holes. "Stand back a bit. Hang on; I'll give you a clue." He switched the light off, returning us to dimness.

I walked a little way away between the swaddled shapes of sculptures, then turned. The disc glowed pale, a burnished moon, complete with shadows and craters.

"It's wonderful," I said.

"It's going to be called *Moon through branches*," he said, turning it round to inspect it. "That's what the holes are for, to hang it up by, but I've got to find some chain that's thin enough not to show too much but strong enough to hold it . . ."

"It was you," I said. "It was you who moved the stones down by the river and decorated the tree."

He looked up quickly. "Did you like it?"

Disappointment flooded through me. Not Mum. Not a message. Deep down, of course, I'd known so all the time, but I hadn't realized how much I'd been hanging on to the merest possibility, a dream to keep by me for comfort. Now my childish fantasy seemed even more foolish. Pathetic.

"You shouldn't have done it," I blurted out.

Philip looked surprised and hurt. He slowly laid the moon down flat. It made a tinny sound as it struck the other sheets of metal. "We're not back to that 'not on our land' thing again, are we?" he said.

"No," I said shortly. "I think I'd better go."

Mick had almost finished when I went back to the work-bench. I stood awkwardly by while he looked out some new screws for the plate on the handle. He handed it over. "It should be easy enough to fit back on now," he said.

"Thanks so much — you saved my life," I said effusively, trying to make up for the bad grace I'd shown Philip.

Philip smiled as Mick and I chatted but his eyes had the puzzled expression of a dog that's got in the way of a boot.

150

"Thanks for showing me your stuff," I said tentatively to him.

He shrugged. "It's only bricks and slates."

He picked the radio up and started fiddling with the tuner, so that it produced crackling noises and high-pitched squeals.

"'Bye, then," I said over the noise, and left.

CHAPTER
EIGHT

Dad came back from the bank looking sombre and disappeared into the office, to work on the cash projection that he said Mr Dixon had demanded to see. When I took him in some tea there were papers spread everywhere. He was working out the monthly balances and writing them in pencil in spaces where grey smudges showed that other figures had been written and rubbed out before. He looked up sharply.

"Don't say anything," he said. "It isn't any of your concern."

I'd wanted to ask him if I could go to the end-of-year dance at school the next night, but I saw that I'd have to pick my moment. I told him that the milking had gone fine, but he just nodded. He was so engrossed in the figures that he seemed to have forgotten he'd meant to make a start on bringing in the hay and I had to remind him.

We worked together well into the evening. Dad drove the tractor and trailer, and I collected and stacked the bales. It was nearly ten o'clock before we decided to call it a day and, looking back at the fields strewn with clusters of bales, we seemed to have hardly made a dent in what needed to be done. For the first time I hoped it wouldn't rain.

Dad opened the big doors of the hayloft, up above the dairy, and I passed the hay up, bale by weary bale.

"Why didn't we get the contractor to bring it in too?" I moaned.

"As you can see, it's very labour-intensive," Dad said between lifting. "At least this saves us a bit of money."

When we were finished and Dad went to put the tractor in the shed, I climbed the ladder and stood back to survey the result of our labours. Half of the loft was now stacked floor to ceiling with bales, dwarfing Tom's makeshift den and filling the air with a sweet smell and dust that tickled the back of your throat. I remembered how, when I was younger, I used to build tunnels and Tom and I used to crawl around, squealing, in the dark. Tom would have a great time enlarging his den with this lot. I'd tell him at breakfast and that would keep him occupied for the day.

I pulled the big doors inwards; the wood was warm from the last of the sun, and flakes of green paint came off on my hands. I pushed the bolts home, closeting the loft in darkness but for the bright cracks around the ill-fitting doors and the pale glow from the hatch to the dairy below. A faint noise, a regular vibration, was coming from Tom's den. Inside, Lolly lay curled up on a pile of sacks, the white streak of her stomach rising and falling in the deep sleep that young animals fall into so effortlessly. I was envious: every bone I had was aching and every nerve fibre longed for rest.

Dad was waiting to lock up as I came in; he too looked drawn and exhausted. Now wasn't the time to talk about dancing, and I stumbled upstairs, pulled off my clothes and slipped blissfully between the sheets.

The next day I was itching to ask, but no good moment presented itself. Dad locked himself away with the books for most of the morning and had a sour face when he came out for lunch. By tea-time I was beside myself with anxiety, and watched every forkful of chicken pie that Dad ate.

"Are you going to The Green Man tonight, Dad?" I finally ventured.

Dad rested his wrists down on the table. "I might be. I haven't decided yet." A smile twitched at the corners of his mouth.

He knows what I'm going to ask, I thought; he's teasing.

"Only," I played along, "you know I've been working really hard, what with the exams . . ."

This produced a gleam in Dad's eyes that somehow made me feel uncomfortable.

". . . and I've been doing a lot to help — the milking and the bales last night . . ."

Dad put his knife and fork down and sat back in his chair.

". . . so I wondered if I could go to the end-of-term dance tonight. Everyone else in my class'll be going . . ." I petered out.

Tom, who had been looking from one face to the other, got up quietly and went into the pantry.

"This dance, it's run by the school?" Dad said, getting up from the table.

I nodded.

"So I could trust you to behave yourself and be back at a reasonable hour?"

I nodded again.

He reached over and pulled a handful of mail from behind the clock, then sat down again and rifled through it. "And you'd say that was your nature, would you, trustworthy?"

I said nothing, unsure where this was going.

He pulled a white envelope from the pile and waggled it at me. "Because this letter," he said, "tells me a different story." He tapped it on the table, turning it round to tap each corner in turn. I could see that it looked official, with a transparent window showing a typed address.

Suddenly he chucked it at me. It landed on my plate in a mess of gravy and burnt pie crust. In faint blue writing "University of Birmingham" was stamped next to the postmark and the envelope had been opened. My hand shook as I picked it up and wiped the greasy mess away.

"Veterinary practice," he said scathingly. "You put your teacher up to that, I suppose."

I unfolded the letter. *Dear Miss Garton,* it read, *I'm delighted to inform you that you have been awarded a provisional place to study Medicine, dependent upon the achievement of at least two A and two B grades at advanced level as follows . . .*

155

I smoothed the letter out on the table, my pulse prickling even in my thumbs. I'd done it! I'd got my chance; it was there in front of me, literally within my grasp. I closed my eyes for a moment, Dad's voice washing over me as he accused me of being devious, selfish and, finally, disloyal.

I opened them again when he had finished. "I'm sorry, Dad," I said, "but it's what I really want to do."

"Well, you can forget it," he said, "and you can forget going out tonight too."

Tom emerged from the pantry, carrying a billycan, and sidled towards the scullery door.

Without looking round Dad said, "Are you taking milk for that kitten?"

Tom froze.

Still looking at me, he added, "If it gets in my way I'll pull its neck." He pushed his chair back from the table and barged past Tom to pick up his keys. "Clear up and then get to bed."

He went out through the scullery and we heard the clatter and click as he locked the door behind him, then the Land-Rover engine sputtered into life and we heard him drive away.

Tom was still standing staring at the billycan as if he were trying to decipher the answer to some puzzle in the pattern of grey-blue chips of the white enamel. I put my arm round his shoulders.

"Don't worry, Tom," I said. "He didn't mean it. It's not you he's angry with."

156

"He's locked us in," Tom said in disbelief. "I've got to move Lolly — he knows where she is." His eyes were wide and anxious.

This was Dad's way of working, I thought, to strike at Tom to hit me, or at the kitten to hit Tom — always at one remove, manipulating you so that if you challenged him you bore the guilt of bringing down his wrath on someone weaker. I gave Tom a hug; this time Dad wasn't going to work me like a puppet.

I took the can from Tom and set it down on the table. I reached across the drainer to the window and lifted the long metal latch off its stop, then swivelled the handle at the side of the window down.

"You know it won't open," said Tom. "It's all painted up."

"We'll see." Grasping both fastenings at once, I gave it a couple of tentative shoves. A piece of putty came away from the top right-hand pane but the window itself wouldn't budge.

"What if the glass cracks?" Tom said.

I kept on pushing with small regular jabs. "I'm not," I said between pushes, "going to be . . . a prisoner . . . in this house."

I fished out a paring knife from the cutlery drawer and began running the blade between the window and the frame, levering it up and down whenever it encountered any resistance, making a gritty crackling sound. A dust of cream paint specks fell on to the sill.

"He'll see the chips," said Tom.

"No, he won't," I said, working away at it. "He doesn't even notice what's on his dinner plate."

I grasped the handles again and shoved and the window gave with a noise like ripped sticky tape. I pushed it wide open, then dusted my hands off, clapping them against each other theatrically to make light of it to Tom.

"Come on, then," I said. "Up you go and find Lolly."

He scrambled up on the drainer, sat on the sill and then launched himself into the yard. I passed the milk out to him and nodded him on. He made for the hayloft, the can swinging as the weight of milk inside it sloshed as he walked.

I started to wash the dishes. I knew that by turning the key in the door lock Dad was saying he wouldn't be crossed. I wiped up the speckled paint and chips of wood, knowing I'd already crossed the line.

An hour later I dropped my handbag over the sill, sat on the edge and swung my legs over. I rested one foot on the waste pipe and lowered myself down to the ground, wobbly on my high wedge heels. I went into the dairy and called up into the loft for Tom. His head and shoulders appeared in the square hatch above the ladder, Lolly clasped firmly against his chest.

"I'm going into town for a while," I said, "so it's time to go in now."

"I don't want to."

"Come on now, Tom, don't mess about." I looked at my watch. "You can watch telly for a bit if you want — Dad won't be back for ages yet. Just make sure you leave the window off the latch for me."

158

Tom shook his head. "I'm not going in. There might be noises again like last time. And anyway, I'm not leaving Lolly."

"She'll be fine. Come on, Tom, be reasonable."

His head disappeared from view. "*You're* not staying in," he said, his voice receding.

Irritated, I climbed awkwardly up the ladder and stuck my head through the hatch. Tom had certainly changed the layout, I thought. A mass of bale tunnels criss-crossed the open half of the floor and his den now stretched as far as the green doors, the bales stacked as high as a standing man and topped with sacks weighted down with bricks to make a taut fabric ceiling. From somewhere in the maze Tom's voice came, muffled and stubborn.

"*You're* not doing what Dad said," he laid down a challenge.

I looked at the bales and decided that I had neither the time nor the energy to chase Tom through them, which was doubtless what he'd like.

"Tom," I said, "I have to go. Go in when it gets dark, OK? There's a good boy."

He made no answer but there was a movement of the bales like a mole tunnelling just under the surface of the earth. I knew that he'd heard. I picked my way carefully back down the ladder and headed for the bus.

The school car park was already full of the kind of jalopies driven by new and learner drivers: beat-up Minis, Morris Minors and tinny-sounding 2CVs. Fathers, driving bigger, sleeker cars, queued to drop off groups of long-legged girls, then drove smoothly away, like big fish moving through a shoal of minnows.

No sign of Nicola. I waved to a couple of girls from a different form, but by the time I reached the entrance to the school hall they were already inside. Two men on the door, probably someone's elder brothers, were taking the money and turning a blind eye to the bottles and cans that, thinly disguised by jackets and jumpers slung casually over their owners' arms, were going in too. I handed over the pounds I'd cobbled together, ignored the beefier of the two bouncers as he asked "All on yer own, darlin'?" and slipped inside.

It was already crowded, and *so hot*. The heat outside was nothing compared with this. The high windows were open but the thick velvet curtains had been pulled across to keep out the light, so hardly a breath of air came in. A big PA system outside the drawn curtains of the stage pounded out Stevie Wonder, and girls danced in tight knots, while the lads sat around tables set at right angles to the dance floor, drinking and shouting to one another over the music. It was dark except for the angular patch of light thrown from the strip light through the bar hatch.

I picked my way over a floor already slippery with spilled beer, to where I'd spotted Nicola dancing. I tapped her on the shoulder and she turned round and squealed "*Jess!*" when she saw me. She drew me into the circle of dancing girls.

"Who've you come with?" she mouthed into my ear. "Skinner brought me in his dad's car; he's just passed his test." She glanced over to where he was sitting and gave a little wave.

"I just came on the bus," I shouted back.

"Well, Martin's here somewhere," she said and gave my arm a squeeze.

"Dad doesn't know I'm here," I started to explain, but gave up. She smiled at me vaguely and obviously hadn't heard a word.

The volume of the music seemed to swell, pumped up to a level that became something more than sound. As I moved I could feel it in the soles of my feet, even in my chest, a rhythm blocking out my own heartbeat.

Nicola disappeared and returned with small glasses full of a dark liquid. "Rum and black," she said and drank half of hers in a couple of gulps.

I did the same and felt a glow spreading through me.

Behind the stage curtains the sound of squealing amplifiers and odd snatches of guitar riffs overrode the records as the group tuned up. The floor filled with more and more people as everyone crammed on to it, jockeying for position to get a good view. Our little group was squashed into a smaller and smaller space and pushed towards the front by the weight of numbers behind. The dancing wasn't individual any more, it was a swaying of the crowd shoulder to shoulder, as if we'd become one big animal.

Arms clasped me around the waist from behind and I turned to see Martin, his hair spiky with sweat. He kissed me, his mouth cool and beery. Someone knocked into him and we lurched to one side and then broke off, laughing. As the tuning-up sounds got louder, everyone turned towards the stage and a slow handclap started up. Skinner gave Martin some bottles and Martin passed me some cider and held on to two bottles of brown ale. I drank the cider quickly with a great thirst, although it was warm and tasted sickly. People were stamping now, the group deliberately keeping us waiting, orchestrating the ritual, playing the crowd along. The wooden floor vibrated and the very building seemed to resonate.

The parents and teachers who'd volunteered to run the bar selling innocuous fizzy drinks and crisps had all come to the hatch and were looking anxious. One of the teachers was shouting something, but no sound emerged; his lips moved like a fish gasping in a bowl. Then *wham*, the curtains shot back and the group launched into their first number with the lead guitar screaming and the drums assaulting our ears. A boy in a vest top knocked into me as the crowd erupted into movement again and I grabbed Martin's arm. Carbon-dioxide snow spilled like smoke over the edge of the stage, a white fog that caught at the back of your throat.

A strobe light came on, turning my white top a strange ultraviolet and picking out specks of white dust on Nicola's black T-shirt. She threw her head back, laughing, and the movement broke into jerky blinks. We were being pushed still nearer to the front, the amplifier on my left was blasting so that I couldn't think and my chest felt tight. I gripped Martin's arm and started to push back against the crowd.

162

"Do you want to get out of here?" he mouthed, and I looked around, unable to see how. He raised a hand to Skinner, then, holding the bottles high above his head to save them from spilling, he laced the fingers of his other hand through mine and pushed his way through the crowd, drawing me after him. The flickering light broke everyone's movements down to black-and-white snapshots, lending a strange distance to the crowd, as though we were elbowing our way through acres of cardboard cut-outs, not people.

At the door the bouncers stopped us to give us passes so that we could get back in again. The beefy one, his shirt buttons straining over his stomach, held my hand in his podgy fist.

"Yer found a feller, then?" he said as he pressed the ink stamp on to the back of my hand. "Just remember me if yer need a lift home, though, eh?"

He rolled the pad from side to side, leaving a smudgy blue number tattooed on my skin. I didn't like his sweaty palm against mine and pulled my hand away, moving close up to Martin.

We went out into the twilight. The air smelt of the hot tarmac of the car park but I took deep gulps of it, filling my lungs with its relative freshness. He put his arm around me and we skirted along the edge of the rows of parked cars and rounded the school buildings to draw level with the netball courts.

"Feeling better?" Martin asked, passing me one of the bottles.

"Mmm. A bit. Those lights made me feel weird." I moved closer into the crook of his arm. Through the criss-cross pattern of the court's wire fencing, the netball baskets loomed like sentinels guarding the quiet grey space and the acres of playing fields beyond.

"I'd started to think you weren't coming," Martin said, then drained his bottle and sent it rolling down the bank. It spun down fast on the dead, frazzled grass and hit the fence with a metallic clang.

"I nearly couldn't. Honestly, my dad's driving me mad. You know what he did? He only went and locked me and Tom in the house."

"How'd you get here, then?" He was leading me along the edge of the bank towards the boiler room and the sports sheds.

"Where're we going?" I said.

"I came with the lads, I'm afraid, so I can't take you home, you know, at the end." He looked at me as though he'd answered my question. We stopped walking. "So you made your escape from Alcatraz just to see me," he said, turning me towards him and running his hands up and down my bare arms. "You didn't come with anyone else, then?"

I shook my head. The hairs on my arms rose to his touch. He kissed me lightly on the mouth, then walked over to the nearest sports shed and pushed the door open.

"How did you know it wouldn't be locked?" I asked.

"It never is."

He went inside. I hesitated for a moment, then decided. I followed him in and pulled the door shut behind me.

We kissed again, his mouth hard on mine, and I found myself clinging to him, holding tight, a drowning girl who's finally found something that might just float. I pulled up his shirt and ran my hands over his smooth back. We pulled at buttons and zips, and sank down among the stacks of hurdles and piles of hockey sticks, coming to rest on something springy. He broke away from me for a moment and turned his back. My heart was thudding and I felt tears welling up. I pulled my top back over me, covering the paler skin of my breasts, but as he turned back to me a voice in my head was saying *Go on, do it, don't be such a baby, you can't stop now.* Then he was on top of me, his mouth on mine, his hands under my hips, lifting me towards him. I cried out as he entered me, not expecting the pain, and gripped on to his shoulders, trying to relieve the weight pressing down on me.

I turned my head and stared at the shed wall, at the knot holes patterning the cheap softwood boards. The pain lessened but my whole body felt clenched and tight against it. I was conscious of the roughness of the material we were lying on, imprinting itself on my back, and the stuffy smell of creosote sweating from the wood. At length he groaned and collapsed on top of me, burying his face in my shoulder. Gradually I let my body relax, then I shifted under him to let him know I was uncomfortable and he rolled off me.

"God," he said, then, as if remembering his manners, "Was it OK?"

"Fine," I said, sitting up to find that what we'd been lying on was tennis netting, a loosely rolled mass of it. I felt my back; it was indented with dots and lines. I felt about for my clothes and put them on quickly; even so, I couldn't stop shivering and I was afraid to say anything in case my voice trembled.

"You should've said it was your first time," he said.

I said nothing.

"It'll be better next time," he said.

I tried to push aside the thought of his knowing that the shed door was never locked.

"My dad'll kill me if he finds out about this," I said, my teeth held tight together as though keeping a lid on something inside.

Martin, who'd been lying back with his hands behind his head, sat up.

"But he won't know, will he?" he said, slipping his arm around my waist and nuzzling my neck.

"He scares me sometimes, that's all," I said. "It's like he has to have all of my life, every little bit of it. I feel like a room that's being painted and there's just this tiny bit of wall left white that I can write on. Do you ever feel like that?"

"Mmm," he mumbled into my hair.

"And what's worse, it makes me so *angry*. That's what's really scary. I don't feel as if I know myself any more, or what I might do. Like tonight, getting out of the house . . . and now this."

Martin was kissing my neck and moving round towards my throat. I shrugged him off.

"Don't you want to do it again?" he said.

I shook my head slowly.

He looked at me strangely. "You worry too much," he said.

"I'm not worrying, I'm telling you how I feel. Don't you ever feel like that, as though you're in the sea and you don't know where the land's gone? Don't you?"

He pulled away from me and started buttoning his shirt. "C'mon," he said, standing up to tuck it in. "It's supposed to be a party, remember." He opened the door. I sat looking dully ahead of me. "C'mon, we're missing the act."

I stood up and dusted my jeans down slowly. I felt as though I was outside myself, looking down at this girl, her hair tousled, a fire of disappointment spreading through her and a shame, as bright and raw as blood smeared on skin. And yet she walked forward, put a smile on her face and followed him back to the dance.

When we got back, the party had spilled out into the corridor and the bouncers were splitting a six-pack with some of the lads. Everyone was red in the face with the heat and the dancing, and people were shouting over the music and over one another. Martin stopped by the bouncers to listen to a joke that the beefy one was telling. Nicola broke away from the group she was with and came over.

"I wondered where you were. I was looking for you," she said accusingly, then peered into my face. "You're ever so pale. Here." She thrust a beer glass at me.

"No . . . I've had enough," I said.

"It's all right, there's nothing in it. It's just Coke."

I took a sip.

The older man's voice was deep and throaty. ". . . So the Irishman said, you can't do it without legs . . ." I heard snatches of the joke from behind me but the punch line was lost in an eruption of laughter as the lads recognized what was coming.

"That's right," said Nicola, "drink up. Have some more." She was fanning herself with her hand and I watched it moving to and fro, trying to concentrate on the movement and fight off the strange detached feeling.

I could see Martin out of the corner of my eye, taking a beer offered by the beefy man. He leant forward to say something to Martin as he passed him the can, and something about his expression, his eyes narrowed to slits of amusement, his fat sweaty face avid for an answer, made me turn towards them, straining to hear.

"What you been up to then, boy?" he said, clapping Martin on the shoulder.

"Yeah," said one of his mates as the attention of the group swivelled to Martin. "You look like a dog with two tails — what you been doing?"

Martin laughed. "Cherry picking," he said, jerking his thumb towards me.

"What's the matter?" Nicola was saying. "What is it?"

But I was turning, walking, released into motion, outside myself, past caring who saw, who heard, what people would think. I gave him the whole pint, full in the face. I didn't just tip it, I chucked it. The dark liquid flew in an arc and caught him unawares. His hands went up to his eyes and he let out a bellow that stopped the rest of the room dead. Brown pools of liquid fizzed on the floor in the sudden silence, and beads of it stood in his hair. A patch spread down the front of his pale shirt, the colour of old blood.

Martin turned aside and stood blinking as people started to laugh and voices returned, animated and high-pitched. I walked away and Martin's mates clustered round him.

"Mad bitch," the beefy man was saying, shaking his head. "Mad bitch!" he shouted after me.

I ran down the steps outside and kept on running. I could hear Nicola calling behind me, but I kept on going. I had to get to the bus. I just wanted to be home.

I walked up the track through the wood, the sound of the river like a hundred voices talking behind my back. I ached all over, as though I'd been in a fight and come out the loser; all I wanted to do was to slink home and bury myself in a safe corner where I could make the world go away. *Stupid, stupid, stupid,* my footsteps seemed to drum as I walked slipshod, my sandal straps rubbing my bare feet raw.

When I heard the sound of the Land-Rover, it took me a second to register what it was. It was coming fast up the track behind me, crunching over pebbles and spitting gravelly dust from its wheels. I was caught on the bridge between its low stone walls and had to run on past the fence on the bend. I slipped quickly into the trees and squatted down among the bracken and brambles. The headlights raked past me as Dad took the turn, and I ducked my head down on my knees. Then he was past and gone.

I straightened up, unpicking the brambles from my clothes, and started uncertainly up the track. The distant sound of the dogs barking reached me and I prayed that Tom had gone to bed and that Dad would just turn in and not notice the unlatched window. I hurried along as best I could, keeping tight into the shadow of hedge and fence posts, but as I approached the yard the dogs let out another round of furious barking as a door banged somewhere inside. I froze in the shadow of the tractor shed and peered round the corner.

Dad came back out of the house and stood in the light spilling from the open scullery door, his hands on his belt and with a face fit to sour milk. He turned to shout to the dogs to be quiet, and in that split second I saw, what he would undoubtedly notice any moment, a thin line of yellow light around the hayloft doors. I took a step forward, then stopped. As if in slow motion I saw Dad scan the yard and then look up. He squared his shoulders and strode across to the dairy.

What to do? Seeing me dressed up like this, obviously having been out despite his strictures, would incense him even more, but what about Tom? I found I was gripping on to the door jamb of the tractor shed like a child in a game of tag, unwilling to leave "home".

There was a thump as if something heavy had fallen, then another, and I was running across the yard and yanking open the dairy door. In the thin blue light of the single strip light above the refrigeration unit I saw

Dad's feet at the top of the ladder to the loft. Two bales were thrown down at the bottom of the ladder, one of which had burst its twine and formed a shapeless hump on the ground. Dad was pulling more bales to one side; they made a heavy dragging noise and a creaking as they crossed the loose boards.

"I know you kids are in there," he was saying. "I know you're in there. Now come out and take your punishment."

There was no answer. Dad, having made himself a space, stepped up into the loft and began clearing his way towards Tom's den in earnest.

"Look at this bloody mess," he was saying as I tiptoed towards the ladder. "This was all stacked yesterday. Little bugger!" He swore to himself as he fumbled his way around in Tom's fortifications. There was a heavy thump as some bales fell. "Tom!" he roared. "Come out!"

In the silence that followed I could just make out the faintest noise, a high-pitched squeak, the noise you make in the back of your throat when your fist is crammed in your mouth to stop you from crying. I pulled my shoes off and went up the ladder behind Dad.

"Right, now I've got you, you little rat," Dad said. He was level with Tom's den and reaching over to pull the bales and sacking away.

I scrambled over the bales tumbled behind him, shouting, "No, Dad, no! Leave him alone!"

Then everything seemed to happen at once. There before us was Tom's den, which was lit inside by a torch propped on a pile of comics. Tom's wet eyes glittered in the light. He had squashed himself up in the corner by the doors and was holding Lolly in his lap, one arm curled around her, the other pressed against his mouth. We looked down into the den as if into a field-mouse's nest pulled apart by a curious boy. Dad put both hands over the bale in front of him and pulled it towards him. I grabbed at his arm but lost my balance as he pulled, falling back against the wall, and Lolly, terrified, broke free from Tom's arms and leapt away. Tom jumped up and pressed himself against the doors.

"By Christ," said Dad, trying to pull the wall of bales out of the way, "you're going to learn a lesson."

Tom's eyes were huge in his white face. I pushed myself away from the wall and scrambled over the bales to get to him, putting myself between him and Dad.

Dad pushed the bales in front of him to one side. "I'll tan your hide!" He made a grab for Tom and I pulled him away.

The face coming towards us didn't look like Dad any more. His colour was livid, his eyes stared. I put my arm up to shield myself from a blow, but instead he grabbed my hair and pulled my head back so that I couldn't move. Behind me Tom was clinging to my clothes.

"Don't you *ever* disobey me again, d'you hear?" He pulled harder and I gritted my teeth.

Tom lost his last shred of control and the sharp smell of urine filled the air. Dad let go of me and stepped back. We stood in silence in the wreck of Tom's den.

"I'm s-s-s . . ." Tom began.

Dad moved his head slowly from side to side, then turned to me. "I was right," he said. "I was right not to trust you. You're turning out just like your mother."

I couldn't say anything. A strange trembling started up inside me as he fixed me with his look.

"I'm going in now," he said. "I don't want either of you in my sight." He looked at the wet mark spreading across the wooden boards. "I wash my hands of the pair of you," he said.

As soon as he'd gone, Tom clung to me, burying his head in my stomach. We sank down against the bales. The torchlight had faded to a weak yellow and would soon go out. I put my arms around him and held him tight against me; I felt terribly cold and began to rock backwards and forwards. A voice, which seemed to come from someone else and yet was mine, was repeating, "We're all right, we're all right," in a strange singsong, over and over to the rhythm of my rocking.

CHAPTER
NINE

Sylvie

7th May 1967. Wrens nesting in the garden again. Same place the cat got the chicks last year. Big hopes. Small foolish creatures.

Sylvie spread her fingers flat on the crisp white cloth and longed for blankness. She felt tired, bone tired; she'd got up at the same time as Henry so that she could clean and tidy before the baby woke up for his morning feed. The christening was to be at two, and already it was noon. She reviewed what she'd done and what was left to do. The sofa in the living room was back against the wall, and she'd hoovered and imported more upright chairs from the kitchen ready for Henry's elderly relatives. She'd rolled out what seemed like acres of pastry, filling Tupperware boxes and cake tins with prawn vols-au-vent, Quiche Lorraine and sausage rolls. She'd ironed Jess's frock and, with the respect due to an heirloom, tentatively pressed Tom's christening robe and hung both up, fed Tom again while Jess ate a sandwich, settled Tom down for a sleep and sent Jess to rearrange her doll's house. She calculated that she had about half an hour of peace left to finish off and get

174

herself ready before Tom woke up. That was if Jess didn't get bored first of course.

She roused herself and twitched the corners of the tablecloth to hang in neat triangular shapes, then stood back to see if they were equal. One side was longer than the other: it trailed a good six inches further down than the opposite corner. She stood staring at it, and suddenly everything seemed too much effort.

Since Tom, her world had been the kitchen and the children, a small domain. The tasks weren't big, or hard, although there were lots of them, so why did it all seem so difficult? She knew what it was: it was because every time her world shrank, she shrank faster, an ant running ever more busily in a forest of grass.

Slowly she pulled the starched cloth straight, then stood with both hands on the smooth surface. It was happening again, that change, barely perceptible at first, as if someone had nudged a mirror and everything around you that you'd thought real and true suddenly wobbled and became as unreachable as a reflection. It had started when the baby came. The midwife had said that it would pass once feeding patterns settled. She had let Henry think this was true.

She could see now that all the things she'd done so far to prepare for the christening were wrong. The food, for instance: too much pastry; everything would look brown and unappetizing. And there wasn't enough. It would look meagre, a few plates spaced out on an expanse of white cloth. As for the christening cake, it looked plastered rather than iced. *Not much of a show,* people would think; *not much of an effort for a christening party.* Rose would say, "I told you it'd be too much for you. I could've helped you make a proper spread," and Henry would say nothing. She cast around for ideas. *Flowers,* she thought, *for a centrepiece, that's what I need,* and went quickly to cut some.

"What're you doing, Mummy?"

Jess's high voice pierced Sylvie's concentration and she looked up. The kitchen was chaotic. Baking trays full of cheese straws and enough sandwiches for a battalion covered every available surface, and the floor was strewn with cut flower stalks.

"What? What is it?" she said, pushing some hyacinth stems through the sharp holes of the chicken-wire curved in a shallow blue-and-white china bowl.

"It's nearly time, Mummy. We've got to get ready."

"It can't be," Sylvie said, trying to prop some tulips up against the hyacinths. They slipped immediately and drooped over the edge of the bowl.

"You said to tell you when it was half past," Jess said, "and it's twenty-five-before now."

"I can't leave it looking like this." Sylvie stuck in some gypsophila in a vain attempt to fill in the gaps left by the droopy tulips. "This is called 'Baby's Breath' ", she said dreamily.

"Come on, Mummy." Jess tugged at her hand. "We've got to put our dresses on!"

Sylvie turned the arrangement round the other way. It looked just as bad. She grabbed the dustpan and brush and swept the flower stalks up and into the bin,

176

leaving sticky trails of sap on the floor she'd been up at five to clean.

"God in bloody heaven," she said, then caught Jess's look. She sighed. "We'd better do your hair," she said.

"Who's coming to the party?" Jess asked as Sylvie sat her down at her dressing table.

She started to brush Jess's springy hair back, ready for the hair band that matched her green velvet dress. Her daughter's face reflected next to her own had the same pale skin, the same expression of worry in the grey-blue eyes.

Sylvie leant towards the mirror. "I wish we could go right through, like Alice through the looking-glass," she said.

Jess reached out and touched it, leaving misty fingerprints behind. "This isn't the right sort of mirror — it has to be in a magic place," she said. "Are our new neighbours coming?"

Sylvie pulled the hair band up and back and tucked a stray strand of hair back under it. "The Swifts? No, they're not coming. Lots of people *are*, though — your dad's friends from The Green Man, and some I don't even know, your dad's uncles and aunts and cousins who farm over in Buckinghamshire. Apparently it takes a christening to get them over here, farming being what it is."

Sylvie didn't mention that none of these people had attended Jess's christening, which had been a quiet affair with close family, and her friend from the village, Sandra, standing as godmother. At the time she'd thought nothing of it, hadn't realized what was usual for a celebration of a new addition to the Garton male line, and so had felt no pique on Jess's behalf. Or maybe, she suddenly thought, it was Rose's disapproval; maybe it had been such a hole-in-the-corner affair because it was a bit too soon after the wedding.

"You look lovely," she said, kissing the top of Jess's head, then spreading her hair out on her shoulders: "like a dark-haired Alice."

She twisted her own hair up on to her head and fixed it quickly with a clip. Tom began to cry, letting out the bereft wail of a baby making the transition from sleeping to waking. Sylvie hurried away, still in her slip and stockinged feet.

"Run a bath for Daddy, Jess," she called over her shoulder, "but don't splash your dress, for goodness' sake."

Sylvie carried a tray of sherry from guest to guest, edging between the powdered aunts in their pleated dresses, the women's bodies yielding and silky as she squeezed by, and the overstuffed dark-suited backs of the uncles.

"Raising beef not worked out too well for you, then, Henry?" a florid man was saying.

"Sweet or dry?" Sylvie interrupted quickly.

Henry was fidgeting, shooting his hands forward in his jacket sleeves to adjust the amount of cuff showing. "Building my new parlour made more sense. You sorted out your drainage problem yet?" Henry said.

178

Sylvie gave a glass to the man. It looked faintly ridiculous in his big hand, like a strongman drinking from a thimble.

"Wet the baby's head," he said, drinking it down.

"Where've your mum and dad got to?" she asked Henry, as she obviously wasn't going to be introduced.

"They've gone home, to pick up some food or something." He turned back to the uncle. "I heard you were selling off some land — because of poor drainage, wasn't it?"

Sylvie left them to it.

"Mind your back, Vi," a younger woman said with a smile at Sylvie as she edged past the broad hips of a woman who stood in her way. "Deaf as a post," the young woman mouthed at her. "I'm Henry's cousin Deirdre. These are my two, Caroline and David." She nodded towards two small children who, together with Jess, were steadily working through the sandwiches, peeling them apart to inspect the fillings. "Oh dear," she said, "shall I take them all into the garden for a bit?"

Sylvie gave an exhausted nod. "Get Jess to look out the ropes," she said. They looked at each other and laughed. "For skipping, I mean, not tying them up."

"Don't tempt me," said Deirdre as she went to round them up.

Sylvie wondered why she hadn't met all these people before. Deirdre and her husband Frank farmed only twenty miles away, an easy trip. Did it not occur to Henry that she and Deirdre might have things in common? That Jess might enjoy playing with her second cousins? No, she thought, it wouldn't have occurred to him; he was solitary by nature, self-contained. These days she wondered if he really noticed whether she was around or not. His nose was so badly put out of joint over having to rent land out to the Swifts after all, that he froze her ever more determinedly out of the business and into the nursery.

"Men aren't any good with babies. Babies need their mother," he said firmly when Sylvie had asked him to take a turn pacing the floor with Tom, who'd had a fractious night. Sylvie had taken Tom into bed with her to quieten him, and there he'd stayed ever since, grafted on to her, clinging closer as if shrinking from Henry's chilly back.

Reminded of him, Sylvie scanned the room for her son. He was being passed from hand to hand like a parcel among a group of old ladies sitting by the door. His bonnet slipped over one eye as he was diddle-diddle-dumplinged on a bony knee and his arms jerked upwards in startled response as he was tipped backwards at the end of the song.

Oh God, don't start him off, Sylvie thought, knowing that if he cried she'd have to rush him upstairs and feed him again. She set down the tray on a corner of the table and went to rescue him.

"Who's a little sweetie, then?" the bony woman was saying, holding Tom's tiny wrists and clapping his hands together. "He's got his daddy's fair hair but he's a dainty one like his mummy," she said to the woman next to her.

180

An ancient lady with a gaunt face the colour of old chamois leather leant forward and tapped Tom's arm.

"Didn't a' bellow in the church, though," she said. "That's the devil coming out of'en, that's what that is."

"Do help yourself to food, won't you?" Sylvie did her best to muster a smile as she swept Tom up and held him tight against her shoulder.

There was a commotion behind her as Henry's parents arrived and were greeted. Rose carried a huge wicker basket with an elasticized floral cover. Smiling benignly at everyone and pressing cheeks with those who proffered kisses, she made a bee-line for the table and began to unpack plates of scones and cherry-topped macaroons, moving the lumpy christening cake and the sausage rolls aside. Pa Garton stood by awkwardly, holding a large cardboard box.

"Where shall we put these?" Rose asked to no one in particular as she picked up Sylvie's flower arrangement. Two tulips gave up the battle with gravity and fell out on to the sandwiches, dusting them with orange pollen. Rose plonked the china bowl of flowers down on top of the record player behind a chair, and took from the cardboard box a three-tiered iced cake, complete with blue bootees in spun sugar. The aunties crowded round to admire it.

"What're those flowers doing in the food?" boomed Auntie Vi.

Sylvie thought she might cry.

Rose came towards her, holding her palms apart. "Where's my little grandson, then? Let's show him his lovely cake."

Sylvie had to let him go.

"Here, let me relieve you of that," she said to Pa Garton, who'd been left holding the box, and took her chance to escape to the kitchen.

Sylvie was blowing her nose as Pa Garton came in.

"All a bit much for you, old girl?" He put his hand on her shoulder.

Sylvie shook her head, unable to speak.

Pa Garton sighed. "She means well, you know. I did tell her I thought you'd have asked if you wanted help, but you know what she's like."

"It's not that," Sylvie gulped. "It's just that I feel so hopeless. I'm no good at all this," she waved her hand vaguely in the direction of the living room, "all this back your own flower arrangement and knit your own icing." She put her hand up to her mouth. "Sorry."

Pa Garton smiled. "Those sugar bootees are bought, you know," he said, squeezing her arm, "though you'd never get her to admit it. It'd mean a lot to her if you said you were pleased. She hasn't been a hundred per cent lately."

"Is it her headaches back?" Sylvie asked, remembering the pallor that Rose's face powder failed to cover. She felt guilty. "Of course, I know. I'll make a big fuss and get her to cut the cake. It's just . . . the flowers. I couldn't even . . ." To her dismay, she started to cry again.

"Come on," said Pa Garton, taking her cardigan from the back of the chair and putting it round her shoulders. "Deirdre's taken the children off over the fields for a run. Let's go into the garden, then you can tell me what this is really all about."

"You've done well with your bulbs," Pa Garton said.

Narcissi clustered around the budding apple tree and the borders were vivid with the strong blue of hyacinths and red tulips streaked with yellow.

"Mmm, it's a spring garden," Sylvie said. "I'd put some roses in for a bit of summer colour if I could get into town to the nursery." She bent and pulled out some ground-elder, then stood dangling it from her fingers. "I can't keep on top of everything, that's the trouble," she said ruefully.

"It's living on a farm," Pa Garton said. "A bit of hedge can't keep out the seeds; the wind blows in and out from all directions."

"Lucky old wind," Sylvie said. "Talking of getting about, how are your legs? Is the doctor pleased with you?"

Pa Garton pulled a comical face. "He says there's not much he can do. He keeps asking how I'm managing with the driving and I say 'Fine'. Well, between you and me, I've fixed a block of wood on the clutch — strictly illegal, I know, but it'll keep me mobile a little while longer."

She walked down the gravelled path to the corner of the garden.

"Peonies," she said, pointing. Glossy green shoots were pushing through the dark earth, the packed buds still bent over like mini Atlases newly free of their load.

Pa Garton followed and admired them.

"Sylvie," he said, "tell me why you're unhappy."

"I love these," Sylvie said, looking determinedly at the plants. "They're so extravagant when they come out: larger than life."

"I might be able to help," Pa Garton said. "There's no shame in getting a little help."

Sylvie folded her arms, tugging her cardi closer across her chest. "I sometimes think I'm going mad," she said, looking straight at him. "Most of the time I'm inside four walls; I can't get far around the farm with the pram. The furthest I ever go is to take Jess to school." She took a deep breath. "Sometimes I don't exchange more than two sentences with anyone all day. Only the milk tanker and the post van ever come up here. I feel like I'm not me any more, as though it's just my shadow moving through the day and no one even notices." She let out the remains of the breath. "There. Now I've said it."

Pa Garton wrinkled his forehead. "Have you talked to Henry about this?"

"As I said, sometimes I don't get more than two sentences."

"What about your friend Sandra?"

"Same problem. New baby, no transport."

"Well," said Pa Garton, "let's look at the practicalities. One thing we can do straightaway this week is to take you to get your roses. I'll pick you and Tom up on Wednesday."

Sylvie blinked. "Thanks. That's really kind."

Pa Garton smiled. "I've had an even better idea. How'd you like to learn to drive?"

"What about Tom?"

"Put him in the back. Babies always fall asleep in the car."

"What about Henry?"

"I don't think he'll want to come, do you?" Pa Garton said with a mischievous look.

Sylvie gave his arm a push. "Stop teasing, you. I meant he'd never lend me the Land-Rover even if I could drive it. He needs it all the time, and we couldn't afford for me to have a car." She shrugged. "It's pointless."

Pa Garton searched her face with anxious eyes. He reached out and took her hand in both of his. "Now listen, Sylvie, it's no good giving up that easily. No effort means no change. Do you see what I'm saying?" He shook her hand as if to emphasize the words. "You learn to drive, and you can borrow the car when you need it."

Sylvie thought of all the things she could do, go to town, explore the country with Tom, visit Sandra, and maybe even Deirdre. "It's a wonderful offer," she said, "but I can't possibly accept it."

"I wouldn't have offered if I didn't mean it," Pa Garton said. "It's not just for you, it's for the whole family. It's no good for them if you're unhappy, is it?"

Sylvie put her other hand on top of his and gave it a squeeze. "You're a good man," she said. "I can't tell you how much that would help."

"We'll start Wednesday, then. Before we go to the nursery we'll find a quiet street and I'll teach you some manoeuvres."

"You'll pick me up, then? I think I'd like it to be a surprise for Henry." She blushed.

Pa Garton gave her a shrewd look. "You've got a right to a life too, love, you know."

Rose appeared at the gate. "What're you two up to? Come on, Henry's about to give the toast."

"Coming," Sylvie said.

The room was stuffy and smelt of whisky and eau-de-Cologne. Henry's cronies from The Green Man were passing round glasses with more than two fingers of Scotch and Henry was standing at the end of the room, holding his tumbler against his suit waistcoat.

"Go on, Henry: 'Unaccustomed as I am . . .' " called out one of the men. Everyone laughed.

Henry smiled benevolently at the company. "I'm very pleased to have you all here with us today," he started. "Thank you for turning out from all over three counties to join us for the christening."

From near the door, Sylvie looked at the back of people's heads, all turned to listen to Henry.

There was a tug at her sleeve. "Your Jess is a wilful one," said the large woman who Deirdre had called Auntie Vi. Unable to hear Henry's speech properly, she seemed to have decided to start one of her own. "What on earth was she doing dabbling her hand in the font like that?"

The ancient aunt joined in. "Vicar were none too pleased — didna give 'er a look!"

Sylvie looked from one to the other, opened her mouth and then shut it again. Vividly she recalled the

186

little party gathered round the font, Tom in her arms, silenced by the echoing space around him, and Jess on the other side of the font, allowed up to the front with the grown-ups to see her baby brother being christened, watching with big solemn eyes.

Jess peered forward to look into the font and saw herself in the dark water. She glanced up and caught Sylvie's eye. Sylvie knew exactly what Jess was going to do: she had found her magic place, and in a ritual of her own making, to mark the solemnity of the moment she slipped her hand into the water to reach through her own reflection and into another world.

"Will someone keep that child in order?" the vicar snapped, and Jess pulled out her hand as if she'd been stung, and wiped it quickly on her dress. One of the aunts had put a hand on Jess's shoulder, as if to restrain her from further sabotage, and Jess had spent the rest of the ceremony staring down at her feet.

The ancient aunt was looking around the group for agreement, and getting the tutting response she expected. No, Sylvie thought, no point saying anything: we don't speak the same language.

Not for the first time, she felt acutely the lack of anyone to represent her side of the family. A revealing word, "side," she thought, like lines joined for battle. No wonder she felt a bit overwhelmed by the Garton clan; she was a newcomer to be welcomed, then stood neatly in her place in the Garton ranks. And where was Tom? She'd half expected — well, hoped — for Henry to be holding Tom. It would have given her pleasure to see Henry show him some tenderness in public — he was just a baby after all, surely not yet in need of "toughening up". She looked around to see who had got him. Deirdre was at the front, holding Jess's hand. Rose was handing out glasses of warm white wine to the ladies. Henry was talking about continuity, about handing on a way of life from father to son. His voice rose with pride as he built up to the toast, despite the fact that his son was nowhere in sight. ". . . So charge your glasses, please, and drink a toast with me, to the next son and heir to Garton's!"

"Garton's!" repeated the family, raising their glasses, then taking a sip and turning back to their conversations.

"Where's Tom?" Sylvie hissed to Rose.

Rose looked startled. "Put to bed, dear — getting a bit fractious."

"Well, that takes the biscuit," Sylvie muttered under her breath. "Shame Tom missed hearing the farm toasted on his christening day."

Rose looked at her blankly, irony lost on her. Sylvie bit down the urge to ask why she hadn't come to find her when Tom had got "fractious". Was she surplus to requirements even where her own baby was concerned? She counted silently to ten.

"I'll get some plates," she said to Rose, "so that you can cut that beautiful cake."

"Oh, I've already done that, dear," said Rose. "I'm just going to wrap it and serve it now." She busied herself undoing a pack of pale-blue serviettes.

Sylvie quietly slipped away upstairs. She lifted her sleeping baby from his cot and held him close, his face

188

warm and damp against her bare neck. She carried him through to her bedroom and laid him down on the counterpane, then kicked off her shoes and lay down, curling her body around him. He smelt fresh as ironed cotton. She put her arm over him and cradled the back of his head in her hand.

The monotone of distant conversation drifted into white noise. She curled tighter. She was a shell, hard and smooth around the tiny creature that she hid. She was a shell, she could feel herself shrinking.

CHAPTER
TEN

Jess

"There's a funny noise in my bedroom, Jess." Tom shook me awake.

I propped myself up on my elbows, woozy with sleep. It was light outside: about five, I thought.

"You've been having nightmares again, Tom," I said. "It's just a silly dream." A week after the night of Dad's fury, the memory was still finding its way like smoke into his sleep. I sat right up and put my arms round him. His shoulder blades felt bony through his vest. "Haven't you got any pyjamas?" I said.

"They're too small".

Sure enough, he seemed all arms and legs. "I'll order some new ones from the catalogue today," I said guiltily.

He pulled away and tugged at my hand. "Come *on*. It isn't a dream — you can hear it."

I could hear Dad letting the cows into the holding yard. "It was probably Dad opening up downstairs," I said.

Tom shook his head doggedly and I let him lead me to his room.

190

We stood listening among the clutter of worn clothes, fishing reels, tennis balls and shoes that covered Tom's floor. There was a flutter at the window as a house martin flew to its nest, and a sudden clamorous peeping from the chicks inside.

"There, you see, it's under the eaves. That's why it sounds so close."

"No, no, no," said Tom, climbing on to his bed and putting his ear to the chimney-breast wall. "It's something living in here."

My skin rose into goose bumps. I couldn't help but think of the time a rat had run across my bare foot when we were playing once in the hayloft. It was over in an instant, but the sensation of fur followed by a trail of skin had stayed with me, ambushing me at any mention of the creatures. Gingerly I clambered across the bed and rested my face against the plaster. Nothing.

"What's the noise like? Is it little scratchy noises?"

"It's not mice," Tom said. "I know what mice sound like."

"Well, I can't hear a thing," I said quickly, not wanting him to reach the same conclusion I had.

"It's a sudden noise," he said thoughtfully, "like something small jumping about." He frowned. "Like something trying to get out."

I shivered. "Well, whatever it is it can't get out here: look." I pulled the bed away from the wall. The skirting board was intact. "Go back to bed for an hour or two — it's not time to get up for school yet."

He stuck out his lower lip.

"Oh, all right then," I said, "you can tuck up with me."

As we trailed back to my room I stopped to check the skirting board on the landing side of the massive chimney breast. Set into the wall, covered by a metal plate, was an inspection hole that you could use to locate a chimney fire. I pushed it to check that the sweep had screwed it back up tight last time he'd been. It was solid. I knelt down and peered through the tiny holes into the cavernous hollow of a farmhouse chimney, as wide as a lift shaft. All that met me was a cool draught and the smell of soot.

He was probably just imagining it, I told myself, as we settled back down in my room. Tom's skinny body relaxed almost instantly once he reached the haven of my bed. Although he'd seemed fine in the daytime, as lively and resilient as ever, the night brought him time and time again to wake me on one pretext or another: he was hot, his covers were itchy, he had a tummy ache; or sometimes he just stood there, speechless, after bad dreams. *I should never have left him*, I thought, for about the millionth time. I watched him now, sleeping on his stomach like a swimmer who's reached the shore and is too exhausted to go any further. I pulled the sheet up lightly over him.

Was that what Dad had meant when he said I couldn't be trusted, just like Mum? Did he mean that I'd left Tom just like she'd left us? I remembered Dad's look, the way he'd stared at me from top to toe. No, it was more than the leaving Tom alone. It was to do with how I'd looked that night; he'd looked at me as though he'd despised me. As though he knew.

My heart beat faster as I thought about my stupid mistake with Martin. A silly little virgin, Martin must have thought — an easy lay. I prickled with shame. I hugged my knees and tried to block out the voice in my head. I don't have to see any of them ever again, I thought. But the anger was still there; the anger wouldn't go away. And if I was honest, Martin was the least of it. This rock of anger I was carrying inside me was for Dad. It was as strong as my need for comfort had been that night; it was as hard as the stony face I'd been met with instead. Every time I thought about that night, the rock's cold surface was polished a little brighter, and every time Dad looked through me as he asked me to do something, as if I was beneath his notice, I was afraid he'd see the flash of it, as if I turned it in my hand.

I put my hands to my face and smoothed my fingertips over my eyes and down over my cheeks. I reached under the pillow to find Mum's bird book, feeling carefully under the cool weight of feathers so as not to wake Tom. I opened it and turned over the pages with their tiny writing punctuated by little ink drawings of Mum's favourite birds: a lapwing with its sweeping black crest; a hawfinch looking pugnacious with its thick bill and bull neck; a pied wagtail, its distinctive markings shaded in black ink.

I found as I turned the pages that the drawings became less frequent, then the entries began to thin out. There was a long gap around the time when Tom was born, then a few entries, but sparse and scrappy. The last entry read: *15th November 1967. Flock of fieldfares in Deeper's field, and roosting in the hawthorn. Winter nomads.* The phrase made me shiver. Then nothing. Twenty or so blank pages to the end of the book. *15th November.* A fortnight later she was gone, just as abruptly. I went through that day again, familiar as a nursery rhyme.

It was a Friday when I last saw her, my day for going over to Gran and Grandad's for tea. We had lemon meringue pie. Afterwards Grandad and I fell asleep in front of the fire, so Gran rang up and asked if I could stay and she must've said OK.

I remember Mum and I had walked over to the house across the fields. It was muddy after raining all day and Gran made me leave my boots outside the front door. Mum gave me a quick kiss and Grandad passed her the car keys. My last view of her was as she backed the red Mini out of the drive. She looked over her shoulder as she swung through the gate, then straightened up and beeped the horn. She was smiling and she mouthed "Be good" at me and waved. That was the last thing she said to me: "Be good". Well, I hadn't made much of a job of it so far.

My mind shied away from the next morning, the whispered conversation between Gran and Grandad in the hall. Then, as the day wore on, every time I asked a question, Gran hugging me so I couldn't breathe, Dad turning up in the Land-Rover, his face a white splodge behind the swish of the wipers.

I closed the book and curled my fingers around its edges, tight. I couldn't remember anyone actually telling me Mum had left. Perhaps I'd blocked that out. Perhaps I just knew.

I slid the book back into its place under the pillow. Tom stirred and opened his eyes.

"What're you thinking about?" he said, looking curiously at my face.

"Lemon meringue pie," I said off the top of my head.

"But you hate it; you always say it makes you feel sick to your stomach . . ."

"Time to get up," I said.

I set to in the morning to clean up Tom's room — not that he would appreciate it, or probably even notice, but it made me feel better; it was a way of making things up to him. Dad went out at about ten, saying something about checking prices for dairy cows at auction, so I was left alone to tidy cupboards and brush down cobwebs from the whitewashed corners of the room. Every now and then I stopped to listen, afraid I'd heard a scuffling in the chimney breast, but the noise of Philip driving the baler in the field below the house drowned it out so that I couldn't be sure. When the baler stopped I banged on the chimney-breast wall and listened again. There was the faintest rustle; it could have been soot falling or a tiny piece of mortar dislodged by my banging, but it still made me feel uneasy.

I went downstairs and settled myself down in the living room to look through the catalogue for pyjamas for Tom. Presently I heard Philip come in to get his sandwiches from the fridge. I kept quiet, idly flicking over the thin pages while he moved about in the kitchen, finding a glass and running the tap.

Suddenly there was a scuffling noise, followed by a rattle and a clatter as a handful of twigs came ricocheting out of the chimney and into the fireplace, and bits of grey mortar pattered in the grate. I squealed and leapt to my feet as a cloud of soot puffed out of the fireplace, covering the log basket and the hearthrug in black smuts.

Philip put his head around the door. "Everything all right?" he said.

"Nothing we can't handle ourselves," I said. "I think we've got rats."

Annoyingly, this seemed to pique his interest. He went over to the fireplace and peered up inside, then picked up the poker.

I retreated behind the sofa. "I don't think you should do that," I said, but he was already poking it into the chimney shaft. Another bundle of twigs and mess came down.

He turned to me with a grin. "Well, I've never known rats make a nest like this before," he said. "I think what you've got is what my grandad would call a grackle."

"If you're trying to scare me with some old folk-tale nonsense . . ." I said.

He knelt down, reached up into the flue and felt around. "We're not going to get it out this way anyway," he said, "not unless it falls."

"But what *is* it?" I said.

He stood up and looked for something to wipe his sooty arm on. Finding nothing, he wiped it on his T-shirt.

"It's a bird," he said. "You've got jackdaws nesting. I've seen a couple of young ones about in the yard over the last few days."

"Well, why doesn't this one fly out too?" I said, coming out from behind the sofa.

He shrugged. "Dunno. Must be stuck for some reason. Perhaps it's fallen out of the nest."

I bent to look past the stacked logs and into the flue. "I'll get a torch," I said, "and a screwdriver, then we can have a look from upstairs."

I showed Philip the inspection hatch. He bent and peered in, then started unscrewing the plate. A sudden fluttering came from below it, then a thump, then silence.

"Uh-oh," Philip said, "we're disturbing him. He'll knock himself out if he tries too much of that." He went more slowly, turning the rusty screws by degrees. "How's the studying going?" he asked.

"I've finished with that," I said. He glanced quickly up. I flushed. "For the moment, I mean. The exams are all over."

He smiled. "Lucky you," he said. "Best summer holiday I ever had was between school and university. No sweat."

I didn't comment.

He lifted the grille out carefully and propped it against the wall, then shone the torch through the hole, angling it from side to side. "There he is!" he said. "Look."

I knelt down and peered along the beam of light. A few feet below us on a ledge on the other side of the chimney, a scruffy-looking fledgeling jackdaw sat blinking its grey eyes in the brightness. It let out a hard *tchack*, and sidled a little way along the ledge.

"At least it's not injured," I said.

Philip swung the torch away from it and around the sides of the chimney. "You can see what's happened," he said. "The parents have built the nest deep in the flue to make it safe, but it's meant it's hard for the fledgelings to fly out — the angle's just too steep." He handed the torch to me.

I looked back through the hole and up to the circle of bright blue above. "How come the others made it, then?"

"They were stronger."

"What'll happen to this one if he won't come out through this hole?" I said.

Philip turned the corners of his mouth down.

I imagined the bird getting weaker, his fluttering jumps diminishing to feeble flaps. The chimney sweep would pull out the remains of the nest in the autumn, along with the bird's small dry body. I put my hand on Philip's arm. "We've got to get him out," I said.

Philip nodded. "Can you find a rake," he said, "or something with a long handle?"

198

Minutes later we had pushed a broom handle across the drop so that one end rested on the thin ledge and the other on the edge of the inspection hole. It sloped at an alarming angle. The bird retreated to the very corner of the ledge, as far away as possible from this new threat.

"He's never going to risk that," I said, despairing.

Philip touched me lightly on the shoulder. "He won't with us peeping in at him," he said. "Let's go away and see what happens."

We retreated to the bottom of the stairs and sat on the last steps. All was quiet upstairs. Neither of us said anything, but I kept craning round to look.

"Nice weather we're having," Philip said facetiously.

"You've got to be joking, haven't you? It's damaging the feed crops and killing off the grass — it'll end up bankrupting us if we don't get some rain soon." I sat quiet after this outburst, embarrassed.

"Seriously?" he said.

"Seriously."

"The river does seem very low," he said. "That stretch where we met, the tree roots are all out of the water now. It looks strange."

The phrase "where we met" hung in the air.

"Dad says it's the Water Board," I said, deliberately practical. "They're taking water from the river since the reservoir dried up."

I thought about the picture of the reservoir in the paper, with the old road across the valley revealed again. People had driven across it again after forty years, and the reservoir floor resembled a moonscape, cracked into hexagons, like a kind of flattened giants' causeway. It seemed that nothing could be relied on any more, not even the landscape.

"Listen, Jess," Philip said, "are you sure things are as bad as you say with the farm?"

I nodded miserably. "I think Dad's looking at selling some cows," I said, "so things must be desperate."

"Only, I know Uncle Mick's interested . . ." Philip started.

There was a movement above us and instinctively we both ducked. The jackdaw was out and was flying from corner to corner of the landing, trying to escape, its neck feathers ruffled and its claws scrabbling against the walls, in its effort to find some purchase. Its sooty wings marked the walls and ceiling with dark bars. We jumped up and ran upstairs. The bird dropped back to the floor and hopped away. Philip made a grab for it but it half jumped, half flew, at the ceiling to escape, then dropped back, stunned.

"Quick," I said, and caught it in both hands. It felt light, like gathering up knitting wool and needles all in one.

"Bring one hand up around its neck," Philip said; "otherwise it'll peck you when it comes round."

Already it was beginning to struggle in my hands, thrashing its feet and jerking its head forward.

"All right, all right, you fiendish grackle," I said as we took him outside. "I'll put him down in the shade somewhere," I said and walked towards the rain barrel. "The parents'll come and feed him. He'll be all right."

"What about the cat?" said Philip. "He'd be safer up high."

I held on to him. "Do you think he can fly properly, though?"

"Well, he was having a good go inside, wasn't he?" Philip said.

I smoothed the grackle's feathers with my index finger, feeling the grey ruff of downy feathers on the back of his head. His beak was dark, but still with a tiny bit of yellow at the corners of his gape.

"Shhh, I won't hurt you," I said.

The bird struggled in my hands. I looked round at Philip, who nodded me on. I lowered my hands, then threw them up, launching the bird into the air. With an inelegant flapping he was airborne, then as he gained height he stretched out his wings wider.

"Yes!" I heard Philip exclaim. Then we clutched each other as the jackdaw faltered, regained a steady beat and flew up to the top of the barn. He folded his wings and stepped from foot to foot, looking unbearably smug, then almost over-balanced, sticking out a wing so that his feathers folded back unevenly, his feet and legs too big for his body. We both burst out laughing and hugged close in the euphoria of the moment. I pulled away first. He let his hands drop.

"I promised Mick I'd help him in the workshop later, and your dad's wanting the baling finished before I go," he said with a sigh.

"See you, then," I said, looking at the ground. "Thanks for the help."

★ ★ ★

I went off to brush up the soot in the hearth and beat the rug, to clear up before Dad got back. The open mouth of the fireplace was dark and silent as a tomb. I was glad to finish there and move upstairs with the stepladders to clean away the dirty wing marks on the ceiling. I stood back and looked at my work with a critical eye. The paintwork looked a bit shinier where I'd rubbed, but I didn't think Dad would notice. It seemed strange that such a struggle for life had taken place today, yet everything looked the same, as though nothing had happened.

I hung the cloth over the rim of the bucket and went to look out of the window. The jackdaw had flown down from the barn and perched on the gatepost next to the cattle grid. It gave a little shake of its wings as if straightening its feathers, then let out a series of *tchack tchack* noises and sprang into the air. With slow wing beats it laboured to gain height, flew towards the dairy, then up and over the hayloft in a long glide, and away beyond my view.

CHAPTER
ELEVEN

Sylvie

15th November 1967. Flock of fieldfares in Deeper's field, and roosting in the hawthorn. Winter nomads.

Sylvie cleared the dishes around Henry while he pored over an Ordnance Survey map spread out on the kitchen table, his pen poised above the stiff paper. Moves were afoot to reopen a public footpath that roughly followed the course of the river, and gave right of way across Garton land. Henry started marking out his field boundaries in blue ink. The lines stood out, imposing angular geometric shapes over the pale-brown waves of contour lines.

Sylvie hung up the tea towel. "You know, now that I'm driving . . ." she said.

"Mmm," Henry said noncommittally.

"Well, I'm getting a job," she said.

He looked up from the map. "What d'you want to do that for?"

Sylvie came to sit down. "I need a change," she said firmly. "I feel cooped up at home and I want to get out a bit more, that's all."

"Well, we all feel like that from time to time," he said, "but some of us have got more sticking power than others." Sylvie held her tongue. Henry drew in a blue line as close to the woods along the riverside as he could. "Do you know," he said, keeping his eyes on the pen, "what it cost me to rent that land to the Swifts?"

"I thought they were paying us," Sylvie said, being deliberately obtuse.

Henry drew a thick line at the boundary of Swift's small-holding. "Look," he said, crumpling the map as he shoved it over to her, "I've done what you were after. What more do you want?"

Sylvie looked at the old boundary line of the farm and at Henry's blue line cutting a sharp V into it.

"It's not really fair to blame me, Henry," she said in a neutral tone. "It's like shooting the messenger. We just needed the money, that's all." She smoothed the map out again. "It's a piece of land," she said, "that we get a living from."

"It's always been Garton land," he said, "and now it's my piece of land."

Sylvie sighed. "You don't own it, Henry, any more than the wind owns it just because it blows across it. You just look after it for a while." She got up and came closer to him. "And it's such a little while, let's not argue." She held out her hand.

Henry sat still, refusing to look at her, and after a moment she let her hand drop.

"The job . . . It'll be a bit more money," she said, "and it's only Friday and Saturday, just in the evenings, so Tom'll be asleep before I go."

"I don't want you doing bar work," he said, staring fixedly ahead. "I'm not having men eyeing you up."

"It's at the cinema," she said, "helping out at their busy time."

"Oh, for God's sake!" Henry stood up. "Selling ice creams — is that the best you can do?"

"You should be pleased," Sylvie said tartly. "No one'll see me in the dark."

Henry walked out and she shouted after him, "The ideal job for someone in purdah!"

The door shut behind him. She folded the map up all the wrong way, then slapped it down on the table and left it there, its accordion folds springing from its covers.

The cinema was a small-town, small-time picture-house with panelled glass doors and a black sign above with stick-on white letters that gave the titles for A- and B-movies and their showing times. It was a family-run business. Mr Burton, the owner, was also the projectionist. His wife and daughter, and now Sylvie too, doubled up to man the box office, shine a torch along dusty rows of plush seats and sell choc-ices and boxes of Smarties at the interval.

Sylvie fell in love with it. Once she'd shown everyone to their places she would slip into a seat by the door to watch for late arrivals. She loved the feeling of celebration, the shuffling and excited whispering as people settled down, the dimming of the tiny lights in the night sky of the ceiling, with its ritual power to produce an expectant silence. She loved being part of the crowd, the way their pale faces all turned towards the screen like flowers towards the sun, the way a theatre full of people with their different lives were caught for a while in the same dream, like the dust motes caught in the widening beam of light.

Betty, Mr Burton's wife, called her "star-struck" as she blundered out, dreamy-eyed, after a love story, then had to rush around as the titles went up, to get the exit doors unbolted. "Cutting it fine again, Sylvie," she said cheerfully as she passed. Sylvie shot back the bolt of the last door and opened it to the car park beyond. The strains of the last verse of the national anthem carried faintly from upstairs and disappeared into the chilly darkness.

After the show Betty made coffee in the back room while Mr Burton cashed up. Sylvie swept up the rubbish from under the tip-up seats, making a neat pile at the end of each row to collect when she'd finished. In the dim, empty auditorium she replayed the best bits of the film in her head, eking out the dream a little longer.

She put the down payment on a TV.

"We can't afford it," Henry said flatly when it was delivered. It sat in the middle of the living room, still in its huge cardboard box.

"I know we shouldn't really," Sylvie said, "but I got it on HP so I can pay a bit at a time, and I've put my first wages into the bank."

"I don't want an aerial up on the house," he said.

"Oh, come on, Henry, don't be such a killjoy." Sylvie started ripping off the parcel tape on the top of the box.

206

"Jess'll love it. She says the kids at school are always talking about the programmes and she just has to keep quiet."

"I don't think TV's good for kids," he said suspiciously.

"What, the undermining of parents' authority by too much *Blue Peter*?" Sylvie looked up at him, laughing. "Or the revolutionary ideas in *Crackerjack*?"

"Something's got into you," Henry said.

Sylvie got up off her knees, grabbed his hand and swung it playfully.

"Life," she said. "Life's got into me." She kissed him on the cheek. "Are you going to help me lift it on to the sideboard?" She pulled the rest of the packaging away and took off the cardboard covers on the tuning and volume dials.

Henry helped her lift it. "Well, you can find the licence money," he said.

Sylvie polished the grey-green screen with her sleeve.

"Mmm?" she said. "You'll enjoy it, you know. It'll take you out of yourself a bit. And it'll be company when I'm at work." She turned back towards him and saw a look of complete bewilderment in his eyes.

"You should've asked first," he said.

She raised her eyebrows. When had he ever asked her opinion about buying anything?

"Let's try it with the built-in aerial," she said, and plugged it in. A fuzzy image of the test card appeared and horizontal lines scrolled slowly down the screen.

Henry said, "I can see Jess'll get a lot out of that."

Sylvie twiddled with the vertical hold. "We could watch something together tonight if you want," she said. "Betty says *Z Cars* is good."

Henry shook his head. "I'm going down the pub tonight. You'll have to watch it on your own."

In the evening Sylvie watched the fuzzy picture determinedly for an hour or two, despite being interrupted by Tom waking, needing comfort. She finally gave up on the TV when she started to get a headache, and went to bed.

"Did you have a good time?" she asked as Henry opened the bedroom door and light from the landing spilled across the bed.

Henry grunted, sat down heavily on the end of the bed and started to undo his shoelaces.

"That bloody Swift man was there," he said, "and he had the cheek to offer to buy me a drink — all familiar, as if we were mates."

"He was probably just trying to be friendly," Sylvie said.

"As if he wasn't my tenant!" Henry said, loosening the laces with irritated jerks.

"What did you do?"

"I said did *he* want a drink? Then he said he was there with his wife and would I like to meet her."

Sylvie sat up. "What did she say?"

Henry started unbuttoning his shirt. "I dunno. I didn't go over. I said I was with a party already, and then . . ." He pulled off his shirt and chucked it over the back of a chair. "And then, do you know what he said? 'Perhaps another time, we could all get together one night when your missis is off work.'"

"He was just being friendly, surely?"

"Too friendly by half," Henry said, emptying his pockets with a chinking noise on to the china tray on the dressing table. "And how does he know about you working? The lads were over playing darts, else they would have heard him."

Sylvie propped herself up on one elbow. "It's a small town," she said. "You're bound to see people you know at the cinema. You say hello. It's called being sociable."

"It's called nosy gossiping neighbours," said Henry, "who should mind their own households and leave me to mind mine."

From Tom's room, a high wail interrupted them. Sylvie sighed, swung her legs out of bed and winced as her bare feet touched the cold floor. She hurried to get there before Jess woke up too.

Tom had pulled himself up by the bars of the cot and was sucking on the crossbar. He had two bright spots on his cheeks. Sylvie picked him up and wiped his snuffly nose. "Poor baby," she said, kissing the top of his head. She walked up and down, rubbing his back and crooning to him. He would quieten for a minute, chewing on his fist and dribbling on her shoulder, then he would take his hand out and give more hiccupping sobs. "Ssh, ssh, now," she said, "you'll wake Jessie up." She picked the teething ring out of the cot and took him back to her room.

"He's not coming in our bed again!" Henry sat up among the rumpled covers.

"Well, what do you suggest?"

"I've got to be up again at half five."

Sylvie glared at him. "And if I put him back in his cot I'll no doubt be up and down with him all night."

Henry grudgingly moved over and Sylvie climbed in. Ten minutes later Tom started to cry again, his legs kicking out like a breast-stroke swimmer, in his discomfort.

Henry burrowed deeper under the blankets. "Can't you do something with him?" he said in a muffled voice.

Sylvie got back up again, pulled on her dressing gown and kicked around under the bed for her slippers. Tom's howls grew louder. As she bent to pick Tom up she heard Henry muttering, "It'd be nice to have your wife to yourself just occasionally." She ignored him and took Tom off downstairs.

She sat next to the remains of the fire in the living room, wrapped him inside her dressing gown and gave him a bottle. At first he just chewed on the teat but then he began to suck, his tight little body began to relax and his eyelids to flicker. The rain pattered against the windows and she wondered how many miles you'd have to go before you found another human being who was awake. Her eyes ached. She could, she supposed, tiptoe up and pop Tom back into his cot, hope for the best, and get back into her own bed. But she felt that if she got one more comment from Henry she would probably scream.

Carefully, she bent forward and put another log on the fire, raising sparks and ash from the embers below.

She tucked a cushion between the arm of the chair and her elbow, to support Tom's heavy head on her arm. She looked at the sleeping face of the child she'd thought would draw Henry and her back together again. His lips were slightly open as he breathed through his mouth, and his pale eyelashes lay against the softness of his skin. She wondered, for the umpteenth time, at Henry's coolness towards Tom, this boychild whom he set such store by as his son and heir. Maybe that was it, she thought: maybe having a son who was going to inherit made Henry feel his own mortality. Maybe he was just jealous that Tom took up so much of her time. She pulled the side of her quilted dressing gown further over Tom. He stirred, rooting against her arm with the old reflex of the newborn. No, she wasn't going to risk going back upstairs. Two children were enough to care for; Henry would just have to grow up.

The next day rain was still pouring relentlessly. It washed gravelly stones and sand into tide lines on the concrete yard, filled the potholes in the track and turned the leaf-fall from trees and hedges into a slippery mush.

Henry came and went from the farm buildings, leaving wet jackets and boots in the way and letting the dogs in to make paw marks all over the floor. When she remonstrated he just looked at her morosely and shut himself up in the office. Tom grew more and more irritable as the day wore on. She gave up feeding him his lunch because he just kept chewing on the spoon and pushing the sieved vegetables out with his tongue. She rubbed his gums with oil of cloves and fed him rusk after rusk to chew on, but he wouldn't be pacified. She paced up and down the kitchen with him, singing his favourite rhymes and lullabies, getting more and more tense as she failed to soothe him and his wails grew more pitiful.

Henry was making a series of phone calls in the hall and she could hear in the intervals of Tom's sobs that Henry's voice was getting louder. Eventually he stuck his head round the kitchen door and said, "Can't you get him to shut the blazes up?"

"No, I can't," Sylvie said shortly. "Who're you phoning anyway? Do you have to do it now?"

"Yes, I do," Henry said, mimicking her voice. "Those idiots at the council are voting for the reopening of that right of way straight across my land. No consultation, mind you, no consideration of the cost of mending stiles and providing a margin for people to walk on."

"You shouldn't let it get you so upset," Sylvie said helplessly, shifting Tom to lean against her other shoulder as he wriggled.

"It's not as if any walkers will use it," Henry carried on. "It'll just be all the boys from the village up here chucking stones in the water and fishing off the bridge. It'll be the young couples sneaking about to do it in our woods and people dumping old tyres and rubbish on my land. We'll have every gypsy and diddycoy for miles around traipsing through my barley and letting my stock out!" He started pulling his jacket on.

Sylvie said, "What're you going to do?"

212

"Never you mind," he said, "but I've told them I'm not having it and I stick to what I say."

"Henry . . ." she started, but he was off out of the door.

She peered from the kitchen window into the rain, and saw him backing the Land-Rover over to the tractor shed and piling boxes and tools into the back of it.

Tom broke off from crying and started to bang his head rhythmically against her shoulder. "Poor little mite," she said to him. "Let's try another bottle, shall we?" Worn out by crying, as soon as he began to suck he fell asleep.

Sylvie turned her thoughts towards the evening, and work. She took her uniform out of the wardrobe and gave it a shake-out. It was shortish, but smart, a blue overall with white reveres, in a drip-dry fabric, modern and practical. She held it up against her and looked at herself in the mirror. With the other hand she lifted her hair at the back: yes, perhaps she'd wear it that way tonight, piled on top. *Chic*, she thought, a movie word. For a moment she was a Bond girl, or Elizabeth Taylor, glamorous . . . She hung the uniform up on the back of the bedroom door. It was *My Fair Lady* tonight. It'd been out a while and she knew lots of the songs already. She hummed a snatch or two. How long was Henry going to be? She was going to need to get Jess from school soon and then take her over for tea at Rose's and pick up the car for tonight.

She stooped to look out of the window. The weather had worsened. The wind was rising; it stripped leaves from the trees and slapped rain at the glass. The Land-Rover was parked a couple of fields away but there was no sign of Henry. She peeped in on Tom. He was flat out, arms and legs spread star-shaped in the cot.

Henry's got a watch, she thought. He knows what time he has to get back so that I can go. She packed Jess's wellingtons in a bag and then checked out the back. The Land-Rover was moving slowly downhill; he was on his way home. She slipped on her wind-cheater, pulled the toggles tight to keep the hood on, and set off down the sodden track. Thank God I'll be driving back, she thought, her hands thrust deep in her pockets and her body bent over to make some headway in the wind. The rain drove against her legs, soaking through her slacks, and wet leaves stuck like plasters to her boots. Down by the river the track was sludgy. The milk lorry must have taken the sharp turn a bit wide in the morning. Sylvie noticed that the bank was churned up and scored with deep tyre marks, and mud was spread over the road. She started to sing to herself, "I could have danced all night, I could have danced all night," to keep up her pace, but her breath was whipped away by the wind and the soughing of the branches moaning with its force.

As she drove back up the drive, having walked Jess round to Rose's for tea and borrowed the car, the light was beginning to fade and the rain was coming in on the slant, driven by an unforgiving wind. She pulled the car up close to the door so that she could nip out smartly when it was time for work, and not get her hair ruined. Already she was beginning to feel excited, suffused with that same feeling she got at the cinema that in her mind she called "curtain up".

"Coo-eee," she called as she struggled out of her wet things.

She went through into the dim kitchen, wondering why there were no lights on. A noise reached her from upstairs, familiar and yet interrupted, stuttering like a motor-bike engine unable to roar into life. She took the stairs two at a time. Tom was puce in the face from crying. His arms and legs jerked with fury as his chest worked in and out to choke out the sobs inside it. Sylvie snatched him up and began rocking him to and fro. His eyes were scrunched up and his mouth was a cavernous "O".

"Poor baby," she said, laying her hand on his hot forehead. "There now, there now, poor baby." His body was rigid, every muscle tensed as he bawled out his need for her. "Shush now, it's all right," she murmured. She fished out a blanket from the tangled mess in the cot and wrapped him tightly in it like a newborn, hoping that the swaddling would calm him. She heard the door bang downstairs and, holding Tom tightly to her, she went down.

Henry came into the kitchen looking like a wild man, his hair tousled, his colour high and his eyes gleaming from the wind.

"Henry," she said, "how could you?"

"What?" He ran his hand over his forehead to push his hair out of his eyes.

"You were supposed to be back at three to look after Tom. What on earth happened?"

"I've got a lot of them done," Henry said, pulling a bag of nails out of one pocket and his keys out of the other. "No one's going to get over them in a hurry."

"Tom nearly screamed himself into a fit!" Sylvie said. Tom's sobbing had subsided to the stage of exhausted lower-lip quivering. "I thought you'd at least got bogged down in mud or something."

"Well, he looks all right to me," Henry said, glancing at Tom quickly. "I'm trying to tell you — I've got more than half of them done."

"Half of what?" Sylvie said coldly.

"The stiles, of course. Barbed wire, three strands each, straight across the top. That should put 'em off a bit." He started to laugh. "And if they put up way markers I'll have them down again."

"You can't do that, Henry. It's against the law."

He raised a finger to her. "Don't tell me what I can or can't do, all right?"

She stood silent. He rubbed his hands together, warming them back to life, then turned his back on her and went to open the fridge to look for something to forage.

Sylvie was trembling with anger. "I'm going to bath and feed Tom and get him down," Sylvie said, "and tonight I'm going to work and you're going to listen out for our son."

Henry swung round. "What about dinner?"

"Bugger your dinner," she said.

A sly look crossed Henry's face. "Just tread carefully," he said.

"Get it yourself," she said.

The phone rang and Sylvie went out to the hall to answer it. It was Rose asking if Jess could stay the night. Sylvie said yes and rang off quickly. It was probably best if Jess wasn't around in this atmosphere anyway. She took Tom upstairs.

When people say they're seething, she thought, as she sponged Tom down, that's exactly it: like a volcano or one of those hot mud baths where the whole surface lifts and boils. She bobbed Tom's boat through the water for him. *Bloody, bloody Henry*, she thought.

She was worried Tom would pick up on her mood and be hard to settle, but he was tired out with teething and bellowing and fell asleep before the end of his bottle. Sylvie washed, splashing her face with cool water to try to calm down. She sat at her dressing table and cleared the rubble that was on it into the drawer — some old face cream, a bracelet, her bird book, stray hair grips, some baby powder. It was getting too full, but she hadn't got time to fiddle with it now, and she gave the drawer a good shove. Expertly she twisted her hair up at the back and fixed it with combs, then back-combed the top a little to give it some height.

It was as she bent close to the mirror to put on her lipstick that she noticed her uniform wasn't hanging where she'd left it. She tutted and changed her trousers for a dark skirt. If Henry thought that hiding her uniform was going to stop her going to work he could forget it. She wasn't having any more of this stupid childishness. She pulled the car keys out of the pocket of her slacks, took a last look at Tom and went casually downstairs.

Henry was sitting at the kitchen table with a sandwich on a plate in front of him, pretending to read the paper. There was no plate for her.

"What have you done with my uniform?" she said.

"In the fire," he said through a mouthful of bread, "since you won't be needing it any more."

She didn't know what to say.

"It went up with a crackle, that nylon stuff," he said spitefully.

"I can get another one," she said.

He turned a page of the paper. "You can if you want, but you'll look pretty stupid wearing it at home."

"What do you mean?" She wanted to shout, but her voice came out in a whisper.

"I'm going to phone him up," he said, "your Mr Burton, and give in your notice. Due to family *commitments*."

She blinked. "But I have to have a life," she said, her voice cracking. "You can't have it all, Henry."

He looked straight at her for the first time and she saw a flicker of uncertainty. "I need you at home, Sylv," he said.

She shook her head wordlessly; she felt as though she could hardly breathe. Henry started to get up and she knew that if she let him he would put his arms around her and tell her this was all for love. She would be tethered and Henry would always be tugging on the rope. She backed away towards the kitchen door, then broke free, pushed past the dogs and ran into the yard.

Outside, the wind was like an assault. It whipped her hair around her face as she dashed to the car. In the doorway the dogs barked at the wind, getting in Henry's way as she started the engine and pulled away. In the mirror she saw him come blundering after her, his palms open towards her in a gesture of appeal. *You've gone too far this time*, she thought, pushing savagely through the gears as she bumped over the track. He was running now, but she didn't care; she hoped he was afraid of what he'd done. She accelerated and his burly figure faded to a smudge in the rain-streaked glass of the rear window.

As she entered the wood, heavier drops shaken from the branches hammered on the roof of the car. Too late she realized that the bend was upon her. She started to lose it, the back end slithering away from her on the muddy surface, slewing sideways, the front wheels unresponsive to her yanking the wheel round, trying to right it. She saw the grey stone wall of the bridge rise up ahead and stamped on the brake and the clutch. She felt the car leave the road and thump the bridge wall on the passenger side; there was a crash and a tinkling of glass as a branch caught the windscreen, then a rushing, breaking noise as she careered through the undergrowth and down the bank. She had both hands off the wheel now, up in front of her face, and she could hear herself screaming. The car jolted as it hit the water and she struggled, pulling at the seat belt. Water poured in through the broken window. She couldn't get her fingers to work; the belt jammed. The cold water hit her like an electric shock. She tried to pull the belt away from her body, to create some slack, and bucked and wriggled to get free, but the weight of water pushed her back.

"Henry!" she screamed out. "Henry!" The swollen river took the car in its current, turning it sideways in a slow arc, remorselessly covering it.

CHAPTER
TWELVE

Jess

It was the hottest part of the afternoon; the air fairly crackled with heat. We were picking up hay bales in the field next to the river: Dad was driving the tractor and Tom and I were stacking. My arms and legs were covered with tiny scratches, which prickled and stung with sweat. I thought about the river, about wading in it up to the waist and then lying out under the trees. Tom was slowing down as he dragged bales over for me to stack. He put the bale down and pushed up his sleeves, his face red and sweaty.

"Can I stop now?" He sat down with a flump on the bale. "It's too hot."

"Soon be tea-time," I said. "Look, have a drink of water to cool down." I reached into the knapsack I'd brought down with us and passed him the flask. He drank and then passed it back. I held it up to Dad as he came alongside us, but he ignored me and gave Tom a withering look.

"I know," I said to Tom, "why don't you go over there," I pointed to the field behind us, back towards the house, "and make the biggest den you can out of all those bales?"

Tom stood up on his bale to see over the hedge. The field, like this one, was dotted with bales in clumps and scatters as they'd been dumped off the end of the baler. At least this way he'd gather some up in one place, making my job a bit easier tomorrow.

His face brightened. "Can I do tunnels?"

"Yes, but it's got to be one big den, not lots of little ones, OK?"

"Dad won't be cross?"

I thought how Dad had cussed at him for standing behind the trailer earlier. I shook my head; as the day got hotter and tempers frayed it would be better if Tom was out of the way.

Tom jumped down from the hay bale, all signs of drooping gone.

"And we can sleep out in it tonight?"

"It's very hot, Tom." My back was really going to ache by then.

"You said we could." He stuck out his chin. "You did. You said I could sleep out and you would come too."

I sighed. It was true. And it would be good to overlay the memory of the fate of his old den with a new and happier one.

"I'll ask Dad," I said. "I don't think he'll mind." I don't suppose he'll care, I thought, as long as we're on the place to get the work done.

Something of how I was feeling must have shown in my face because Tom suddenly gave me a hug. "It'll be cool later," he said. "It'll be real camping, you'll see."

222

He was right: the nights stayed clear in this drought and the air cooled. I imagined taking a top bale off above us so we could look up at the stars.

"You'll need to get some things when you've built it, then," I said. "Blankets, a torch, food — that sort of thing." This could keep him busy for the rest of the day.

With a quick nod he set off for the gate between the fields, breaking into a trot. I hauled another bale up, the pink baling twine sawing against my fingers.

A tall figure was approaching along the field margin on the river side. I pushed my hair back from my face with my forearm and squinted into the sun. The man raised his arm in greeting and I recognized Mick Swift, both from the gesture and his long ambling stride. Dad saw him and pulled the tractor up, but kept the engine running, its deafening clatter modulating only slightly to a throaty growl. Dad sat with his sleeves rolled up, one arm resting casually on the steering wheel, the other hand on the gear stick, as though he was taking the merest pause for the sake of good manners in the middle of a busy job.

Mick looked up at him with an open smile. "Henry," he said.

"Mick," Dad replied, tilting his chin up in a small act of recognition.

Mick stood waiting and Dad was forced to turn the engine off. The noise died with a sputter and a heat haze of diesel fumes hung over the bonnet.

"You've got a good helper, then," Mick said, smiling at me.

"When she does what she's told," Dad said heavily.

I kept quiet.

Mick looked nonplussed, then started again. "River's very low," he said. "Lowest I've ever seen it. Alice and I wondered how you were all doing over here, what with the radio saying some folk are having to sell stock."

Dad shifted in his seat. "No danger of that," he said with false joviality. "We've got fields full of hay and the river's still running. I think we'll manage."

Mick looked dubious. "Well, I'm glad about that," he said. "There's been such a fuss on the radio about the amount the Water Board is pumping out of the river. People are saying they're going to sell it back to farmers at eighty quid a tanker and there still won't be enough to go round."

Dad glanced pointedly around at the bales dotted across the field, still to be collected.

"I'll not keep you long," Mick said. "The point is, I've got a proposition to make. I know when we took on the small-holding you were keen to rent rather than sell . . ." I saw Dad's back stiffen. Mick carried on: ". . . but circumstances change, and I wondered if you'd like to think about it again."

"Whose circumstances do you mean?"

Mick kept up his light tone. "Well, in the current climate, no pun intended, a lot of farmers are feeling the pinch a bit."

"Whereas, no doubt, you're doing very nicely, thank you, working on my land out of my buildings."

"Well, we're not doing badly," Mick admitted hesitantly.

"So, not here to gloat, then," Dad said with a smile that belied the rudeness of his words.

Mick scratched his head. "Certainly not. We just wondered if this might be a good time to renew our offer, what with hearing that the water shortage was putting your stock at risk."

Dad shot me a poisonous look.

"Well, thank you for your neighbourly concern," he said to Mick, "but if you think you can beat me down on price just because of a long hot summer, you can think again."

"I didn't say anything about changing our bid," Mick said. "All I wanted to say today was that the offer's still there."

Dad gave a disbelieving snort.

I stepped forward. "I think what Dad means," I said, "is that we'd need time to think about it."

"No, I don't," Dad broke in rudely. "I don't know who gave you the impression we needed any help from you, but they're wrong. That land's worth a lot more to me than a couple of oily rolls of banknotes."

Mick laid his hand on the tractor bonnet. "That remark was uncalled for," he said, giving Dad a sharp look.

"So was your offer." Dad turned the ignition key and the tractor roared back into life, drowning out Mick's next words.

Mick stepped back sharply as Dad pulled away. Dad moved on towards the next set of bales, his jaw set and his shoulders hunched.

"The stubborn cuss," Mick said to himself.

I flushed. "I'm so sorry," I said. "He doesn't mean to be like that."

"Oh, I think he does," Mick said, looking grim, "but playing the hothead doesn't sit well on a man his age." He sighed and patted my arm. "You're a good sort, Jess," he said, "and you're welcome at our place any time."

He pressed his lips together and set off to walk back the way he'd come.

Further down the field Dad kept his back to us as he jumped down to start loading, leaving the tractor running. When he'd finished he moved on to the next stack rather than coming back to me and I trudged after him. We worked for a while.

"I've decided to sell most of the hay," he shouted over the noise.

"What if we don't get rain?" I shouted back. "Then we'll need it."

Dad shrugged. "Better sell the feed than sell the stock," he yelled. I knew better than to argue when he was in this mood. "And I'll tell you this much," he went on: "hell would have to freeze over before the Swifts or the bank or any other conniving bastards get their paws on my land."

Later, after he'd rung the feed merchants and then the bank to give excuses yet again for not having put in the accounts for their inspection, we ate and then Dad went to cool off and look through the paper. Even he was feeling the heat and had decided we'd done enough for one day.

226

I didn't want to hang around in the house, especially as it was hard to hold my tongue about the day's events. I thought I would go down to the river and follow my earlier plan. By the time I got back Dad would be off to the pub.

I picked up a book, one of Grandad's old P. G. Wodehouse novels, and, remembering my funny turn in the heat down there before, put on a shapeless old gardening hat.

I set off for the shallow stretch, through the gluey heat. Alongside the track the grass was bleached to brownish yellow and wild barley stalks rustled against one another as I brushed past. Everything was dry as bone and my feet raised little dust devils as I walked, which covered my sandals and toes with a gritty powder. To the left, dominating the field, stretched Tom's den, a long tunnel of bales with offshoots and switchbacks and a large square structure at the end. It must be like a mole's workings in there, I thought: all passages and dark chambers. There was no sign of Tom. A few bales were scattered nearby as if he'd decided his den was big enough now and had gone off elsewhere until the temperature was cool enough to play in it.

On the other side of the track, a couple of fields away, the cows were gathered together under an oak, seeking its scanty shade. The earth was practically bare beneath it, where the tree's root system sucked all the moisture from the ground, producing a circle of packed soil that replicated the shade of its branches. The cows stood dreamily chewing the cud, preferring shade even to fresh grass.

I cut across the fields and under the wire to arrive at the riverside near Philip's hanging art. The thought of the twirling shapes seemed comforting, although I couldn't have said why.

When I reached the river I was shocked by how much the level had fallen. The water had dropped back so far that the trees at the edge of the banks had their roots exposed, all ungainly and tangled. It was like seeing a swan on dry land with its huge flat feet spoiling the elegance you usually took for granted. I climbed down on to the roots of a willow and perched for a while with my feet in the water. A water rat sculled along under the opposite bank, its nose and ears just breaking the surface in a V-shaped ripple. It disappeared into a dark hollow under the cavernous roots, and I shivered and tucked my feet up under me.

My book stayed unopened in my lap; it seemed too much of an effort to read. In the quiet I noticed that even the note of the river had changed: it was higher, with more tinkling noises overlying its low gurgle, as the water surface was broken in more places by the forest of roots. In the shade of the bank a little downstream, the barred shapes of trout hung still in the brown water.

I began to feel thirsty and decided to go back to the house to get a flask of something cold. As I moved, my shadow fell across the water and the small black dashes of fish fry flicked away, startling me. I began to go back the way I'd come, then decided I'd stay in the cool of the trees as long as possible and walk instead alongside the river to meet the track at the bridge.

The river was sluggish. A twig floated down beside me and I followed its progress as I walked, watching it fetch up against islands of other twigs and debris, then wash free and continue its journey, tracing the flow and twirling eddies of the current. I remembered how Mum and I used to race sticks through the bridge, Mum always throwing hers over to one side so it would get caught up, and how she'd hold on to me so that I could lean well out and pitch mine right into the middle of the current. Then we'd rush to the other side to watch the stick shoot between the steep concrete sides of the culvert that squeezed the water into a deep fast-flowing channel.

I came nearer to the bridge and braced myself for the scramble up the steep bank to get back on to the track. The water was so low that the ugly concrete sides were partly laid bare, a dirty grey, streaked with river weed drying to a dull brown in the sun.

It was only because I was thinking of our game that I saw it. I just ducked my head to look through the arch of the bridge; it was so unusual to see a big patch of daylight on the other side. Something was jutting out of the water, silhouetted against the brightness, something big and angular, and I think I knew, right from that first moment, but I wouldn't let myself think it, didn't want to see. That was why, when I began to scramble down the sloping concrete, I had to steady myself with my hands against its ridged surface because my legs were trembling as if I'd just done a hurdles race.

I worked my way along, crab-style, until I came up against the edge of the arch, then turned round so that

229

I could peer into the dimness underneath. The top of a car stuck out at an angle from the water, wedged against the stonework of the bridge, not red, but a dark rusty brown, like an old tin can. The windscreen was smashed and on one side the metal was crumpled and misshapen. Bile began to rise in my throat but I made myself look. A Mini. And just visible below the water line, a bundle inside, a dark shape . . .

Then I was climbing, scrabbling back up the slope, slipping and grazing my knees on the concrete. I dropped the book and it skittered away into the water. I waded into the bracken and doubled up, retching, my whole body trying to throw out what I'd seen. *It's not possible. It can't be true.* I let out a cry like a child, a cry of distress meant to bring a parent running, a wail of pure loss.

The trees towered above me in a mesh of dizzying green. I stumbled through the undergrowth to the fence and leant against it, sobbing, holding on as though it was the only solid thing in a world turned to water. The track stretched back towards the village road, empty and silent, a long tunnel of green boughs, endless. Then I was clambering over the fence, turning away from the void, running, back towards the house. I ran with my mouth open, gulping for breath in the thick bracken-scented air, the trees above me closing in, suffocating. I got clear of the wood, my hat flying off into the dusty grass, and still I ran, past Tom's deserted den, my chest wrenched by pain as I struggled up the hill. At last, gasping for breath, I reached the yard and

230

swung into the dairy. I clasped the sides of the ladder to the hayloft and rested my head for a moment on a rung, praying that Tom wouldn't be there. I climbed into the dusty darkness and squeezed myself into a corner between two bales, like an animal gone to ground.

I pressed my palms over my ears to block out the noise of the river that ran in my head. I screwed up my eyes, but the dim shape of the car outlined under the arch of the bridge was there whatever I did, wherever I looked.

I couldn't, I wouldn't, believe it. I tried to stop the pictures forming in my head: a car careering out of control, the smash of glass and metal against stone. The impact seemed to shudder through me as I saw Mum thrown forward, heard her head hit the steering wheel with a horrible thud, then the splintering sound of branches as the car ploughed down the bank. Was she gone in the instant of the impact? I tried to block out the sound of screaming, the thought of the car hitting the freezing water. I was gripping the bale next to me, digging the sharp straw into my hand in an effort to block out the thoughts.

Why had she been driving so fast? She'd only just learnt to drive; she was still so careful, always reminding me to put on my safety belt. But it was so wet that night. I remembered how the rain hammered on the window at Gran's as we sat eating tea and how it made it seem so cosy to be inside with a bright fire and the smell of beef stew and baking pastry. I felt so special as Gran let me serve out the food, Grandad exclaiming and asking for more. I wanted to stay, pretended to fall asleep after tea so that they'd let me just lie there on the sofa, warm and comfy, listening to the rain beating down outside . . .

The thought was unbearable. I laid my head on my arms and sobbed. I saw again, with awful clarity, the image in the shadow of the bridge, the low water moving slowly, barely breaking into ripples as it flowed through the rusty car, passing a formless shape slumped against the door.

I knew about death. I had seen plenty of it on the farm. I'd picked up birds frozen stiff in a hard winter, their featherweight frames made heavy by frost, as if death had its own weight. I'd lifted still-born calves with lolling heads and stick-like legs, seen the look in the eyes of sick beasts as they went down, too weak to stand; seen rows of carcasses at the abattoir. I knew that death is hideous. But none of that had caused me real pain. This was different. This was revulsion, an utter rejection of something so *wrong* it must surely be impossible, a travesty my mind couldn't contain. My mum, my beautiful mum, turned into a thing, a mass of dark stuff, decayed and ugly.

The scent of straw and hay was in my nostrils. Outside, the birds were singing and the faint sound of a plane reached me through the clear air. Everything went on as before, when it should be cracking, splintering, breaking into a million pieces. How could everything just be carrying on as normal? With a horrible shock it struck me that all the days since her death had been just like this; that I too had carried on, oblivious, passing daily over her very grave.

Did Dad know? Surely, he must do. I remembered him putting up the fences at the sides of the bridge where the walls ran out, his grim face as he leant on the stakes, testing them with his weight, his strictures that we were never to play at the bridge, that the river there was deep and dangerous and *out of bounds*. And I had even felt offended that he'd think I'd be stupid enough to take Tom to play there, where the water ran like a mill-race in the winter and the bridge cast a deep shadow filled with dancing insects in the summer months. When was that? Was it weeks after Mum went, or months? I couldn't remember; that time had blurred into one awful, empty feeling.

There were things here I couldn't understand. How had it happened? If Dad did know about it, how could he leave her there? There, in the dark? A creeping cold spread through me as though my blood was shrinking back from my limbs, its warmth sucked back to the centre, just to keep my heart beating. My lips and fingers felt numb and my sweat chilled on my skin. I thought of Mum's clothes that had gone to the charity shop, the books that Dad said would never get read again, the dressing-table drawers I'd found empty of Mum's most personal things, drawers stuffed with old magazines instead of her trinkets and scarves, cleared of the mementoes I'd been so sure I would find. Wiped out. No evidence that she'd ever been.

My mind shied away from this new, most awful thought. They were my parents; they had loved each other. I'd watched them dance, seen them lace their fingers together as they walked. *They had loved each other.* That was before, though. There were other memories too: silent mealtimes when I'd willed them to ask me something, anything, about school; raised voices in the night when Tom woke up. Mum picking up a broken plate and trying to smile when she saw me, calling herself a baby to be crying over a cut finger and saying that it had got knocked off the table, that it was an accident. A cold logical part of me took a tally of the ways Dad had changed towards her.

The thought of confronting him made me feel nauseous. What kind of daughter could think such things of her own father? I would be wrong and he would never forgive me for doubting him. Then I would have lost them both. It had been an accident, a terrible accident. Dad had got rid of her things because he thought she'd left him and he couldn't bear to be reminded of her. Of course, that was it. And now I would have to find a way to tell him and hope that he wouldn't completely fall apart. I didn't think I could do it, couldn't think how to frame the words. I began to shake. *Mum and Dad loved each other,* I said to myself again and again; Mum wasn't unhappy and they loved each other. I repeated it like a charm to keep off evil spirits, a child's secret spell against the dark.

I curled up tighter, curving my body around the empty place inside me. My mother was unreeling like a film pulled off its spool, my fantasies of her return to us, her plans to get Tom and me back, imagined messages and rescues all blacked out, reeling backwards to a single picture, a smile, a raised hand behind a car window smeared with rain.

CHAPTER
THIRTEEN

Hours later the hayloft had grown dim; the bar of light from the crack between the two great doors had moved across to the far side of the dusty floor. It quivered slightly as the doors rattled. I passed my hands across my face. A breeze was getting up and it was dusk. I listened but there was no other sound. I had a dizzying sense that I was completely alone and I longed for another human face and to hear a familiar voice, to have arms around me.

I climbed stiffly down the ladder and crossed the dairy. The Land-Rover was gone from the yard and I went quickly to the house to find Tom. The house was empty and Tom's bed was stripped of blankets, left only with a rumpled sheet. On the floor lay the torch casing, a clutter of useless batteries emptied out beside it. Of course: his plan to sleep out. He must've got tired of waiting and gone on without me, thinking I'd let him down yet again. I wondered if I would find him already asleep, curled up in his blanket nest, worn out with waiting. I pulled a blanket and a pillow from my own bed and rolled them into a ball under one arm. I prayed that he would be asleep so that I could simply crawl in beside his small, warm form.

As I crossed the yard the breeze still felt warm against the back of my bare legs and arms. Small gusts seemed to suck and blow against the outbuilding doors, rattling them on their hinges, and the barley stalks sawed against the barbed-wire fence beside the cattle grid. The sky was streaked with pink and lemon and a few wisps of cloud and a sliver of moon had begun to show, pale as pasted tissue paper.

I sniffed the air for rain. Nothing: this was a dry, warm wind. I sniffed again: no sign of freshening, but the faintest trace of something, a tang that the breeze carried away again, down towards the river, familiar, elusive. I stood still at the top of the track, peering out over the fields. The dogs started to bark. It came again, this time unmistakable, acrid: the smell of smoke.

I walked forward a few steps uncertainly, scanning the fields, my heart quickening its beat. At first nothing seemed amiss; the haze that lay across the fields was golden, as the last of the sun passed through the dust-laden air. But in one spot the haze was thicker, paler, forming itself into a rising cloud by the second as I watched in disbelief, my limbs immobile, stricken; Tom's den.

Then I was dropping the blankets, running, shouting at the top of my voice, "Tom! Tom!" No answering cry came and I stopped calling, needing all my breath to run, focused only on reaching him. Grey-white smoke rolled lazily along the top of the den. As I reached the field boundary I heard the sound of the Land-Rover revving as it pulled out of the river turn. It emerged from the trees and I waved my arms as I ran, but Dad must already have smelt the smoke. The Land-Rover accelerated and shot along the track, its back end bouncing as it bumped and jounced over the potholed track.

Dad swung round to the field gate. I ran on, ignoring the burning in my chest, taking great gulps of the dusty air. Dad jumped down from the cab, took a few strides towards the gate, then hesitated for a second and returned to pull a tarpaulin out of the back. He pushed the gate open and then ran towards the bales.

I tried to cut off the corner by squeezing through the hedge, its prickles catching on my clothes, and then ran diagonally across the field, both of us aiming to converge on a single point. I had never run like this before. This was no sports-day measured sprint, this was flat out; muscle-wrenching, lung-stretching, life-or-death speed.

When I was still a hundred yards away, Dad reached the den. I could see what he was going to try to do and I shouted to him, but I had so little breath left that my voice was too faint to carry. He threw the tarpaulin on to the top of the chest-high pile of bales, then ran round to the other side to pull it tight and smother the fire.

"No! Dad! N-o-o!" I shouted as I reached him.

He glanced at me uncomprehendingly, still intent on tucking in the tarpaulin to starve the fire of air. I grabbed the other side and pulled.

"Tom's in there!" I yelled straight at him.

Then everything around us seemed to slow. Dad's face paled and he let go of his side. I saw everything in detail as if a camera lens had suddenly brought it sharply into focus: the shiny green surface of the tarpaulin, the glint of the brass eyelet holes at its edges, the curls of dense, choking smoke around it and the trickles emerging from the cracks between the bales.

I yanked the tarpaulin towards me and there was a noise beneath the den's bale roof, a dull *woomph* like the lighting of a gas oven. I stepped back. Between the bales there was an orange glow and small yellow flames came licking at the sides and corners, leaving the hay charred and smouldering. I dropped the tarpaulin just as Dad lunged forward and grabbed two bales off the top. He picked them up as though they were as light as cardboard boxes and threw them down behind him. In the moment that Dad reached over to pull down the side of the bale wall, the fire met the air full on. The effect was like a bellows. There was a noise like the igniting of a hot-air balloon and flames leapt into life, shooting feet into the air as if greedy for more. Then as the breeze caught, the flames flattened and smoke rolled out across the field towards the river in a dense dirty white cloud.

I ran round to Dad. The smoke stung my eyes and choked at the back of my throat. At first I couldn't see him and groped towards the place where I thought he'd been standing. Then I heard coughing and retching and turned to see a humped shape on the ground. I reached to help him up and as I touched his arm he let out a cry of pain. Holding his arms awkwardly across his chest, he rose heavily to his feet and stumbled away to get clear of the smoke, only to collapse again and sit with his knees up, moaning. There was something wrong with the way he was sitting. His elbows were tucked in close to his sides, as if cradling something to his chest, but his palms were upwards, as if he was holding his hands and forearms away from him.

"Go on," he said through gritted teeth, "keep looking."

I ran back to the long tunnel entrance that Tom had built to the den, praying that he would have crawled along it to escape. I left a gap between me and the fire, which rustled and crackled as it ate into the pile of bales, in the hope that I could avoid drawing it along the tunnel. Nonetheless as I pulled the first bale off I felt a scalding pain, casual as a dog's lick, a sly tongue of flame across my hand. The bale fell to the ground as I nursed my hand, the flames catching hold and the baling twine snapping, then wriggling and shrinking as it melted. Already from each bale we'd dropped new fires were starting, fanned by the breeze, at first just creeping, then running along the ground as smouldering pieces of hay tumbled and rolled. Sparks from the main fire flew and burning wisps of hay were carried on the updraft and borne away on the air.

I cast around in a panic; already another stack downhill towards the river field had caught and added its crackle to the din.

Bale by bale I hauled the top off the tunnel, only a few yards in front of the fire and smoke, forcing myself to keep ahead of it as if in some macabre race. At last as

I pulled a bale away I saw a shape and bent forward to feel something hard: Tom's foot in its sandal. I shoved the next bale aside and clambered into the trench. He was lying on his side, one hand over his mouth and the other arm flung across his face. I lifted him, his head lolling and his limbs limp. I kicked the bales away and carried him uphill to the back of the field, where Dad had dragged himself and now sat propped against the hedge bank. Behind me I heard a muffled thud as the main chamber of the den imploded, the pile of bales falling softly into itself.

He's still warm, he's still warm, I said again and again in my head. I could feel his bare legs warm against my arm as I carried him across me like a baby.

As I laid him down beside Dad he rolled on to his side and fell into a fit of coughing until he vomited. I rubbed his back.

"Come on, Tom. That's right, get it all up," I said as he began to cry.

He balled up his hand and pressed it to his chest. "It hurts," he said, "it really hurts," then fell into another bout of coughing.

I held him, one hand on his shoulder and the other at his forehead, to steady him as he coughed.

Dad was sitting again in his strange position, like someone begging for alms. His head was thrown back and his eyes were shut tight, his lips pressed together as if trying to suppress the low moan that he couldn't help making. I laid Tom's head down and put him back on his side, then shifted across to look at Dad more closely.

His hands were red raw, blistered and shiny, and the nylon of his shirt had shrivelled and melted across his lower arms, sticking to the burns beneath. His hands wouldn't keep still, but trembled as if with a life of their own.

"I'm going to have to go for help," I said, but neither of them answered.

I stood uncertainly between them, then turned to look back down the valley. The breeze ran behind the fire, carrying smoke and sparks towards the field beside the river. Already the hedge at the field boundary was alight in places, the wood of hawthorn trunks standing out dark against a glowing red frizz of burning twigs and leaves. Suddenly three or four rabbits broke cover and scuttered from the hedgerow, running wildly hither and thither among the burning ricks until they found their way to the edges and out to other fields.

The bale den was burning down to an irregular patch of blackened ground. Even if the wind turned round there would be nothing left to burn on its return path.

"I'll be as quick as I can," I said to Dad, then bent over Tom and whispered, "Be a brave boy. Jessie'll be back soon."

Then I ran.

Later I waited with them for the ambulance; I sat between them, cradling Tom's head in my lap. He was coughing less but his breath came in wheezy gasps.

"They'll be here soon," I said. "Don't worry, it won't be long now."

I wished I'd brought water down with me from the house; it might have eased him a little. My own throat was so tender I tried not to swallow, and the taste of ash was dry in my mouth.

Dad said nothing. His face had an unnatural pallor beneath the grime of soot and dirt. He stared straight ahead across the valley. The fire had crossed the second field now, eating through our hard work like orange rust, crumbling the bales to powder. The first hedge had been reduced to a line of blackened stumps; the second now crackled, dry tinder going up like a torch.

There was no sign of help. The woman on the phone had arranged an ambulance but said that all the county's fire engines were already out; she would do what she could but a field fire was low priority when in other places buildings were involved. Anyway, I thought, it's too late to do anything now; soon the fire'll meet the river. It was wide and shallow here, with broad stony banks; the fire would never cross it. Then it'll all be over, I thought. The hay's gone.

We sat with the breeze at our backs and watched a clump of trees beside the river bank catch alight. Bits of burning debris caught in the branches; the light was almost gone from the sky now and they glowed like strange, gigantic fireflies, then flowered as they found fresh wood to feed upon. The flames grew and joined, roaring through the boughs that turned grey-white with heat, the bark powdering to ash. The trees creaked and groaned; an aspen branch suddenly broke, splitting away from the trunk and falling with a thud to lie across other branches below. I turned to Dad but couldn't find any words to say.

He made no response but closed his eyes against me. There were pale tracks down his face through the grime. I put my hand on his shoulder and felt the tremor still running through him.

At length we heard the wail of a siren in the distance and I got up and laid Tom's head gently down again. He pulled at my arm.

"Have you seen Lolly?" he said in a croaky voice.

"She'll be fine: cats have got nine lives, remember? We're going to get you off to hospital now, but I'll look for her for you, OK? I promise."

I could see the blue light of the ambulance as it turned off the main road and on to the track. I started across the field and as I went I heard the lower wail of a fire engine, which approached the field on the other side of the river, then manoeuvred to get through the field entrance. The men spilled out and walked along the far bank, calling to one another. Their lack of haste confirmed my earlier thought: the river was containing the fire; there would be nothing for them to do but wait to see that the prevailing wind held until it was all burnt out. The ambulance came on up the hill and drew in at the field gate and the siren and flashing light stopped. A man and a woman jumped out and I waved my arms.

Now that someone had arrived to take over I suddenly felt very odd; my legs felt weak and my head was spinning. I bent over and held on to my knees, putting my head down, the blood rushing in my ears. Then there was an arm around me and a man's voice.

"All right, love, what's your name?"

I pointed back up the field to where the others were. I opened my mouth to explain, but nothing would come. I leant against the bulk of the man as he directed the woman towards them.

"Tell me your name, love," he said again.

"The hay's all gone," I said. "He's never going to forgive us for this."

I sat in the corridor outside an examination room in the Emergency department, where a doctor was looking at Tom. I'd had a dressing put on the side of my hand for my brush with the fire and had been given a coffee in a vend-pack cup. I sat sipping the lukewarm brew, which seemed to have taken on the chemical undertone of the hospital air. A row of blue plastic chairs stretched out on either side of me, all empty.

I felt wiped clean, see-through like glass. The noise of the hospital, the distant squeak of trolley wheels, the gurgle of the pipes that laced the corridor ceiling, and the repetitive whine of the lift around the corner, all seemed somehow muffled, part of another world. Everything here was painted the same colour, a creamy beige: the walls, the pipes, the ceiling, all the same. Blank. My eyes started to close. I wondered if anyone would mind if I lay down across the seats for a while, then I thought, no, I mustn't sleep, I must wait for news. Yes, that was what I was here for; I must just wait.

Dad had gone down to theatre. A man in a white coat who said he was the houseman on duty had explained to me that they had to remove the pieces of nylon material that had melted in the fire. They had to do this in sterile conditions because some skin would come off too. They would keep him in and skin grafts might be needed. When they took him off in a wheelchair he was still trembling.

A nurse in a pale-blue uniform came down the corridor, her flat rubber-soled shoes squeaking on the polished floor. She smiled at me as she turned in to the room where Tom was. I craned forward to see him as she opened the door but all I saw was the doctor's back.

I finished the coffee. I didn't know where the bin was, so I put the cup down under the seat. Eventually the nurse came out again; she said something over her shoulder to the doctor, who laughed. His laughing made me feel better; surely it couldn't be too serious if he could laugh like that. She sat down beside me, looking at her watch.

"Right, then," she said, "here's an update."

I straightened my back and tried to concentrate.

"Your brother's suffering from the effects of smoke, as you know. We're going to give him oxygen, which will help his breathing a lot."

"Can I see him?" I asked.

She smiled. "You can look in on him in a minute."

"When will I be able to take him home, do you think?"

"We're not sure yet. We need to keep him under observation in case of lung damage." Seeing my face fall, she touched my hand. "Kids are very resilient, you know. More than likely, he'll be out within twenty-four hours."

"What about my father?"

"Don't know yet. Same thing really: it depends what we find in theatre. Basically it depends on how deep his burns are. He was in a lot of pain, wasn't he?"

I nodded slowly. "Except he told the ambulance man that his left hand was numb."

"Well, I know it sounds strange, but the pain is the good news. If the burns are third-degree the patient feels no pain because the nerve endings are destroyed. That's more serious."

The doctor came out and hurried off down the corridor and the nurse ushered me into Tom's room. He was propped up on a mound of pillows; he looked so small in the high hospital bed with its barred metal back. The nurse had washed his face and put him in a gown. He looked wan, pinched with worry lines that should never be on a nine-year-old face. I sat on the edge of the bed and gave him a hug, but it made him cough. I let go and held his hand instead.

"I'm really sorry," he said, his eyes filling. "It's just that it was so dark in there, and you didn't come." He fell into another coughing fit and reached for the metal tray the nurse had left beside him.

"It's all right," I said. "Don't try to talk."

"I was careful; I put the candle in a jar," he said. "I knew not to just light a candle."

I sighed.

"It wasn't me," he said. "It was Lolly; she kept patting at it as if it was something to play with."

I squeezed his hand tight.

"Then when she made it fall over the candle came out and I panicked and I . . . I . . ."

"Shh," I said. "It's all right, it's all over now. You did the sensible thing after that, you got yourself out of there. That's the only thing that matters."

Tom swallowed hard. "No . . . no, it's not that bit, it was before that." He rubbed at his eyes miserably. "I think I might have hurt her. I was trying to stamp it out and she was getting in the way and I grabbed her and sort of threw her behind me, down the tunnel. But then I couldn't find her." He looked at me with a question in his eyes.

I shook my head. "Not yet, but she'll turn up, I'm sure."

A porter came in with an oxygen cylinder on wheels.

"Do you want to stay?" the nurse said. "We could probably rig up a comfier seat in here while we wait to get him on to the ward."

"I can't," I said. "We've got cows needing to be milked and there's no one else to do it. I'll have to come back later."

I kissed Tom on the top of his head. "Listen," I said, "I'm sure Lolly will be fine — cats are fast and wily. What's more, she won't remember anything about you being cross, you know."

I waited while the nurse explained to Tom about the oxygen, then put a clear mask over his nose and mouth. The elastic of the mask made his hair stick out over his ears. I smoothed it back and got up to go. She walked with me towards the lift.

"Have you got some money for the phone?" she asked. "Is there someone who could come to fetch you?"

"Yes," I said, thinking of Grandad. I felt in the pocket of my shorts. "That's a point."

"Here," she said, reaching into her breast pocket. "Take this." She gave me a handful of coins.

"Thanks. It's really kind of you."

"Phones are in the foyer," she said over her shoulder as I stepped into the lift. "Good luck."

It wasn't until I got to the phone and started to dial the number that I remembered about Gran and Grandad being away. I pressed the button and the money came clinking back out. There were some cards pinned up on the wall beside the phone. I picked a number and rang for a taxi. I'd have to explain on the way that I needed to get money from the housekeeping tin to pay the cabbie.

"The Infirmary," I said to the girl who answered, "to Garton's Farm, Lastcote."

People stared as I passed through the busy admissions department. I stood at a dark window at the hospital entrance and saw that my hair was wild, my face dirty and my clothes streaked with soot. I looked through myself into the darkness, waiting for the car, waiting for a light.

CHAPTER
FOURTEEN

The alarm woke me from a sleep that had been troubled with dreams, not of fire but of water. Dark and treacherous, it flowed through tunnels and caves, filling and flooding them, stealing the last of the air. I sat up with a gasp and slammed my hand down on the alarm clock. I got dressed quickly, then hurried down to let the dogs out, as if I was afraid to look back over my shoulder at the night.

I made tea and drank it hot, then made myself eat some cornflakes before going out to let the cows into the holding yard. It was going to be a long job doing it solo. The brightness of the dawn that gave everything to the right of the track freshness and sparkle, simply revealed more sharply the devastation on the other side. As though a comet had swept diagonally across the fields down to the river, a large swathe of land was blackened and burnt. By some fluke of the wind a few piles of bales stood untouched in two of the corners, a poignant reminder of a harvest wasted.

The Land-Rover still stood abandoned at the field gate, sticking out at an angle into the track. The landscape was broken by the lines of charred stumps that were once hedges full of hawthorn and elder. The skeletal remains of trees at the river's edge stood out stark and black against the morning light. From other fields the sound of birdsong reached me, but in the burnt acres there was no sound, nor the pale flash of a rabbit's tail. I felt grief rising again and was afraid. This was a ruined and desolate place.

I opened the gate to the holding yard with a clang. I must concentrate on practicalities, I told myself, and set my jaw. I must be glad that there was some hay left to supplement the grass that was becoming ever thinner and browner in the drought. I must focus on what needs to be done to keep things going. Everything else will have to wait.

The dogs returned from their run and flopped on to the parlour floor, panting. It comforted me a little to have them there, even if they'd only come to find some coolness; the way Kelpie rested her chin on her paws, looking at me with mournful brown eyes, made me feel less alone.

It was mid-morning by the time I'd finished milking and sluicing out the pipes and the day was turning into another scorcher. I had a good look for Lolly but with no luck, so I put a saucer of water out for her in the hayloft in the hope that she'd return to the place where she was most often fed. I went to pick up the pillow and blanket that I'd dropped last night beside the track. The stink of smoke on them made me shiver.

As I returned to the house the phone was ringing and I rushed to get it, suddenly afraid that it would be the hospital with more bad news. It was Mrs Swift calling.

"Jess," she said, "I just wanted to know if you were all safe."

I told her about Dad and Tom and that Tom, I expected, would be let out soon but that they were keeping Dad in.

"What a terrible thing," she said. "Can we do anything? Philip's away, baling over at Farnsbrook for a few days, otherwise I'd send him over."

"It's really kind of you," I said, "but I'm managing fine."

"Oh . . . well, if there's anything you think of. How about eating with us tonight?"

I didn't think I could bear answering any more questions, not even from Mrs Swift, who meant kindly. *Especially* from Mrs Swift, I thought. She had a way of making you say more than you meant to without even realizing you'd done it.

"It's fine, honestly. I'm a bit . . . I don't know what time I'll be back from visiting."

Mrs Swift still sounded doubtful. "As long as you know you only have to ring."

I thought of Dad's attitude to Mick yesterday in the field and the way he'd scowled at me to make me shut up, unwilling to let me even be civil.

"Tell Philip we're OK, though, won't you," I said anyway. I took a deep breath. "I'd be glad of some help when he's back."

"All right, then. You take care, and send our best to your dad and Tom."

252

We said our goodbyes and I rang the hospital to see when Tom would be able to come home. The consultant's round was at one, they said, so they'd know by afternoon visiting and that I should bring in some clothes for Tom in case.

For the umpteenth time I wished that Gran and Grandad were back from holiday. I had no way of contacting them — "somewhere in Spain" wasn't going to get me very far — and there was another whole week to go. I went into the kitchen, opened the housekeeping tin and shook the contents out on to the table: a ten-pound note and a handful of coins; that wouldn't last long for cab fares, and there wasn't much food in the fridge.

I sat still, listening to the quiet in the house. It pressed on my ears. The thought of going down to the river to fill the bowser made me feel sick. I remembered the dark tree roots exposed above the water-line. I didn't want to go near them again, with their damp shadowed caverns and the rustle and splash of scavenging creatures moving among them.

I took the crumpled ten-pound note and smoothed it out on the table, trying to focus on its sepia pictures. Since childhood I'd seen the river as exciting and special, coming from who knows what mysterious springs up-country, flowing through our land and on, out into the wider world. I'd imagined it moving through the town, through green parks, or at the bottom of children's gardens, then out again through other farms until it spent itself at sea. I'd always felt its quiet tug, a gentle reminder that the world was out there waiting to be discovered. Now it felt like a boundary; a silver loop enclosing me on an island I wanted to escape from. There was only one way to drive off the farm and that was over the river.

I thought about all the times I'd crossed the bridge, every day back and forth with Mrs Jones. I imagined the rock and tremble of its foundations as she drove the car over it, vibration transmitted through the water like a touch. And what had we been doing? We'd been talking desultorily of the day ahead, or Tom and I had been bickering quietly under cover of the engine noise, or just staring out of the window, worrying about some pointless school test or other. And every time we passed, the car below would have settled a little deeper into the mud. Grimly, I started to count up the coins, then lost my concentration and began again.

The sound of the milk tanker reached me as it turned on to the track, making me jump and knock the table. The small pile of coins went skidding across the shiny wood. I steadied myself, made myself gather them up. He would drive straight over the bridge — he had no reason to stop. In any case you'd have to climb right down as I had to see anything. I broke out into a sweat. I hoped that no village boys would come to gawp at the effects of the fire; they poked their noses into everything with their fishing and swimming.

A loud blast of the tanker's horn made me jump up and go to the window. The driver had stopped behind the Land-Rover, unable to get through. I let myself out, raised a hand to the driver and forced myself down the track to move it.

The keys weren't in the ignition and my heart sank; then I saw them in the seat well, where Dad must've dropped them in his haste. I climbed in and pulled in tighter to the gate to let the tanker pass, then drove back up the track after it. Well, I'm just going to have to grit my teeth, I thought. I'm going to have to take the Land-Rover in this afternoon; I haven't got enough money for fares. If I can just get over the bridge it can't be that much more difficult to drive on the road than around the farm, and as long as I don't bump into anything no one's going to ask any questions.

I knew the tanker driver who was working that day, a tall well-built man with a rather dour expression, and had to endure all his questions about the fire and all his tutting and sucking of teeth. I skirted round the cause of the fire, knowing that if it got out Dad would feel he'd been made a laughing stock. "Could've been anything," I said. "Everything's as dry as tinder. We get village lads up here leaving cans and beer bottles around; we even find butt ends sometimes."

The tanker man nodded sagely. "Well, tell your dad I asked after him, won't you." He looked down at me. "You've got a lot on your hands. I wish you luck with it."

He climbed back into the cab and began the tortuous business of turning the tanker within the confines of the yard. I saw him out and watched until he emerged again from the trees and drove on and out to the main road and the quiet settled once more.

I tried to steel myself to get the tractor out and take the bowser down to the waterside. "Come *on*," I said to myself, "you're not going anywhere near the bridge." I just could not do it. Breaking every rule, I set it up to fill from the tap in the yard, even though it would take ages.

I dreaded seeing Dad. I knew he would be furious with me already about the hay. I was afraid to say anything to him about Mum, but it would be so hard to act as if everything was all right and keep my feelings locked away. If only Tom could come home, I thought. Just having to get meals for someone else and having to provide reassurance would create an illusion of normality that I might be able to pretend I believed in.

It was a different nurse on duty when I finally tracked Tom down to one of the children's wards. "He's much better," she said with a smile. "His chest sounds clearer and he's eating again." She gave me a paper bag with Tom's clothes in it. "When you get him home let him rest if he wants to, but in a day or two you'll probably find he'll bounce back."

They had found him some pyjamas and he was sitting curled up on a leatherette sofa in the play room, watching *Tom and Jerry*. I sat down beside him and took his hand.

"Have you found Lolly?" he said.

"Not yet, but we'll have another look together, shall we?"

He buried his head in my shoulder and my arms went round him.

"Guess what," I said into his hair, "you're coming home, OK? We'll be back in time for tea." I felt him nod and guessed he couldn't trust his voice. "Listen," I said, tilting his face up to me, "I'm going to see Dad now, but I want you to stay here until I come back."

"I don't have to come?"

"No," I said firmly. "All I want you to do is to get dressed in the clothes I've brought you so that you're ready when I come back for you. All right? Will you do that?"

Tom nodded vehemently.

The cartoon theme tune blared out and another episode started — cat-and-mouse games of catch and escape in which no one ever really got hurt. On an impulse I kissed him on the cheek. "Enjoy the show," I said.

Dad had been moved to a side ward in the burns unit on the third floor. There were four beds, but I could see that he was the only person in there at the moment and my step slowed as I approached. He was propped up in bed with his hands laid, palms up, over the bedclothes. His arms were heavily bandaged, right to the elbow. His head was turned away towards the window, although all he'd be able to see from the bed was a rectangle of hot blue sky.

I stood at the end of the bed. "How're you feeling?" I said. "I brought you some things — slippers and your dressing gown and stuff." I slid the bag along the floor towards him.

He turned slowly to look at me. "We're done for," he said. "You do realize that was this month's loan payment that went up in smoke?"

I looked down at the chart clipped to the end of the bed.

Dad lifted his hands towards me. "Then there's this," he said. "What use am I to anyone like this? I can't even grip a pen, never mind drive or milk or do anything useful."

I fiddled with the shiny bulldog clip on the chart. Dad reached across to his locker, where a jug of water and a glass stood.

"Here, let me do that." I stepped forward to pour him a drink and my hand knocked the jug handle. Water spurted from the lip and ran down the side of the locker.

"Oh, for God's sake," he said, holding his hands up hopelessly and sinking back into his pillows.

"I should've brought you some flowers," I said helplessly, looking at the bare locker top.

"Where were you, Jess? What were you thinking of, leaving Tom to play around with matches in the hay?"

"He wasn't playing with matches ... I ..." I stopped, unable to explain myself without talking about Mum and those were words that I didn't yet know how to utter.

"I used to think I could rely on you," he said, "but you've changed." He shook his head. "I had to sit and watch my last bit of cash burning up in front of me and you won't even tell me what happened."

I didn't answer.

"See," he said. "You keep secrets from me. I can't trust you any more."

258

"That's unfair!" I said, stung. "I've been up since five keeping things going at home; you can't say I'm not to be relied on."

"Not fair!" Dad sat forward, scowling. "I'll tell you what's not fair. It's struggling to keep a livelihood against the odds of bad weather and no money; it's trying to keep a lid on a teenage daughter who's got more lip than sense; and it's landing up in here just when I need to be fighting my corner with the bank, because of your irresponsible stupidity! That's what's not fair!"

From the corner of my eye I saw a nurse get up from the Sister's station and walk towards our ward.

"You never even asked about Tom," I said. "Well, in case you're interested, I'm taking him home."

Dad snorted and turned his face back to the window. The nurse put her head round the door.

"Is everything all right down here?" she asked.

Neither of us replied.

"Only, it's about time to change your dressing, Mr Garton."

"It's all right, I was just leaving," I said. "I was just telling Dad I won't be able to visit every day because there's only me to do the farm work." I picked up the bag of Tom's soiled clothes.

Dad stared fixedly out at the blank, blue sky.

"I'll ring," I said.

When Tom saw the Land-Rover he stopped dead.

"You drove on the road!"

"Shh," I said. "Don't tell everyone. I'm not meant to really."

"How fast did you go?"

"Just the same as everyone else. I didn't go breaking any speed limits." I didn't tell him that the first three times I'd met a roundabout, I'd stalled. I would be better on the way back; I was getting the hang of it now.

We stopped off at a supermarket in town to get a few iron rations and I let Tom choose some raspberry jelly as a treat. It would slip down easily and soothe his sore throat.

As we turned on to the track for home and drove towards the bridge, I gripped the wheel tight.

"Are you all right?" Tom said. "You look funny."

I fixed my eyes straight ahead as we rumbled across the bridge. "I'm fine," I said, changing down a gear for the tight bend with an awful grinding crunch. As we emerged from the trees I managed a weak smile. Tom turned away and stared out of the window. I decided that I must try harder.

As we pulled into the yard I saw that someone had left something beside the door — a basket. I helped Tom down from his seat and we went to see.

The cover on the basket was pulled askew. Inside was a card and a Pyrex dish covered with tinfoil. The card read: "Hope your menfolk get better soon. Ring me if there's anything I can do. Love, Elaine, Ray and Ralphy." There was a row of Xs at the bottom. I read the card again, although the second time it blurred before my eyes. Blinking, I bent to pick the pot out of the basket.

"Here, Tom," I said, "something's been at our dinner." One side of the foil had been pulled away.

Just then Tom let out a piercing squeal, as a familiar black-and-white form came darting round the corner of the house. He swept Lolly up in his arms and, kissing her and stroking her, his face wore the biggest smile I'd seen all day.

"Well, will you look at that!" I said. Lolly's coat was sleek and clean, her eyes bright and alert — a far cry from the bedraggled, soot-stained creature I'd secretly expected to find somewhere licking its burns.

"You were right! You were right!" Tom hugged her tight. "They do have nine lives!"

"I think you were right," I said, unlocking the door. "She hasn't been back for food until now. You said she was going to be an ace mouser and that's just what she must be."

CHAPTER
FIFTEEN

I was glad to have Tom home for company; things only got harder over the next few days. His first day home he hadn't much energy and I made him lie on the sofa and read or watch TV, until he got his strength back. By the second day he was almost back to normal, but then we heard from the hospital that Dad needed a graft on his left hand and would be staying in for a while.

I went in to see him. He seemed tired and listless. By mutual consent we stuck to safe ground in conversation: the state of the stock, what the milk yield was like. I told him as little as I could get away with; my farming at the moment was unconventional, to say the least. And then, on top of it all, the temperature soared.

I felt worn out. The early milking was a trial, but at least it was cooler before breakfast; the afternoon milking was a killer. Doing anything at all in the heat made me feel dizzy and sick. In the papers it said that the temperature had reached ninety-seven degrees and the hospital was full of people suffering from heat exhaustion. It was so hot that the tar on the roads had melted and begun to move downhill. I hosed the cows down outside the parlour, just to give them some relief.

The heat was finishing off the grass. It was patchy, fading to a brownish yellow. Another day or two and I'd have to start them on what was left of the hay, regardless of Dad's intention to sell it. There was hardly enough left to make it worthwhile anyhow. To me it was no longer a case of making a profit from a deal. Everything had dwindled to one simple aim: to keep the farm running by keeping the beasts alive.

Lugging water around in this heat was no longer an option. I had stiffened my resolve and Tom and I had moved the cows down to the field nearest the river, not far from the shallow "beach". We'd heaved out a portion of the fence and blocked the opening with old planks and a single strand of barbed wire to form a makeshift gate. It was a bodge job and had to be rebuilt each time we used it, but it was better than using the bowser. Together we just about managed to keep the herd from straying off into the trees and got them down to the river to drink. After the first time, they knew their way and keeping them from wading into the water was the only problem. Dad would have been furious if he had known the risk we were taking: the Ministry was hard on farmers who let their stock foul the water. The lure of the coolness and an escape from the interminable flies was too much for the cattle, and Tom and I had a busy time paddling about in the shallows and waving our arms to keep them on the bank.

At first I'd thought that Philip might turn up, that he must have been back from Farnbrook by this time, surely? Stupid, really. I should have known he'd stay well clear after Dad's falling out with Mick. That was just the way things worked round here, wasn't it, whatever overtures of friendship the women might make. Daft even to think he would have helped me anyway — why should he?

Tom, to be fair, had been doing his best, had been a real help, until now. I stood in the dairy and stared at what he'd done.

"What's happened?" I said to him, looking up at the glass pipes. The water pumping through them in regular spurting rushes was *going the wrong way*.

"I didn't do anything!" Tom wailed. "I turned the valve just like you said."

"You must have turned it in the wrong direction," I said. "That's the trouble, you just don't concentrate."

The colour of the water was turning from watery milk to a bluish grey, but instead of flushing everything out, ready for the morning milking, the dirty water was flowing not down the drain, but directly into the milk tank. I moved quickly to switch the pump off.

"It won't matter," said Tom. "We can switch it over and clean everything again, can't we?"

"It's not that," I said wearily. "What on earth am I going to do with all that spoilt milk?" I didn't add, how am I going to explain it to the dairy, or that all my work sweating away in the parlour had now been wasted.

"Can't we just not tell anyone?" said Tom.

"No, we cannot. I'm not going to be responsible for making the whole area sick, on top of everything else."

I couldn't put it down the drain either, because of tainting the water supply. There was nothing for it, we were going to have to find a way of rigging a hose up to run it out on to the field, well away from any ditches so it wouldn't get into any water course, and then I'd have to clean the whole system through ready for tomorrow. Yet more hours of back-breaking work. I could have wept.

I kicked the dairy door open with a resounding thud. "Come on," I said, "we'll have to find all the hoses we've got and then I'll phone the tanker man."

Tom didn't move.

"Tom, I can't do it without you," I said in exasperation. "Don't go getting in a sulk just because something's gone wrong."

"I don't like Dad not being here to help," he said in a small voice. "Why can't Grandad come?"

"Grandad's still on holiday, Tom."

"I want Grandad," he said.

I went and squatted down to his level and held his hands.

"Please, Tom, I'm asking you. I promise Dad'll be back soon. Please."

"Well, Philip, then."

I sighed. "We can't really ask him to get involved. We don't know him well enough. It's just you and me, I'm afraid, kid."

Tom hesitated. "As long as I can have chips for supper and Lolly can sleep in my room."

"Yes, yes," I said. "Now, let's get going."

When we eventually finished, there was a strange quiver in the air, a heaviness with a shimmer running through it, as though the heat had built up to a point where something had to give. I made Tom chips, and left him eating them while I made the necessary call to the dairy, then stepped outside again to smell the air. The sky had turned milky, trapping a humid heat between earth and cloud.

"Come and look at this," I called indoors to Tom.

When he didn't answer I went back in. There was no sign of him. There were no chips left for me. I called upstairs. No answer. The little rotter, I thought, he knows I've got to water the cows for the evening and I need him to help.

"Tom!" I called into the yard. "I need you to give me a hand!" I hadn't got the energy to go and look for him. "Tom!"

I decided to just get on with it. Feeling light-headed from hunger and the heat I tramped across the fields towards the cows' new pasture. The air was now so humid that the sweat stayed on my skin in beads, making my clothes feel clammy and heavy.

Then, from the direction of the town, came the deep grumbling of thunder. Only a week ago a cloud had sailed whimsically across acres of farmland to dump its entire contents on King's Melford village fête. As the thunder rolled round again I let myself imagine the freshening of the air before rain, the first huge drops splattering on the hot roads, then hundreds, thousands, of them, skating on slate roofs, bouncing off the paving stones, sending people, squealing, into doorways, holding newspapers over their heads. The rain would run in rivulets down the gutters and rush away uselessly down storm drains, leaving only a few puddles where the road needed mending and the smell of dog rising from the pavement.

Here, the air was thick and heavy, charged with static and full of thrips, the tiny harvest flies that got everywhere, even behind the glass in picture frames. They covered my white T-shirt and tickled my face and arms as they crawled across my skin.

The cows were behaving very strangely, as if the heat had finally driven them crazy. Every now and then one of them would jump skittishly and take off across the field, to be followed by the others, their normally placid gait electrified to a gallop, their muscles tense and stiff. I quickened my step. Perhaps my arrival would calm them down with the expectation of a long drink.

I lifted the rope loop off the gatepost and slipped into the field. The cows were still again, some of them grazing, some swishing their tails against the flies. Then Pirate startled and was off again, her tail stuck out straight behind her as she galloped away towards the river and then slowed to a trot, then a walk and then stopped again. I walked gingerly forward towards the herd, then saw what the problem was: warble flies.

In front of me an insect about the size of a bee hung in the air. I batted it aside with my hand, but it returned to its original position; the hovering action of these flies drove the cattle wild, making them gad about.

Pirate jumped again, kicking up her heels, but this time, trapped almost in the corner of the field, she had no way of putting a good distance between her and the insect. She ran straight at our makeshift gate and, head down, barged right into it. The planks fell with a clatter and her hoofs slipped on the tumbling wood as she tried to push her way through.

I ran towards her. Heaving herself forwards but unable to get through, she seemed to be stuck. She pushed her neck out straight and gave a deafening bellow. I caught up with her and saw that the barbs of the wire had caught in her back, piercing her tough hide. As she struggled forward the sharp steel just embedded itself more deeply.

"Whoah there," I said, coming round to her side and ducking under the wire. I lost my footing on the loose boards and scrambled to right myself. I put a hand on her neck to try to steady her but she responded by backing up and bellowing even louder.

I got my arm around her neck and braced my shoulder against her chest to try to keep her still long enough to look at the cut. Moving backwards had only meant that another prong had gone in, and the wound was bigger.

"Hold still, you stupid animal," I said as I tried to pull the wire free. Frightened and in pain, Pirate moved back and forth, struggling to keep a foothold on the loose planks beneath her. My hands were covered in blood and hair, but still I couldn't get her loose. As the blood flowed quicker and began to soak into my shirt, I started to panic. I couldn't work the wicked points free.

There was a shout behind me and Tom came running across the field, followed by Philip. For once I was truly glad that Tom had disobeyed me. His eyes grew wide as he saw the blood on me and the dark wet stain on the animal's side.

"What can we do?" asked Philip.

"I don't know," I said, almost in tears. "You come and hold her head, Tom."

Philip stepped up beside me on the wood. "You hold the skin flat and I'll try to slide the barbs out," he said.

I laid my hands either side of the wound. "Right. Everyone hold her *still*," I said.

We all braced ourselves against her and Philip quickly slid the wire towards her tail, up and out. Pirate gave a wild kick that sent the wood flying, then Philip yanked the wire up as high as he could bend it and Tom and I pushed as hard as we could against her chest, forcing her back into the field, her eyes bulging in her effort to escape.

She quieted as Tom whispered to her and I rubbed her neck. The blood was drying on my forearms and had soaked through my shirt, warm against my belly. My legs seemed not to want to hold me up. Fumbling, I took the belt off my jeans and looped it into a makeshift halter.

"I need to get her patched up," I said. "Can you block the hole up, Tom, after you've taken them down for a drink? Make sure you plug it up good and tight."

Philip stayed to help him and I led Pirate away. Every now and then she stopped dead, her skin twitching as an involuntary shiver ran through it. We made slow progress as I persuaded her along, heading for the yard. I took her through the gate at the side of the cattle grid and into the calf housing, where we had a spare stall.

As I got out some hay for her Philip arrived, out of breath. "Are you all right?" he said.

I nodded.

"You look a bit white."

"Fine doctor I'd make," I said. I held my arms out to show him where the blood was drying in brownish streaks. "This makes me feel sick."

"What made her try to get through that gap?" he asked sympathetically.

"Warble flies," I said. "Well, you can't blame her really." I spread the hay out in the trough. "They lay their eggs on the cow's body and the larvae bore their way right inside. So they've got the instinct to run if they see that characteristic hovering."

Philip pulled a face. "Disgusting."

"The whole herd has to be treated against them twice a year."

Philip looked more closely at Pirate. "D'you think she needs stitches?"

I shook my head quickly. The last thing I needed was the vet up here asking questions. "I've got antiseptic powder and dressings," I said. I washed the wound, still feeling nauseous as the water changed from clear to pink. I quickly blocked out the picture forming in my mind of Mum's head against the steering wheel, a dark stain streaming in the water around her. I hoped that Philip wouldn't notice my hand shaking as I applied the dressing.

"Why don't you ring the hospital and ask to speak to your dad?" he asked.

"Why? Do you want to talk to him?" I said rudely. I rested my hands on Pirate's flank. "I'm surprised you're here at all after that run-in between Dad and Mick the other day."

He stepped towards me and put his hand on my filthy arm.

"You're a bit too hard on yourself, you know," he said. "Anyone would be upset having to deal with an animal hurt like that."

Sympathy was the one thing I had no defence against. I turned to him and buried my head in his shoulder. His arms went round me as I broke down.

"It's OK," he said. "It'll all be OK. Things'll come right again in the end."

"Dad's still angry," I choked out. "He's always angry . . ."

"Sshh," he said. "Come on, let's leave Pirate to it. She'll be all right now." He shut up the stall behind us, then took my hand. "I don't know what's going on," he said, "but I can see you're at the end of your rope."

"I'm so tired," I said, giving in.

"Bath first," he said, "then food; then you'll have a proper sleep."

I let him lead me indoors.

Philip ran me a bath while I sat on the hall chair outside. I felt ashamed of our budget coal-tar soap and the holes in the towels. As no one ever visited it had never seemed to matter before. He looked big and ungainly in the tiny room, and I noticed how a man moves differently, squatting down to stir the hot in with the cold, rather than bending over it. I watched his hand moving through the water, the curve of his forearm.

"There," he said. "You'll feel miles better when you've got all that off." He avoided saying "blood".

"I'm all right, you know," I said. "You don't have to do all this."

He came and helped me to my feet. "You'd do it for me," he said.

I made no answer. I was unused to such openness; my defences were loosened by his words, like a wall that's stood so long that a finger can scratch out the mortar. Each time he offered friendship he caught me by surprise — a thump, as if another stone had fallen into the grass. He clomped off downstairs to the kitchen and I closed the bathroom door behind me.

My shirt had dried on me. I peeled it off like a giant plaster, stripped off the rest of my clothes, then slid right under the water: a baptism. I held my breath, then came up, releasing it slowly in a sigh.

I tried to blank out thought; it was dangerous to be alone. When I was with someone else I had to put on a show, which had its own kind of strain, but at least stopped my feelings bursting through. No, the dangerous times were when you woke alone to the shock of memory, when you passed your own face in a mirror or locked up the house and glanced out at the night. Now, with nothing to see but the flaking distemper of the ceiling, and nothing to hear but the rippling of the water as I stirred, the pictures began again. I felt as though I was looking down on myself.

The pale oval of my face was the only part of me breaking the surface; my naked limbs were loose in the water and my hair had spread out like dark waterweed. I sat up, knocking into the side of the bath, my breath taken away by the picture that had flashed across my mind, hair streaming in a current, and the sound of river water in my ears.

I heard footsteps pounding up the stairs.

"Are you all right?" Philip's voice came anxiously through the door.

I rocked myself, with my head on my knees. That was the trouble with cracking walls: they let things in.

"Yes," I managed to call out.

"You're not going to faint or anything, are you?"

"No."

"Well, if you're sure . . . I'll get you something to eat."

I heard him go away again. I bathed quickly, leaving no more room for thoughts, scrubbing hard at my skin to get the marks off, then wrapped myself in a towel and let the filthy water out.

I was in my dressing gown, sitting on my bed, combing the tangles out of my hair, when Philip tapped on the door.

"Come in," I said, and put the comb down.

He came in carrying a tray with two mugs of tea and a huge cheese sandwich. I tried a smile.

"You could keep the barn door open with that."

He looked sheepish. "I've eaten mine already."

I raised my eyebrows.

273

He said, "Well, Tom's had two."

As I ate he sat down at the bottom of the bed and started sipping his tea and looking around at my stuff.

"Crikey, look at all your books," he said.

My textbooks were still lying about in piles on the dressing table; I hadn't had the time or the inclination to tidy them up. They seemed to come from another world, when I was a different person.

He put his head on one side to read the titles. "Has your grant letter come through yet?"

I shook my head. "I don't see how I can go."

He looked at me curiously. "Don't you want to any more?" he said.

"It's not that," I said. "I really do want to do it, to help, you know, mend a bone, prescribe a cure. To prove to myself that some things can be put right, I suppose." I swallowed hard. "The weather's changing," I said, looking towards the open window.

The air was cooler and a restless breeze was moving through the barley field, where the ears were heavy, necked and ready to harvest.

I leant forward to put down the plate and was aware of my nakedness under my dressing gown, the way my body moved beneath the fabric.

He stared into his tea. "Will you be all right now?" he said.

I said nothing and he didn't look up.

He put his mug down carefully. "I think I'd better go now."

"Don't," I said, reaching for his hand. "Don't go."

274

I wanted to touch him, as if I were frozen and could absorb heat from his touch, his warm arms, his quick pulse. Our hands met and I drew him towards me. He held me and I clung to him. I'm alive, I thought as we kissed, *I am alive.* We undressed without letting each other go, and the feeling of his skin against mine was like a homecoming.

From outside came the sound of Tom's feet running, then a whooping and a hollering as the rustle of the first drops of rain moved across the fields and swept into the yard. I imagined the big drops falling on the ground between the barley stalks, turning the earth from its dun colour to a rich red-brown, filling up and bubbling from the crazy cracks, soaking into the thirsty soil. Not the dark water of my mind, with its endless flowing through cold spaces, the caves and tunnels that I dreamt about, but clear living water, falling from the sky like jewels, like a blessing.

We lay face to face, entwined. The rain intensified, drumming on the corrugated iron of the barn roof. Its rhythm entered us as we moved together, ebbing and flowing as the wind blew veils of rain against the house bringing fresh, cool air into the room with the scent of rain on its breath.

Afterwards I told him all of it. He listened in silence as we lay together holding hands, the pressure of his fingers on mine the only sign I needed, encouraging me to go on. When I'd finished he hugged me to him.

"What can I do?" he said. "Just tell me and I'll do it."

"There isn't anything anyone can do. I think I just have to keep going." I drew back to look at his face. "You could come over when you can — when you're not working, I mean."

He nodded, frowning. "It's not just the work, though, is it?" he said. "It's the knowing. No one should have to carry that all on their own. You need to be able to talk about it."

I gazed at the ceiling, thinking about what silence had done to Dad, his absolute refusal to talk about Mum or his own feelings. How he'd grown a hard exterior to protect himself from the outside world, to give what was inside time to harden up, like a horse chestnut's prickly shell protecting its fruit.

"Don't you think you should tell someone? You shouldn't have to deal with this alone; someone older would know what to do."

I hesitated. "I don't know. I'm afraid of how Dad might react."

The thing was, bringing what had happened to light would be like stamping on the shell to split it right open; sometimes the force could smash the inside to bits.

With a shiver I realized that what I felt when Philip pushed me to look straight on at what had happened, this cornered feeling, was a taste of what Dad must have lived with for years: the mention of Mum's name waiting to ambush him; Mum's things a reminder smouldering in a drawer, too dangerous to keep; Mum's presence in the house, in the fields, in the woods; not a day when he wouldn't have felt it. Not a day in all those years. And now, if I confronted him with what I'd seen . . . The sides of my throat seemed to close up. For eight years he'd barely allowed us to mention her name. If he was brought face to face with everything he had been trying to turn his eyes from I didn't know how he would react in his effort to escape it.

Philip leant up on his elbow. "Have you talked to him about it? Does he know . . . about what you've found?"

I shook my head violently.

"It's not going to go away, Jess," he said gently.

I rubbed my arms.

"You're cold."

He got up and held the covers back for me to get right into bed, then went over and shut the window. The sound of the rain seemed to drop a key. Muffled behind glass it was a vibration, a steady thrumming joining earth and sky.

"You don't have to go, do you?"

"Not yet. But I'd better not be here for breakfast or Alice will come looking for me." He gave a rueful smile.

From downstairs came the sound of gunfire from the TV. Tom was watching a thriller, but I wasn't going to quibble about it tonight.

I pushed the covers back and moved across. He slipped into bed, his body warm and smooth.

"You should sleep now," he said and bent to kiss me on the forehead. "I'll watch for you for a while."

Watch for what? I thought groggily as sleep began to take me, but I guessed what he meant. He would watch over me in case the bad thoughts got into my dreams. He wouldn't go until I was sleeping a child's sleep, the deep unconsciousness that follows too long a day. I felt my breathing steady like the rain, my eyes stilled under my eyelids and my limbs grew languorous. My hand crept underneath the pillow to its familiar place. There was no book there. I roused myself long enough to remember that, with Dad away, I'd been reading snatches of it downstairs. It was on the kitchen table, I thought drowsily, or maybe the window-sill. Anyway, Philip was here. Now everything was going to be all right. I slept.

CHAPTER
SIXTEEN

It was the light streaming in through the open curtains that woke me. Just as well, I thought, sitting up and yawning. I'd not set the alarm the night before and the clock said quarter to six. I hoped that Philip had taken Tom up to bed — he was bound to have fallen asleep in front of the television.

On the dressing table a page torn from an exercise book was folded in half and propped against the mirror. I picked it up and read it. *Back as soon as I can. Don't you think you should tell someone? Love, Philip.*

I put it down on top of the books and quickly dressed. I was almost out of the door when I turned back and folded the note into a tiny square so that it would fit into my jeans pocket. I checked on Tom; he was in bed sleeping so deeply that I didn't have the heart to wake him for milking. He could feed the calves later instead.

When I went down to get the cows, you could hear the river from the field, the rush and roar of a body of water moving fast. It ought to have made me feel easier in my mind: nothing now for Tom to see, a terrible thing, sunk and secret again. Instead I felt sick and stirred up, and still afraid.

All through milking I thought about how Philip and I had talked. It had been such a relief to confide in someone; for a little time I'd allowed myself to let out some of the confused feelings that churned inside. But it had also disturbed me. Although I tried not to hear them, his words kept coming back. He was right, it wasn't just going to go away and I couldn't just keep hiding my eyes like a child. An awful thing had happened and I needed to know how and why. The chill of the stone parlour floor seemed to strike upwards through my soles.

I was going to have to talk to Dad.

Tom came into the parlour, his hair standing up like a brush. The dogs trailed in behind him. "Can I go down as far as the bridge?" he asked. "I want to see how full the river is."

"No," I said sharply. "Absolutely not. You know how dangerous it is in full spate." One of the dogs pushed its nose into Tom's hand. "I tell you what," I said more gently, "take the dogs up over the back for a walk and see if you can find us some mushrooms. There should be loads after all this rain." I shoved the next cow over to give myself room to put on the teats. "Off you go," I said, forcing a smile into my voice, "then we can have them for breakfast. There's a shopping bag behind the kitchen door you can use."

"If I get a lot, I can give some to Gran and Grandad. Remember, you said they'll be back tonight."

He slapped his thigh to call up the dogs and set off. I worked on steadily; I needed time on my own to think.

Later I rang Mrs Swift to ask if Tom could go round to her for the afternoon while I visited Dad. I wasn't going to leave Tom on his own at the farm ever again, and there was no way I could take him with me to see Dad this time. I dropped him off with Lolly. Mrs Swift seemed pleased to have him and said he could stay for tea too if I would pick him up about seven. She wanted me to stop for a drink but I made the excuse of having to fit in with visiting hours.

I found Dad in the day room for the first time. It was a small room at the end of his corridor with a coffee table piled with out-of-date magazines, a scatter of seats and a TV on a trolley. He was still unshaven and the gingery-blonde stubble made him look older. The arm with the graft was still heavily bandaged but the other was patched with dressings now rather than bandaged all over and the skin between looked tight and shiny with marks like ripples in places and livid, red scars. His hands were still in an awkward curved shape as if he were cupping an invisible ball.

He was reading an old copy of *Motorsport*, the magazine laid flat across his lap. He looked up to acknowledge me when I came in but then returned to his article. I sat down opposite him on a plastic-covered seat that stuck to the backs of my legs.

"You're feeling a bit better, then?" I said.

He gave me a long look and then scuffed at the page with his bandaged hand, taking several goes to turn it.

"I think they've taken the bandages off a bit early. This arm's still weeping." He raised it slightly but didn't show me.

"Do you think they'll let you home soon?"

"Who knows." He shrugged. "Anything from the bank?"

"Not yet. There are some window envelopes that look like invoices. I just brought them for you to see — I can take them home again and keep them in a file until you're back."

I took out some post and opened them one by one to show him.

"Look," I said, "the cheque from the dairy's come through. That's something."

"Bank that," he said. "Do it on your way back. Do you know how to get round the one-way system?"

I nodded guiltily.

He said drily, "Well, don't go and prang the Land-Rover. I saw you come into the car park."

I blushed and bent to gather up the papers.

He watched me. "That cheque won't go far," he said.

I took a deep breath. "At least we got the rain last night," I said, then found that I couldn't go on.

Dad stiffened, all his attention now on me, and instantly I realized that he knew. His face tightened: there was no smile of relief, no exclamation or celebration.

"Didn't rain here at all," he said.

I struggled to contain my worst fear, that Dad had known all along, had done nothing, had somehow been involved.

"Dad, please . . ." My chest felt as if it held a great weight as I forced myself on. "We need to talk."

He froze for a second, looking at me intently.

I said, "We need to talk about Mum."

He leaned towards me in the chair. "No, we don't," he said. "You need to listen." His face had drained to a putty colour. "I'm going to say this once and once only. It was an accident, what happened. The car went into a skid. There was nothing I could do then and there's nothing we can do now to bring her back." I raised my hand as if to stop the words, but he carried on in the same flat tone. "No one knew about it then and no one needs to know now."

"Why?" I broke in. "Why didn't you tell anyone?"

He looked at me sharply. "I had to be strong. I was afraid there would be . . ." he searched for the word, "enquiries . . . blame. People would ask how it happened and why she was driving so fast. Then everything would come out about how being on the farm, being with me, made her unhappy."

"What do you mean? You said it was an accident." I dug my nails into my palms. "You let me think all this time that she'd left us, left me," my voice began to tremble as I fought for control, "and all the time she never meant to, she was . . . she was . . ."

Dad stared at me as I stumbled to a halt. "I'll spell it out," he said. "Your mother and I had a row and she walked out. I tried to follow her, to stop her leaving, but I just made it worse. She was driving too fast because she wanted to get away. That's how it happened, and I have to live with that. But that's my business, nobody else's, and that's how I want it kept, right?"

I wanted to shut him up, stop him saying these things, but my voice stuck in my throat. He looked at me hard, as though weighing this up.

"I'm sorry you've had to find out, Jess, but you're not a child any more. You're strong like me, you've had to be."

"Where are her things?" I said.

"She walked out on us, remember."

"She didn't take her things with her. There were things she would have taken if she was going for good: clothes, photos, her make-up. I remember, I used to look at them and you wouldn't let me have them. Where are they now?" I asked doggedly.

"She left, Jess. No one was even surprised. She never really belonged on the farm."

"What did you do with her things?"

I met his eyes. They held a blank determination as he stared me down. He said nothing.

I shook my head. "She did belong," my voice came out in a whisper, "and she's still there, no matter what you throw away. I see her every day, everywhere: in the kitchen, in the yard, walking the fields," my voice began to break, "down by the river. You can't just wipe someone out as though they've never been."

Dad looked at me with a level gaze. "You can't bring her back, Jess." He got up and went over to the window, turning his back on me, and stared out. "The dead are gone and the living do everything they can to survive. Every beast knows this. Best to start again."

My eyes blurred. "You know that's not true," I said. "Even a cow will call all night for its calf."

"I want your promise, Jess," he said. "This goes no further than us."

I sat mute.

He walked across and stood over me. "I have to have your promise, Jess." His voice took on a coaxing tone. "We're a family; we have to work together." He squatted down beside me.

I sat very still in the silent room. It would be so easy to lay my head against his shoulder, to let it all out, be his little girl again.

"Jess?" he said, trying to get me to answer. He bent round to search my face as I tried to muster the strength to stand against him.

I was unable to speak; my eyes filled with tears. I broke away and he let me go, satisfied with what he'd seen. Leaving the papers strewn on the table, I slammed out of the room and ran down the corridor past the Sister's station, where a nurse got up as if to follow me, past the lift, and clattered down the stairs. I pushed past visitors queuing for the vending machine in the foyer and out to safety.

I sat in the Land-Rover with my head down on the steering wheel and wept without restraint, my hands over my face.

When I was all cried out I sat for a while to try to get calm before setting off to drive home. Then I drove slowly to the exit and stopped at the barrier to show the porter my visitor's pass. In the mirror I could see a figure standing at the last third-floor window. As the barrier rose, he turned away.

It was early evening before I got the chance to stop working and get away on my own properly to think. I went to the woods, but out of sight of the river, turning not towards the bridge, but the other way, keeping a distance between myself and the agitated rush of the water. I went slowly along the narrow path, pushing through the bracken and gingerly picking aside brambles, which shed water drops and a dusting of seed on to the earth.

Philip's note was still in my pocket and his voice was still in my head, urging me to tell someone. But the way it had turned out, talking to Dad had only made things worse. I could still barely believe that he had known all along and had done nothing. He said he'd followed her but it was too late. But when you saw, when you knew beyond a shadow of doubt, that it was too late to save her, wouldn't you still want to hold your wife in your arms to say goodbye? If you loved her, if you loved her at all? I didn't understand, would never understand, how he could leave her there in that horrible place, as though once the spark of life was out a person was worth nothing, just so much matter left to rot. And for what? So that he could present it as all Mum's fault, the townie wife who'd found the farming life too hard, who couldn't cope with her responsibilities and ran off leaving her kids and her husband to manage on their

286

own. Yes, I thought, it certainly plays better than the truth, that whatever he did or said that night made her get out so fast that she lost control of the car. And now, after all these lies, he wanted me to "keep quiet". *Keep lying*, I thought, that's what it amounts to, whatever he called it. I pushed on through the bracken. In places it grew so thickly that its springy stems tangled across the path, forming a wet mesh that soaked me as I shouldered my way through.

Dad expects too much, I thought; I can't carry this for him. At the same time the thought of his anger if I crossed him made my stomach churn. And I was afraid to get anyone else involved. There would be questions and outsiders, a grown-up world that I knew next to nothing about. Even in my mind I couldn't utter the words to explain about Mum, could think of no form of words to say.

To the side of the path, in a small clearing, stood an old beech tree where Mum and I used to picnic. I struck off the path, for a moment dazzled by low sunlight as I crossed the open space, then entered the tree's shadow, moving from dappled to deeper shade. I sat down with my back to the trunk and put my head in my hands. Pictures of us here together came back as clearly as the sun through stained glass, memories illuminated by grief.

I saw Mum kneeling on a rug, opening dumpy paper parcels of sandwiches, me knocking over a jam jar of tiddlers and running back to the river with an inch of water left, the jar swinging from its string handle. I remembered bending close to watch her hands as she showed me how to make a bark boat, her slim, quick fingers spearing a beech leaf with a twig to make a sail. She said we had to give them names when we launched them. Mine was the *Dawn Treader* and hers was the *Mary Rose*.

Once we lay on the rug, looking up into the tree, and watched the movement of the lace of twigs and the new leaves at their tips, the brightest, youngest green as the sun shone through them.

"Happy?" she said, and I didn't even have to answer.

I sat up and wiped my eyes. How had it come to this? I remembered an evening when I'd come downstairs because I had a headache and found Mum and Dad dancing. One of Grandad's old scratchy '78s was playing: a man's voice and a piano. Mum had her arms around Dad and her head turned sideways against his shoulder, and Dad's arms were clasped around her waist. There were no set steps to their dance; they were swaying, moving in a slow circle, their bodies touching all the way down, and they both had their eyes closed. I stood hanging on to the doorknob, not wanting to go in, not wanting it to end. I felt like the moon must do towards the sun, as if they gave me their light. Dad bent his head a little to say something to her and, as they turned together in their dance, I saw her smiling. I remembered how quietly I crept away.

I put my head back against the trunk of the tree. The roughness of the bark pulled at my hair as I looked up into its cool branches.

One time I'd climbed the tree and gone so high I'd got scared. Mum had called out, "Don't look down.

288

Feel with your feet." And it had worked: I'd stared up into the first break in the branches at the sky and I'd felt as though the air beneath me was no longer a dizzying void through which I would inevitably fall, but an element to move in, which I could choose to travel through, to climb higher into the breeze and a clear view. She must have been petrified for me, I thought, looking back on it, but she never showed it. She followed her own advice. *Don't look down.*

The roaring of the river was distinct from the shushing of the trees. Look at me, I thought, afraid to go right down to the water, afraid to see the mud stirred from the bottom by the rain, its current writhing like twisted ropes drawn across its surface. No place to mourn her, nowhere to lay flowers, nowhere to find some peace.

Fear had shaped my steps and planned my route today. Could I really live my whole life like Dad, turning my face away? If I did nothing, that's what it would amount to: one long walk away from the bridge.

I got quickly to my feet and set off through the wood back towards the house. I knew now what I was going to do: trust my instincts. *Don't look down.* I cut back to the fields and broke into a run; I had to do this quickly before I lost my nerve. I reached the house and rushed through to the hall.

"Grandad," I said breathlessly into the phone, "I need to come over."

"Are you all right, love?"

"I'll come straight over," I said, forcing out the words. "I'll explain everything when I get to you."

CHAPTER
SEVENTEEN

I drew up on the gravel drive. The front door was open and I went straight in, squeezing past the suitcases that were still piled in the hall. Grandad was in the snug, standing with his hands clasped behind his back, looking out into the garden, where Gran was pegging out the first batch of washing. The room was cluttered with the debris of a holiday — Thermos, picnic rug, souvenirs spilling from half-open bags.

He turned and held out his arms. We hugged, then he gave my face a long searching look.

"It's a bad business, I can see that," he said. "Where's Tom?"

"Oh God," my hand went up to my mouth, "he's still round at the Swifts'. I'm supposed to collect him at seven."

"Don't worry," he said, suddenly businesslike, "I'll ask Rose to get him. Then you and I can get to the bottom of this."

He went out to the garden and spoke to Gran. I saw her face grow more serious and she glanced towards the house. Grandad said something else and looked at his watch. Then Gran put down the peg bag and set off briskly around the side of the house.

Grandad returned and motioned me to a chair. "Now," he said, "what's been going on? Where's your dad?"

I picked up the cushion from the chair and sat with it clasped on my lap. As I told him about the fire, about Dad being in hospital, about trying to keep the farm going, his face grew grave. I told him about the bank pressing Dad and how we'd lost the hay that he was intending to sell. I told him how I'd had to water the cows at the river and how, before the rain, the river had fallen very low . . . and then my voice petered out.

"Is there something more, Jess?" he asked gently.

I picked at the fringe on the cushion, twisting and untwisting it as I told him what I'd seen.

His face was grim.

"And you're sure, you're absolutely sure, about what you saw?"

I nodded miserably. "Dad knew about it already," I said. "I asked him about it this afternoon."

Grandad sucked in his breath.

"It was an accident," I said quickly. "He said they'd had a row and Mum was driving too fast."

"But why didn't he tell us?" Grandad was shaking his head in disbelief. "I looked for her. When Henry rang us and said she hadn't come back from work, he was in such a state I drove all over the county — the hospitals, everywhere." He was silent for a moment. "Poor Sylvie, poor dear girl."

"He didn't want me to tell anyone, even now. He wanted me to promise . . . He said we had to forget Mum and move on . . ." I tried to swallow the lump in my throat.

Grandad took my hand. "Are you very angry with your dad?" he said.

"No . . . Yes . . ." I stared fiercely at the clock on the mantelpiece. "I could never understand how Mum could've left without me and Tom. I was always wondering what we'd done that was so bad she could leave us behind — and then Tom was just a baby," I faltered, "so that meant it was something *I* must've done. For years I've been wondering." I hugged the cushion to me. "I don't think I can forgive him for that," I said, looking back at Grandad.

Grandad had closed his eyes as if to shut out my words. "Henry, Henry . . ." he muttered under his breath.

Dad's his only son, I thought: it must be hard for him to hear this. For a moment I felt a stab of envy for this real fatherly love that could respond in sorrow rather than anger — the kind of love I'd missed and would never have again.

"I'm sorry," I said. "But it isn't just about me and Tom and being lied to. And it isn't just about Dad, and him wanting to hide from what happened. It's about Mum. She deserves better."

Grandad nodded slowly. "She needs to be laid properly to rest," he said, "but it's not going to be easy, Jess. There'll have to be an inquest."

The sound of voices reached us from the hall as Gran and Tom, Lolly in his arms, came in.

"Are we having tea here?" Tom was saying.

I got up and went to meet him. "We're staying overnight," I said. "Now Gran and Grandad are back we're going to stay with them for a little while."

Gran looked anxious. "Tom tells me Henry's in hospital?"

Grandad said, "Jess, would you give me the Land-Rover keys, please. Rose, get your bag: we're going in to see him."

I felt dread in the pit of my stomach. Dad would see this as a betrayal.

Gran reached up to get her bag from the hallstand. She gave me a hasty peck on the cheek. "There's not much in, because we were away. Make a big omelette — we've got eggs," she said as they went out.

"I'll tell you on the way," Grandad was saying to her as he helped her into the Land-Rover. "It's serious, Rose. We're going to need to support each other through this, and I don't mean just Henry."

"Come on," I said with my hand on Tom's head. "You can eat an omelette can't you? Not too full of Mrs Swift's tea?"

We watched some TV, Tom eating steadily and never taking his eyes off the screen, while I toyed with the food, staring at the screen without seeing it. Gran and Grandad still hadn't come back by Tom's bedtime. I took him up to the spare room and put a camp bed up for myself. Looking around at the room I hadn't slept in since I was a child, I sat beside him until he fell asleep. There was a crocheted bedcover, patterned with neat squares and a picture I remembered of Paddington Bear worked in cross-stitch. On the dressing table stood a brush and comb set, together with several lumpy clay models of houses and farm animals that I, and later Tom, had done in Miss Turner's class. I left the lamp on in case he should wake from one of his dreams and need to find me. As I came downstairs I heard the key in the lock.

They both appeared worn out. Gran's eyes were red rimmed behind her glasses. I looked from one to the other for reassurance.

"He'll calm down," Grandad said. "Anyway, you kids can stay here as long as you like."

My heart sank.

Gran hung up her bag. "He's got a bit of a temperature so they're taking a swab and putting him on antibiotics. He'll be kept in for a bit, I think."

She walked past me to the kitchen and shut the door. She wishes I hadn't said anything, I thought. I went into the snug and sat down in one of the fireside chairs.

I heard Grandad pick up the phone in the hall and dial, then in a stiff, formal voice I'd never heard him use before he asked for the duty sergeant. Then he said, "Ah, Ken, I'm afraid I've got to report something serious." He lowered his voice and spoke quickly and quietly so that I heard only odd words: "accident . . . storm . . . tomorrow." There was a click as the phone went down.

"What'll happen to Dad?" I said when Grandad came in. "They won't understand why he didn't say anything before now." My voice was rising.

"Now, Jess," Grandad sat opposite me and leant forward to hold my arms, keeping me grounded, "seems to me we have to take this one step at a time."

I forced myself to take slower breaths.

He went on. "By tomorrow the river should have calmed down enough for the police to recover the car." I felt my body stiffen as he spoke. "So you and Tom will stay here with Rose. I'll deal with the milking and suchlike."

I rocked from side to side in Grandad's grip as if to get away. "Dad's going to kill me for this," I said.

"Is this what it's come to, Jess, between you and your father? Is it as bad as this?"

I closed my eyes up tight.

"Now listen," he said. "All my life I've believed that honesty's the best policy and I've tried to live that way, but I'm old enough and wise enough to know that there's an exception to every rule."

"Do you mean I shouldn't have said anything?" I said in a small voice.

"No," he said firmly. "You did absolutely the right thing. What I mean is, I think we should let your dad keep quiet about the fact that he already knew. Do you think you could do that, Jess? It's still a big secret to keep."

"I don't want to get Dad into trouble. I only want to do the right thing by Mum."

"It's going to be hard enough on him facing up to the past, without having a charge for withholding information as well," Grandad said.

"But that's what we'll be doing."

Grandad looked thoughtful. "That's true," he said. "I've got no right to ask you. You must do what you think best."

"I wouldn't have to tell Tom that Dad had lied to us then, would I?" I said slowly.

Grandad waited.

"But we could still have a proper service for Mum."

"I know you're angry with your dad," Grandad said gently, "but hiding what happened, as he did, is the sign of a weak man, not a strong one. He must have felt guilt and shame for that cowardice every day of his life since. Don't you think he's been through enough?"

I thought of the closed look that came over Dad's face if Mum was ever mentioned, of the photo albums locked away in the sideboard, of the silences on anniversary days.

I nodded.

"You've got a good heart, Jess."

Gran brought in the tea and set it down with a heavy sigh. She sat at the table to drink hers. They talked for a while of practicalities, of what time to get up for milking and what Gran should get from the village shop to keep us going until she could get into town to the supermarket. I sat quiet but was aware of Gran watching me.

"He'll come round, Jess; he won't stay angry for long," she said.

Yes, he will, I thought. There are no grey areas with Dad. Everything is sharp edges, with no softness where forgiveness can seed. I said nothing, just sipped my tea.

She turned to Grandad. "Have you two spoken about being discreet?" Grandad shot her a warning look but she carried on. "There'll be talk as it is, everyone in the village wanting to know our business. It doesn't take much round here to turn a misfortune into a scandal; there are always some that can't wait to get a bit of gossip on a land-owning family like ours."

"Rose . . ." Grandad said.

"What?" Gran said testily. "We're a family. We have to close ranks, stick together."

I put my cup down carefully on the hearth. "I really don't care what people think," I said. "I'm not going to say anything, because I don't want to make things worse for Dad, or Tom, but don't think for a moment that it's to save Garton's getting a bad name. That's how Dad thinks and look what it's led to."

Gran stared at me as though she couldn't believe her ears.

I stood up. "I'm done with all of that." The clock on the mantelpiece ticked into the silence that followed. "I think I'll go on up now," I said.

"Jess . . ." Gran said as I went out of the room

"Leave her," Grandad said in a low voice. "It's all been too much for her. Let her get some sleep."

I went upstairs, peeled off my clothes and switched off the lamp. I lay down on the rickety camp bed and stared into the darkness. I heard Gran and Grandad come up and get ready for bed, then they talked for what seemed like a long time. Eventually it was quiet except for the regular sound of Tom's breathing. I would have to tell him tomorrow that Mum was never coming back.

I have to sleep, I have to sleep, I said to myself again and again, like a mantra.

Outside in the night a dog fox barked: a harsh, lonely sound. Then there was silence covering everything, complete as dewfall. I closed my eyes and let the hot tears brim and spill down my face, for my mother, for myself, for all of us.

CHAPTER
EIGHTEEN

The next day was hard to bear. We stayed off the farm while the police were there recovering the car. Gran tried to keep us busy, giving us silver to polish and weeding to do. Grandad had taken sandwiches with him and intended to check over the farm and feed the dogs as well as do the milking.

In the afternoon Gran said she was going up for a lie-down but if we needed her she wouldn't be asleep, just resting. Tom and I sat under a tree in the garden, shelling peas for tea, with Lolly asleep in the dappled shade. Tom had been quiet and withdrawn all day. Now, looking at his head bent over the bowl of peas, I could see the tension in his neck and shoulders, sense his wariness. I took a deep breath and told him that we'd found out why Mum had never come back. He kept his head down over the bowl in his lap all the time I was speaking, but I saw his fingers fumble and grow still. I told him what Mrs Swift had said about Mum loving us both very much.

"I knew she wasn't coming back," he said, taking me by surprise. "Did you think she would, Jess?"

"I suppose I just hoped," I said, choosing my words carefully.

"I can't really remember her very well," he said thoughtfully. "Except I think she used to play 'This is the way the lady rides . . .' bumping me up and down on her knee. I can remember her laughing."

I opened my mouth to speak and then stopped. He looked at me curiously, as I fought to keep what I felt out of my face. Then his self-possession seemed to waver.

"Can I go and see Gran now?"

I nodded. "That's fine; I'll finish these."

I picked up the bowl and started running my thumbnail along each pod, trying to concentrate on the regular repetitive movement, the ping of the peas into the metal bowl. The words of the game played through my mind.

This is the way the lady rides, trit-trot, trit-trot,
This is the way the farmer rides, gallopy-gallopy,
gallopy-gallopy,
This is the way the drunkard rides,
He stayed behind to finish the wine and ended up
in the ditch!

I'd played the game a hundred times with Tom, but not until he was old enough not to cry at the end when I tipped him backwards and caught him again. And that was at least a year after Mum had gone.

Later, I tiptoed up to look in on them and found them both asleep on Gran's big double bed, a story-book open on the bedspread beside them. Tom hadn't asked for a story for years. I was glad he had Gran to turn to. After all, it's hard to take comfort from the person who brings you bad news. I was glad she'd baby him a bit; God knows it was something that he'd missed.

There was a tap on the front door and I went down to find Philip waiting on the step.

"Are you all right?" he said. "Alice told me you'd come here. Does that mean you decided to tell?"

I nodded. "Grandad."

"I'm glad," he said. "How are you feeling?"

I kissed him for an answer. He slipped his arm round my shoulders.

"Can you come out?" he asked.

"I don't think I can. I need to wait and see Grandad."

He leant his head against mine. "I wish you could," he said. "I don't want to waste any of the time we've got."

"How d'you mean?"

"I'll be in Germany in September," he said, "and you'll be here, and we'll both have no money. We'll never get to see each other."

I was quiet for a moment. "Maybe later," I said, "when Tom's gone to bed. Where'll you be?"

"I'll come to the gate at the bottom of the lane," he said, "about nine o'clock, and then I'll just wait."

We untwined our fingers. "Later, then," I said, smiling.

★   ★   ★

Grandad came home in time for supper and took me off for a talk. The police had said that the damage to the car suggested that it had hit the bridge at speed and the coroner's report was likely to record a verdict of death by misadventure. I felt as though a huge weight had been taken off my shoulders.

Grandad had spoken to the undertaker and the vicar and the burial service would probably be on Tuesday. He thought that Tom and I should stay on with him and Gran for a while but I could come over with him from tomorrow in the daytime and we'd work together on the farm.

He didn't say anything about Pirate's injury or using the river for watering the cows. He just gave my shoulder a squeeze and said that he was really proud of me and Tom for having kept things going. The only mention he made of the fire was to say that he'd phoned the tree surgeon to set a date to take down the remains of the burnt trees along the river bank as some branches were likely to fall.

When he got up he had to place his hands carefully on the arms of his chair and lever himself up. Suddenly he seemed older, frailer.

"I'm going in to see Henry again," he said.

"Do you want me to come?"

"Probably best give it a while," he said.

The burial was awful for all of us. There was a memorial service at the village church and then she was buried in the little cemetery on the edge of the village, backing on to Grange Farm fields. Only close family came to the graveside. We stood sweltering in our black clothes. Grange Farm was harvesting, and we were covered in dust and were barely able to hear the vicar over the noise of the combine in the background. After a while Grandad walked over to the field boundary and flagged the combine down. He spoke to the man, who stared over at us and then nodded and went off to take his tea break.

The sudden silence seemed eerie. I became gradually aware of the noise of bees as they busied themselves over the funeral wreaths. I watched them crawling in and out of the trumpets of the lilies, collecting pollen and leaving it too, uselessly pollinating flowers that were already dying. I felt desolate. Tom cried and Gran and I stood either side of him, holding a hand each. At the end I gave Tom a flower and took one myself and we dropped them together into the grave. There was some weird fake grass material draped over the sides of the hole, to hide the rawness of the newly dug soil, but before we went Grandad stepped forward and took a handful of earth. He put it into my hand and helped me crumble it into the grave. It pattered on the wood like stones. He put his arm around me. "Steady, girl," he said. "Now you've said your goodbye." He steered me back to the car, nodding to Tom and Gran to follow.

I went back there in the evening. I wanted to say my goodbye properly on my own. I took a bottle of water and soaked the florist's stuff that the flowers were arranged in, to keep them going a bit longer. Then I rearranged them to cover the lumpy turfs on the mound of earth as best I could. I sat for a long time looking out over the newly cut field, until I felt calmer.

A figure approached over the field and I shaded my eyes against the low sun to see. It was Philip.

"I thought I'd find you here," he said. "Come for a walk? Or do you want to be on your own?"

I climbed over the fence and we walked in single file at the field margin between the barley and the edge of the wood, until we came to the river, more or less on the border between Swift land and ours. He looked very solemn. We walked together under the flickering leaves of the aspens.

"I've made something for you," he said, as we climbed the stile leading to the river path. The sun was going down, the ripples on the water alive with the last of the shaking light, darkness already gathering under the trees. "Look," he said, pointing at a willow leaning out over the water.

Suspended in its branches, catching the light reflected from the water's surface, was the huge disc of the moon, as if it had dropped to earth and been caught in the arms of the tree.

"It's for you to remember your mum by," he said. "I didn't do the wrong thing, did I? I know you didn't like me doing that stone spiral, but this just felt right somehow."

"It's beautiful." I put my hand in his. "It wasn't that I didn't like the stones, you know; it was just that when I found them I had this strong feeling of Mum's presence, and I built it up in my mind as if it was some kind of message. Then when I found out it was all a sort of false hope . . ."

"Maybe she was there in a way," Philip said. "I mean, in your memory she's all along the river, isn't she, everywhere you ever walked together." We watched the drooping willow twigs move across the moon's face in the breeze. "I thought you could come here sometimes when you wanted to be on your own to think about her. And I thought . . ." the words came out all in a rush, "well, you can see it from the bridge. In the daylight it's like a big shining ball, so I thought if you were ever there and you had black thoughts you'd only have to look downstream, and it might help somehow."

We sat down on the grass and I laid my head on his shoulder. For the first time that day I felt the tightness in my chest relax. Downriver on the opposite bank the flock of Canada geese was gathering, some on the water, bobbing gently in the current, and some on the bank, pecking over the grass.

"Yes," I said. "This is a good place to remember Mum. A very good place."

We sat in a companionable silence until the light began to fade, and then Philip walked me home. He kissed me at the gate, then said, "Alice says, do you want to come for tea tomorrow, about six?"

I hesitated for a moment; I would have to tell Gran and Grandad where I was going if I was going to miss a meal. I was so jangled up over Dad not wanting to see me that I didn't think I could bear any more disapproval.

"You don't have to. I can meet you at the gate again."
He looked uncertain, vulnerable.

"No, 'course I'll come," I said quickly, and in that
moment realized just how much I felt for this gangly
boy who held my secrets safe and understood me
before I understood myself. I didn't want to give him
even a moment's hurt. I kissed him again quickly. "See
you tomorrow," I said and ran up the drive.

As I let myself in, Grandad came out of the front
room.

"Are you courting, Jess?" he said. "The Swift boy?"

I coloured up.

He patted my arm. "No, no," he said. "Nothing
wrong with that. He's a good lad."

Gran came out of the kitchen, frowning. "What's
that?" she said. "Mick Swift's nephew? Honestly, Jess,
did you have to choose him? I sometimes think you set
out to cross swords with your father."

"He's the kindest person I know, and I don't care
what Dad —"

Grandad cut in. "Leave her be, Rose; not everything
revolves around Henry." He turned to me. "There's no
ruling over matters of the heart. Just be discreet around
your dad, that's all."

Gran let out one of her heavy sighs, the sort where
she pressed her lips tightly together afterwards.

I started to go upstairs, glad of Grandad's
peace-making. As I reached the top I heard him say to
Gran, "We should be glad she's got someone to lean
on. She's had what I'd call a long walk in a north
wind."

CHAPTER
NINETEEN

Dad would be home in the afternoon. Grandad had gone to fetch him. With mixed feelings I'd moved back to the farm to get things ready. Grandad and I had mended the fence properly down by the river and were using the bowser again, so we'd moved the cows back to Five Acres. Dad need never know the short cuts we'd taken with watering while he was away. Gran and Tom had come over to help clean the house and Gran had been playing with him while they changed the bed linen, throwing the sheets up in the air so that they'd come down over him and pretending not to notice that she was making the bed with him in it. His laughter made me smile too; it was a long time since I'd heard him laugh out loud. Gran had roasted a chicken and baked an apple tart so that we could celebrate Dad's homecoming together. I wished with all my heart that it would turn out as she pictured it, the Garton family reunited. I kept my misgivings to myself.

As I finished clearing out the fridge to make room for the fresh food, Gran and Tom came down and went off to feed the calves. Tom ran back to give me the afternoon post he'd picked up from the mat, then caught up again with Gran.

There was a letter for Dad that was bigger than usual, with the address typed on the front, rather than showing through a window. Not a bill, I thought, but not a cheque either; the envelope was thick, stiff and official. I took it into the office, where Grandad had put the mail for Dad to look at when he got home.

I suddenly remembered what Philip had said, that the university grant letters should be out now. I sorted through the pile and my heart gave a leap when I saw that two letters were addressed to me. I opened the first one carefully and a computer-printed sheet fell out: my exam results. I picked it up and had to smooth it out on to the desk to read it, my hand was trembling so much. I couldn't believe it: three A's and a B; even the awful chemistry paper hadn't been a complete flop. I read it again and again. It was enough to meet my offer from Birmingham, if only I could find a way to go.

Quickly I tore the other letter open; it said that I had been awarded full coverage of tuition fees but would have to cover living expenses and accommodation costs myself. I could do some part-time work, but it'd never be enough to keep myself in hall, and then there were books and travel costs and food. My excitement shrivelled like a punctured balloon. And anyway, Dad would say he couldn't cope without me. I might as well be wishing for the moon.

I tucked the letters into the pocket of my work shirt. A few moments ago I'd been ready to ring Nicola to swap results and congratulations with her. Now I didn't want to speak to anyone about it — wouldn't until I'd worked out a form of words that would mask my disappointment.

I heard vehicles on the track and went to look out of the kitchen window. Dad and Grandad had turned up in the Land-Rover, closely followed by the tree surgeon's truck. Both vehicles drew up into the field and Dad and Grandad stood talking to the boss while two other men got out ladders, chainsaws and tackle. With a sigh I put the kettle on. As Grandad drove into the yard, the whining sound of the saw started up and, as they opened the door and came in, the noise increased to a pitch that jarred your nerves and put your teeth on edge.

Dad had a long-sleeved shirt on, buttoned down over his wrists so that only his hands showed. His left hand was still bandaged but the right one was open to the air, still a little swollen, the skin tight and pink with some scarring, but he held his hand open now, not curled or carried protectively in front of his chest. He looked pale — all his tan had gone after such a long spell indoors — and his stubble had thickened to a full sandy beard.

I stood uncertainly for a moment, then stepped forward as if to kiss his cheek.

"Mind my arm," he said.

Grandad gave him a sideways glance. "How about that tea, love?" he said. "Kettle's boiling."

I busied myself with laying out the teacups while Grandad gave Dad an update on the stock and the need to have the burnt trees made safe. While he was talking, Dad kept glancing over at me, until finally he couldn't hold his tongue any longer.

"And where were you, Jess, while your grandad was doing all of this? I thought I left the farm in your charge?"

"Now don't start getting at her, Henry," said Grandad. "She kept things going beautifully until we got back from holiday and she's either been helping me or Rose ever since. Where is Rose anyway?"

"She's with Tom, feeding the calves," I said.

"Right, well, I'll go and tell them we're back," Grandad said. "Your mum's cooked up your favourite tea, Henry, to be a bit of a welcome party."

As I spooned the tea from the tin into the pot I began to tell Dad that we'd had to move the cows down to the bottom field, but that now the rain had come the grass was recovering and we'd been able to move them back. I kept glancing over at him, almost hoping that he would tell me I'd done something stupid; anything would've been better than this awful silence. I poured the water into the pot and stirred it noisily to fill the quiet.

I carried the pot over to the table and took the top newspaper from a pile of magazines and free papers, to use as a mat to put the hot teapot down on. Underneath it was the bird book. It was lying on the top now; its blue and green cover seemed to flare at me in the moment that I saw it, as startling as a shout in the quiet room. I put the pot down clumsily, rattling the lid and spilling a little tea on to the paper. Dad looked up at the noise and followed my gaze. His eyes rested on the book.

I picked up the whole pile of papers as if to tidy them away. I held them bunched against me, the book sandwiched between the papers and my body. I thought that there was a moment of recognition in his eyes, that he started, made a slight movement towards me, but I couldn't be sure, so quickly did he relax back into his seat. His eyes slid away from mine as he reached for a teacup and awkwardly put it down in front of him.

"Has the bank rung?" he asked.

I shook my head. "No one's rung," I said, "except I had to ring the dairy to cancel the tanker on one day because we spoiled some of the milk. They weren't too pleased and we had to get rid of it after." I finished in a breathless rush, offering up this misdemeanour in the spirit of a prayer. *Shout at me, rage at me, call me a fool, only don't ask for the book, please, don't ask for the book.*

He looked at me coldly. "Are you going to pour me some tea, then?" he said.

I put the pile down on the draining board for a moment, with the book safely hidden at the bottom, and poured the tea. The others came in and Gran began fussing round Dad: wouldn't he be better in an armchair? Surely the least I could do was to make him comfortable. Why had I given him such weak tea? Didn't I know he liked it stronger? She swilled the tea around in the pot and poured Dad a fresh cup, muttering that she still had a lot to teach me about running a household and nursing a patient.

Tom and Grandad were helping themselves to cups and saucers, so I took the pile of papers upstairs.

In my room I dumped the papers on my dressing table and spread my palm for a moment over the smooth cool surface of the book's marbled cover. It seemed strange to think that this was all I would ever have of Mum. I had begun to accept that now. It's better than photos anyway, I thought fiercely. When I read Mum's words it was as though I could hear her voice, speaking directly to me, letting me see the world we shared through her eyes. It was like being given a whole boxful of memories you thought you'd lost for ever. I tucked the book back into its place under my pillow.

When I went back into the kitchen Dad was insisting that Grandad take him to see the stock and Grandad was trying to argue him out of it.

"They're all perfectly healthy, Henry; they've been in good hands," Grandad was saying. "Look, why not give yourself a couple of days to rest up a bit? I can help Jess with the milking for a few days; you need to pace yourself; no need to pick up the reins again straight away."

"I'd just like to get my feet under my table, so to speak," Dad said. "I know you will have done everything that needed doing but I've got my own ways of doing things and I want to see what's what."

Grandad paused as if counting to ten. "All right then, we'll do the rounds just quickly before tea. You'll call us, Rose?"

They walked off over the fields and Gran and I started to prepare the salad and whip up some cream to go with the apple tart. Tom sat at the table, doodling on a scrap of paper with a stubby bit of pencil.

"Would you set the table, Tom?" Gran asked. "Give the glasses a nice shine with a tea towel first, there's a good boy."

He put the pencil back in his pocket and set to straight away without a moan.

"Where have you put Lolly?" I asked.

"Well, I couldn't bring her over here, could I?" Tom said grumpily.

"We left her in her nice new basket, didn't we?" said Gran. "Have you got any shallots, Jess? I never think a salad's got much flavour without."

"'Fraid not — only chives." I passed some over.

Gran sighed. "I didn't think Henry looked himself at all," she said. "So pale. You should cook him up some casseroles; they never give you enough meat in hospital, not for a grown man anyway, and he'll need strengthening. Now, this is a proper square meal." She nodded at the dishes spread out on the table, then added: "You make sure you look after him properly. You need to be keeping things comfy for him on the home front, not gallivanting off out with a certain lad. Your father needs rest, not more aggravation."

"He can't be feeling too bad," I said. "He seemed to be holding his own with Grandad."

"There." Gran sprinkled the chopped chives over the salad. "Tom, go and give them a shout, love, please."

Tom went.

Gran picked up the tea towel and busied herself rubbing a shine into the knives and forks.

The others came in, and Grandad stood back in mock amazement at the laden table. "My word," he said, "it's a feast!"

"I'm a bit tired now," Dad said. "I think I'll sit in an easy chair and have it on a tray, Mum."

"I'll bring it through," Gran said, ushering Dad into the lounge, "and I'll come and have mine with you. You don't want to eat on your own, do you?"

Grandad sat down at the table. "Come on then, Tom," he said. "The three of us will just tuck in."

"See," I said. "He won't even sit down to a meal with us."

"He'll come round. Give him time."

We ate in silence for a while.

Tom said, "Can I come home with you again, Grandad?"

"It depends what your dad says."

I said, "I think it'd be a good idea; only one of us is in the firing line then while Dad's 'coming round'."

Gran came in carrying the tray, unstacked it into the sink and started to wash up.

Grandad said, "I think we'll go home now, so I can have a bit of a rest before milking — that all right?"

"You don't have to come back again. I can manage," I said. I didn't add that the more I had to do, the easier it would be to keep out of Dad's way.

"All right if I take the 'Drover, then? If your dad won't be driving anywhere for a bit?" Grandad picked up the keys. "Tom's coming back with us, Rose."

Gran looked round from drying her hands, her face brightening. "That's nice," she said. "You can come and read to me while I have a little toes-up, then we'll go and pick some blackberries down the lane. How about that?"

After they'd gone, the house was quiet except for the odd click and clatter as I finished putting the dishes away. I left Dad where he was in the lounge and set about giving the kitchen a good clean; the dust was thick on the dresser and mantelpiece after our time away. Afterwards I took the washing-up water out to the garden. Down by the river the tree men had gone for their tea break, leaving the landscape altered yet again. Two thirds of the clump of tree skeletons were down, so there was a new gap leading to the fields on the other side of the river. Through the charred mess in the burnt fields, a faint blush of green was beginning to show.

In the garden some of the plants were starting to recover from the drought; some were dying back as if it was autumn. The grass around the apple tree would have to be reseeded: the tree had sucked up all the moisture there was and even then the leaves looked curled and blighted. Mum's roses had pulled through, though; some had late buds forming and one had even bloomed, a creamy yellow, tinged with a dark pink at the edge of the petals. I bent to smell the delicate sweetness that reminded me of raspberry canes. A memory of planting bulbs together in the garden came back to me with the scent: how she loosened the earth first for me with a spade and then gave me an old dessert spoon to dig holes for the whiskery bulbs; how she laughed when I put them in upside down and told me they'd come out in Australia; how we'd patted the earth down with our hands. I poured the water gently around the roots of the flowering rose. All of it. Perhaps it would keep its flower for just a little longer.

When I went back indoors I heard Dad moving around in the office and I thought about the letter that had come that afternoon. I tapped at the office door and pushed it gently. Dad was sitting at the desk, surrounded by papers. Wads of receipts and invoices were spread out in front of him, in drifts like fallen leaves. As I opened the door, two or three lifted in the draught and floated to the floor, flimsy as a child's tracing paper. In the middle of it all, Dad was trying to write, painfully slowly, in his large looping hand, bringing the ledger up to date.

"Can't stop," he said without looking up. "Got to make up the books for the bank."

I stepped closer to look over his shoulder. "But, Dad, I can do this," I said. "You could read the figures out to me."

He shook his head. "You don't know how to make them add up," he said.

I bent to pick up some fallen papers.

"Leave them!" he snapped.

"You won't make the sums come out in the black," I said stubbornly. "All you're doing is making a mess."

"I said leave it!"

I straightened up again. "If I can't help, why don't you wait until Grandad comes over tomorrow?"

He pointed to a letter among the jumble of papers, a letter on stiff, thick paper folded in three.

"*This* is why I have to do it now," he said, "and, no, I do not want my father involved."

"What is it?"

"A foreclosure notice."

I wasn't sure what that meant, so I said nothing.

"It's the knock-on effect of losing the hay." He pushed the letter towards me. "I didn't meet the last payment on the loan and, unless I can rectify that, they're calling it in."

"You mean they want all of it back?"

He turned to face me full on. "Yes, they want all of it back," he said as if I was simple-minded. "And unless I can find a way to convince them otherwise, that'll be the farm gone." He stared at me. "Do you understand, you stupid, stupid girl? That's what's come of you leaving Tom to his own devices when you should have been watching him."

"So now it's all my fault!"

"Of course it's your fault!" he roared at me.

Shaking with anger, I shouted back. "The only reason I wasn't with Tom was because I'd just had the shock of finding my mum . . . and that wasn't my fault . . ." I broke off.

We stared at each other in silence.

Dad's voice was icy when he spoke again. "You're never going to let me forget it, are you? You're always going to be whining on about the past."

"At least I admit I've got one," I said, "and that it's part of me. I don't try and pretend things didn't happen. I'm not afraid of feeling something, even if it hurts."

"Hurt?" Dad said. "You've still got lessons to learn — you don't even know the meaning of the word."

I turned to leave the room. "I think I do," I said.

As I came away I was aware of a background noise, a low mournful calling. The cows. I was late for milking.

The herd was crowded up against the gate, lowing pitifully. Even Pirate was pushing from the back. I let them into the holding yard and then worked as fast as I could, my hands moving automatically through the routine as I muttered to the beasts to soothe them. I couldn't accept Dad's determination to wipe out the past. Couldn't he see that to try to deny it was like dismantling part of yourself? It wasn't healing, it was amputation. And it was useless; he could as soon cut himself adrift from the past as he could cut off his own shadow. By the time I'd finished, turned the cows back out to grass, cleaned the parlour and sluiced the pipes the sky was growing dim outside.

I went inside and stood in the hall. The sound of voices on the radio came from the living room and a light showed under the closed door. He needn't have shut me out, I thought; I wasn't going to sit with him anyway. The day had left me feeling drained and I didn't want to be with Dad in a room full of awkward silences. I realized that I was hungry — I hadn't eaten much at tea — and went to the fridge to get cheese for a sandwich. I buttered the bread and cut the rind off the cheese, then opened the door of the cupboard under the sink to chuck the pieces of rind into the bin. There, on the top of a bin full of rubbish, was Mum's bird book.

I dropped the rind and squatted down to lift the book out. Bits of food — chicken skin and scraps of salad — had stuck to the covers. My eyes filled with tears of fury as I picked the greasy mess off the beautiful marbled covers. The stink of the bin clung to it, a fermented, vegetable smell. I stood at the sink, dabbing it carefully with the dishcloth, trying to get out the worst of the marks. So, this was a punishment; he'd put it where he knew I would certainly find it and couldn't avoid his meaning: "You care about this? To me it's just so much trash". There was no way I could dress this up as thoughtlessness. This was intentional; he had meant to cause me harm. This was the lesson I was meant to learn, what it felt like to really hurt.

I fetched the shopping bag from the back of the door, wrapped the book carefully in a clean towel and put it in the bag. I took a last look around the kitchen: there was nothing else that I wanted to take; the book was the only object of real importance to me in the whole of the house. I wondered for a moment if this was how Mum had felt, this resolve forming, tensing, like a creature feeling its own strength, this sudden lightness as your mind was made up. I pulled the handles of the bag up over my shoulder. I walked out.

CHAPTER
TWENTY

"Henry's such a stubborn cuss," Grandad said as he and I were working on the allotment together the next evening. We'd been sent by Gran to get some carrots and potatoes and Grandad was taking the opportunity to talk to me about seeing Dad earlier in the day. He stood resting his foot on the fork. "I told him, it's no good ranting and raving at me. That won't help you get out of this mess."

"Has he spoken to the bank yet?" I asked.

"No, but I have. Dixon was my banker for thirty years. He knows the farm's business almost as well as I do, and he agrees that the obvious thing to do is for Henry to sell that parcel of land that Mick Swift wants."

I carried on pulling up a row of potato plants ready for Grandad to dig the patch over. Tiny potatoes clung to the roots and I picked them off and dropped them into the bucket.

"Dad's dead set against that," I said.

"Well, frankly, he hasn't got any choice now," Grandad said. "In my time we managed fine with an overdraft. I knew my limits and stuck to them — never had a cheque bounce. Henry shouldn't have taken that loan out, far less secured it against the farm." I stood back and Grandad drove the fork into the earth at the beginning of the row. "Didn't think my advice was worth having, you see. Thought he knew best."

"So he's going to have to sell it?"

"Yep. It's a case of sell a bit or lose the lot, now. The solicitor's coming over with me tomorrow so Henry can sign the papers." He turned the soil over, shaking it loose so that the potatoes rolled out. "I told him, 'It's no good getting angry with me, my boy. That's just so much bluff and bluster. What I'll do is I'll cover two instalments on the loan while the sale goes through. What I won't do is stand by and let you bankrupt the farm I worked my whole life on.' That gave him pause for thought."

I bent down to the soft earth and picked it over carefully, looking for the golden gleam of more potatoes among the clods. "Did he say anything about me?" I said while Grandad couldn't see my face. When he didn't reply, I looked up again. He was frowning.

"That's partly why I'm so disappointed in him. I don't know how to say this . . ."

"What? What did he say?"

Grandad sighed. "He doesn't want you to come back, Jess. He says you've done nothing but damage."

I bent to carry on working, so that my hair would fall across my face. "That's fine with me," I said. "I wasn't intending to go back anyway."

"Rose has been round too, trying to talk some sense into him. It's breaking her heart to see the family split like this. She told him he needs a woman about the house. He's not used to looking after himself; he's always had Rose or your mum or you at home. But he wouldn't listen, not even to Rose."

We were quiet for a while, brushing the worst of the dirt off the potatoes as we picked them out. I tried to sort out my feelings, finding it hard to understand how I could feel so angry with Dad and yet he had the power to hurt me still. I was conscious of Grandad glancing at me every now and then, trying to gauge my reaction.

"Well," I said at length, "Tom's happier with you."

"He's really shaping up a treat, that boy," said Grandad, quickly taking up the change of subject. "He's coming fishing with me next week. He'll make a fine countryman yet."

"You don't find him clumsy, then? Dad's always saying he's got two left thumbs."

"Clumsy? No! No more than any nine-year-old whose brain's trying to catch up with his arms and legs. No, Tom'll be fine with us. I haven't seen Rose so sprightly for years. She was talking of taking him to the swimming baths in town the other day."

I gave a half smile. "Well, if you're sure."

"But what about you, Jess? That's more to the point." He rubbed his chin. "What're you going to do?"

"I don't know," I said simply, "but I can't stay on your camp bed for ever."

He leaned closer to me. "You know you're welcome to, child. You can stay as long as you like. Henry's getting a couple of youngsters on work placement from the agricultural college in September. You know you could always get a job and use us as a base."

I nodded but said nothing. I thought of Nicola and everyone else from school going off to start the lives they'd planned. And there would be no Philip. It seemed as though all the best bits of my life would end with the summer.

"What is it, Jess? What is it that you want to do?"

"Go to university," I blurted out. "I've got the results I need and I've got a place and I want to go. I'm supposed to tell them by the end of next week if I want the place." I stopped and dumped the potatoes I'd got in my hands into the bucket, still dirty. "I know it's impossible," I said.

"You never said about your results." Grandad looked surprised. "Didn't you need to get two A grades or something?"

I nodded. "I got three As and a B."

"Is that so? Well, you're a very clever girl." He patted my shoulder. "Don't know where you get it from," he said. "Did you tell your dad?"

"No point," I said, "and I can't do it on my own. I didn't get enough grant to be able to keep myself, even if I work part-time."

"Hmm, three As, eh? That's quite something." He carried on filling the bucket and I gathered up an armful of potato stalks and took them off to the compost bin. When I came back Grandad said, "How much do you want to do this, Jess?"

"It's what I've always wanted to do," I said, "right from when I was a little girl."

"And you can't see any way . . ."

"I've racked my brains about it," I said. "I'm not bothered about new clothes, or records, or anything like that — those aren't things you need — but even without them, even on the bare minimum, I wouldn't make enough waitressing or whatever to cover the hall fees, never mind eat."

"Henry should really help," Grandad said thoughtfully. "You shouldn't miss an opportunity like this."

"He was against it even when I was doing everything he wanted," I said. "He's not going to change his mind now."

Grandad picked the bucket up. "You're right," he said with a heavy sigh. "Tell you what, let's go home and have a look in the *Advertiser* for a job in town. At least it'd stop you brooding and give you a bit of spending money to cheer you up." He led the way back to the lane, then held out his arm for me to take. "Come on," he said, "sometimes one door closes and another one opens."

I found a job more quickly than I thought I would. Philip was still working at Lasenby's, doing contract harvesting. It was their busiest time and they needed extra help in the office too.

"I can do filing," I said uncertainly to Mrs Swift, the evening before I was due to start. "I've seen Dad do that . . ."

"And you can make a wonderful cup of tea," Philip said cheekily, as he came into the kitchen in his work clothes. "That was a hint, by the way."

I flicked the tea towel at him.

Mrs Swift said, "Typing?"

"Never tried it."

"I've got a portable upstairs. I could show you the basics, then if they ask at least you'll be ready."

She brought the typewriter down and I spent the evening typing "the quick brown fox jumps over the lazy dog", until I could find all the keys for the letters of the alphabet with my eyes closed.

"There," she said when I'd finally mastered it. "If you get some practice at work you'll soon speed up. Then you'll be able to apply for better-paid holiday jobs when you go to university."

"*If* I go to university," I said.

"*When*," she said. "It might not be this year, but you can start saving, can't you? Get your speed up: that's the answer."

"I'd better go," I said. "Get some sleep before the big day."

"I'll walk you," Philip said.

Mrs Swift put the lid on the typewriter. "Here," she said to Philip, "you can carry this for her."

"Are you sure you can spare it?" I said. "Won't you need it?"

She waved us away. "Bring it back when you hit eighty words a minute," she said. "That's my challenge."

Although I wanted to sleep to be fresh for the new job in the morning, I found it hard to settle down; my mind was too active wondering what would be expected of me and what the people in the office would be like. I couldn't have the lamp on to read because Tom was already asleep, so I lay in the dark, fretting, until I finally fell into a troubled sleep.

In the small hours I had one of my dreams. I dreamed that Tom and I had been blackberrying and we were happy. We were walking down the track at the farm and we both had carrier bags heavy with fruit. We were approaching the bridge on our way back from the fields where the best brambles were. Tom's bag had a tiny hole in it and drips of juice were falling on to the dusty ground, leaving a dark trail.

I was telling him that making a crumble is just like for pastry except you don't put any liquid in with the flour. He soon lost interest and ran on ahead to lean over the parapet of the bridge. I became half aware that I was dreaming and was trying to wake up, yet in the dream I walked quite leisurely up to join him and we looked over the edge together.

The river was a little low and it was flowing lazily through the culvert, not in the rushing torrent that it would become as autumn drew on. Tom lifted one hand from the stone parapet to point and I saw that it was stained a dark red.

"Look, Jess," he was saying, "look, there's fish!"

I looked more closely and saw that beneath the surface of the water something was glinting, catching the light. Then I knew.

I woke and clamped my hand over my mouth. I sat up, the camp bed creaking under my weight, and glanced across at Tom's sleeping form, all rolled up in his sheet despite the heat, with only the top of his head showing, the way he'd taken to sleeping since all the trouble began. He didn't stir. I swung my legs over the side of the camp bed and sat for a while, getting my breath back and letting what air there was get to my skin. My mouth was dry and when my heart had slowed I got up and tiptoed downstairs to get a drink.

In the kitchen I snapped the light on and caught the swift movement of tiny silverfish darting away to the cracks between tiles and cupboards. I shivered, hesitating on the threshold, still feeling halfway between dreaming and waking, then walked across to the sink, the floor cold to my bare feet. I ran a glass of water and there was a groaning and a ticking from the pipes. I turned the tap off again quickly, still unused to the night sounds of this house that were all so different from home.

As I drank the water in one long draught I saw myself reflected in the window. The blackness of the night pressed against the glass; it seemed to press against me. I pulled the blind down; I didn't want to see my anxious face or to look beyond it into the dark. Surfaces were treacherous. I rinsed the glass slowly, in a trickle of water, afraid to go back to bed.

I took milk from the fridge and Ovaltine from the shelf and I was mixing them together in a saucepan when I heard the door open behind me. Grandad stood, blinking, in the bright fluorescent light, his hair all ruffled up and his tasselled dressing-gown belt trailing on one side.

"You all right?" he said. "I heard a noise."

I held up the Ovaltine jar. "Want some?"

Grandad looked at me for a moment, then nodded. He sat down at the kitchen table and passed a hand over his eyes. "What woke you up?" he said. "Was it Tom again?"

"He's sleeping like a baby tonight," I said. "It was me this time."

I lit the gas and stirred the pinkish-brown mixture slowly with a wooden spoon.

"Do you want to tell me about it?"

I quickly shook my head.

Grandad waited. The phut-phut of the gas drawing and the scrape of the spoon on the bottom of the pan seemed loud in the silence.

"It's just . . . I get these times when I see Mum so clearly, or hear her. The other day I heard her calling me and Tom in for supper, and it was *her* voice. I mean, it used to happen before when I was missing her . . ."

"But now it happens more?"

"It worries me a bit. I don't want it to stop — it's all I've got left of her — but when it happens now," my voice became husky, "it hurts, you know?" I left the spoon in the pan and turned towards him.

Grandad got up and came and took my hands. "It's hard, Jess. It's going to take a long time." He squeezed my hands tight. "I know it's difficult to believe now, but it won't always be like this. It won't exactly get better but you'll learn to cope with it."

I looked up at him. "I don't know how I will," I said miserably. "And then there's Dad. The place in me that was for him is all scooped out, leaving this big empty hole. It makes me feel bad."

Grandad's arms went round me.

I said, "I keep having these awful dreams."

He looked down at me, his face full of concern. "Perhaps, if you told me about them?"

"I can't," I said miserably. "It'd be like going through it all again."

Suddenly feeling terribly weary, I sank my head down on his shoulder, my cheek against his prickly dressing gown.

He patted my back. "I know, I know." He sighed. "I wish I knew the right thing to say. If I could, I'd take all your troubles off your shoulders — you know that, don't you?"

There was a rushing, sizzling sound and we both turned to see the milk spilling over the top of the pan and burning and spitting on the gas. I stood looking at it stupidly.

Grandad turned off the gas ring. "Do you want me to make some more?"

I shook my head. I felt as though all the fight had gone out of me and I couldn't do another single thing.

"Go on," Grandad said. "You go back to bed and I'll clear this up. Go on, you look about done in and you've got a big day tomorrow." He reached behind the blind and opened the window to let out the smell of burning milk; then, seeing me still standing there he gave me a kiss on the cheek. "Night, night, love," he said.

As I went I looked back. "That's what Mum used to say."

"I know," he said. "I remember."

It was hot and stuffy in the Lasenby's office. The desks where the girls sat were arranged in two long rows with a narrow aisle, with the office manager, Mr Wakeham, sitting at the top, facing down the room so that he could see everyone working. I was given the desk next to the window, in full sun. The office fronted the street and sometimes people stared in as they passed by outside. I was so close that I could hear snatches of their conversations.

I spent most of the morning typing, filing and running errands for Mr Wakeham. I went for cigarettes for him, then biscuits at coffee time, then later a newspaper. "Why can't he ask for it all at once?" I wondered as I trailed back from the news-stand.

At lunch-time Mr Wakeham went out for a while, leaving the chief clerk in charge. She was a big woman with a pair of glasses that went up at the corners as if they were frowning and she sat at Mr Wakeham's desk to answer his phone while he was out. The girls took it in turns to man the other phones when the rest ate their lunches. One of them showed me where the mugs were and let me have some of her coffee powder so that I could make myself a drink. They were all a bit older than I was and I sat on the edge of the group and quietly got on with my lunch. Another girl was just back from her honeymoon and they chatted about the wedding. She was just about to get out some photos to pass around, when Mr Wakeham came back. Everyone returned to their own seats and I quickly shut up my sandwich box and went back to my filing.

In the afternoon Mr Wakeham seemed to think that I'd passed my apprenticeship and let me take some phone calls. I was just getting the hang of it, when I answered the phone to a familiar voice querying his account. I listened until he'd finished.

"Dad?" I said. "Is that you?"

There was a silence, then a click and the long hum of the dial tone. I held the receiver in both hands for a while, then put it slowly back on its cradle.

A moment later, Mr Wakeham's phone rang. He answered it in his normal way: "Lasenby's. How can I help you?" Then his face became serious. "Certainly, sir," he said, "I'll be right on to it. It won't happen again." When he put the phone down he came over to me looking awkward.

"Mr Garton . . . erm . . . your father would prefer it if someone else dealt with his account."

The other girls had stopped what they were doing and were all staring over at me. One nudged her neighbour and whispered something. My face burned.

Mr Wakeham reached over and picked up a batch of timesheets from the desk of the girl behind me and held them out to me. When I didn't take them straight away he shook them and gave an irritated sigh. I took them and began to type up a bill, my head low over the keys, letting my hair swing forward to hide my burning cheeks. Mr Wakeham stood looking at me for a moment then he moved away.

As I paused to find a new sheet of carbon paper, I heard him talking in a low voice to the chief clerk. "Untrustworthy, apparently," I heard him say, then she said something about "checking her work" and "typing duties only." The normal buzz of conversation in the office had completely stopped and no one was typing. Mr Wakeham added something in a very low voice that ended in "unreliable". My eyes pricking with tears, I bent over the bill I'd just typed. It was full of mistakes. I crumpled it up and started again.

I worked steadily on through the afternoon until my fingers were sore. No one spoke to me except the chief clerk, who took my work away, then returned it with two corrections circled in red. She stared at me with open curiosity as she handed them back. When five o'clock came I asked Mr Wakeham if there was anything else. The other girls were crowding in the aisle between the desks to look at the wedding photos before they went for their buses and lifts. They were oohing and aahing over the dress, but they stopped and moved aside as I picked up my bag to leave. No one said goodbye.

When Mick picked me up from the bus station on the way from getting Philip from the depot, I sat quietly in the back and rested my head against the car window. My head ached from trying to decipher other people's scribbled handwriting on files and letters. I felt as though I'd been cooped up like a battery hen, with typewriter keys to peck at. And tomorrow, maybe all my tomorrows, would be the same.

"You're very quiet," Philip said. "Was it all right?"

My heart ached from what Dad had done. I would never, ever, trust him again.

"It was fine," I said. "I'm just tired."

When I got in, I heard Gran and Grandad having words in the dining room. As I hung my shoulder bag over a peg in the hall, Gran came out saying, "I haven't got time to talk about this any more now. I've got to go and get Tom from his swimming lesson." She glanced at me and went out through the kitchen without saying anything.

I stood for a moment, wondering whether to follow her, then Grandad came to the door.

"Ah, there you are," he said. "How was your day?"

"What's up with Gran?" I said, following him back into the room.

"We had a disagreement. Nothing to worry about." He pulled out a chair for me. "Come on, tell me how you got on while you eat your tea."

I took the upturned plate off my meal and laid it to one side. "It was all right," I said, trying to sound convincing. "One of the other girls seemed nice."

Grandad nodded. "And . . .?"

"It's a bit boring, but I expect I'll get faster at typing eventually and that'll come in useful." I started to eat.

Grandad picked up the newspaper, fidgeted with it, folding it smaller, and put it back down again. "When do you get your first pay packet?"

"End of next week."

"And what are you going to do with it?"

I shrugged as I took another mouthful.

334

"Jess?" Grandad brought me back to the subject.

"I was going to put it straight into the bank actually . . . unless . . . Do you think I should offer Gran some housekeeping?"

"No, love, we don't need any housekeeping." Grandad gave a broad smile. "Are you thinking of saving up for university?"

"Mmm," I said. I imagined the number of mornings I'd start by taking the cover off the typewriter, the number of evenings I'd finish by standing to stretch my back before bending to zip the cover on again. The way I'd always be the girl whose own father didn't trust her. I took a deep breath. "It might take me more than a year. I'm going to do it, though."

Grandad was nodding. "Good answer," he muttered, "yes, good." He was leaning forward on the edge of his seat like a kid about to open a birthday present. "You're going," he said, then slapped his hands down on the table, making the cutlery rattle. "It's being sorted out and you're going this year."

"But Dad wouldn't —"

"Not your dad," he said. "*We're* going to send you. You won't be flush, mind; you'll have to be very careful, but we can pay your bed and board if you can save all your money from Lasenby's and cover anything else by working part-time once you're away."

"I won't mind working; I'll do anything," I said, not daring to hope. "But how can you afford it? I can't take money from you when you're retired."

"Now, don't go worrying about that," Grandad said. "I stayed behind and had a word with Mr Dixon after

I'd sorted Henry's business out today, and Rose and I can take out a small loan."

"But you don't agree with borrowing," I said, confused. "Is that what you two were arguing about earlier?"

"Not exactly," he said. "With your gran it's more about 'what Gartons do', which is: stay at home, stick together and run the family business." He gave a snort. "Oh, and 'no one in the family has ever been to university before'. I pointed out that if that was everyone's reasoning we'd still all be living in caves and wondering whether the wheel would ever catch on. Then one word borrowed another."

"I really want to go," I said, "but I don't want you two to argue and I'm worried about the borrowing. It's not safe; look what nearly happened with the farm."

"This is different," Grandad said firmly. "Next year the mortgage finishes on this place and we've got an endowment from it, so we'll pay off the loan and have money in hand to be able to help some more."

"I can't let you put yourselves in debt," I said uncertainly.

"I want to do this, Jess, and I'm putting my foot down to Rose for once." He reached across the table and took my hand. "You're not too proud to accept a little bit of help, are you?"

I got up and went round to give him a hug. "Thank you," I mumbled; I couldn't find the words for my feelings. "This is the *best* thing," I said, "the *best*."

"Go and get those entry forms, then," he said gruffly. "Let's get them filled in and in the post."

336

It was September, the tail end of what had turned out to be one of the longest, hottest summers we'd ever had. There had been a hundred days without rain before the downpour came, and afterwards many more dry days to follow. The river had dropped back after its roaring spate but was full enough to almost cover the tree roots, taking away their bare, eerie look; it would take months before the reservoir returned to normal and the old road across it was submerged again.

Those last weeks of summer were special. Somehow, when you know that everything is about to change, it invests even the most ordinary things with new significance. I played old games with Tom, counting "one elephant, two elephants", to let him find really good hiding places, and helped him build a tree-house in Gran's garden. I was going away. *The last time, the last time,* sang in my head and it was both sad and exciting at the same time.

Philip and I met whenever we could and grew closer all through those weeks. We were both painfully aware that for us time was running out.

As it turned out, my term was due to start before his. The evening before I was due to go, we met by the edge of the wood, near to the place where Philip had hung the moon. We walked together, both of us quiet and serious.

Ahead of us the metal surface of Mum's moon glinted between the branches.

"This is a special place," I said.

"Do you come down here on your own?"

"Sometimes," I said. "I think about Mum." I fell silent.

He held my hand and took me over to the stile that led to the river path. He climbed up and then helped me up alongside him. We sat for a while in silence, watching the river; it was broad and slow here, brown and peaceful. Willow branches leaned out over the surface, making pools of shade, where midges danced.

"What are you thinking now?" he asked, turning to me.

"I was thinking that when I've gone, Mum won't really exist here any more," I said. With my fingernail I traced the grain of the wooden crossbar, weathered grey by the rain and shiny by the touch of many hands. "There'll be no one to put flowers on her grave, or prune her roses in the garden, and she won't . . . be walking the farm. No one will see her here any more the way I do. So this place will be empty and she'll be truly gone."

"She won't be gone," he said. "You'll be taking her with you, that's all." He touched his forehead. "Here. Same as you'll take this whole place with you."

In the shade of the bank a fish took a fly, the surface of the water breaking for an instant, then ripples spreading, flattening back to smoothness as if it had never been disturbed.

I sighed. "What if I can't keep it clear in my head? It'll all be different in the city. Grey. Millions of people. Sky shrunk to strips between buildings."

Philip nudged my arm. "Yeah, yeah, and not a blade of grass. What about parks? And then of course all the

338

shops and cinemas are a real disadvantage. And parties — well, who wants them . . ."

"Oh, shut up," I said, giving him a push back, making him grab at the stile to keep his balance. "Anyway it's not just that."

"Well, what, then?"

"Oh, nothing much really. It's just that I've only ever lived here; this is all I know." Suddenly everything came out in a rush. "Everyone says cities are really lonely places. And I bet everyone will be cleverer than I am and they'll be all right because they can come home whenever they want, like Nicola; her dad's already bought her a rail pass . . ." I took a deep shaky breath. "And I won't have anyone to talk to."

"You'll soon make friends; you'll all be in the same boat."

I looked at the ground, as if studying the mixture of nettles and docks at my feet. "No, I mean really talk to," I muttered.

He put his arm around me and bent to look at my face, his eyes full of concern. "I'm sorry we're going to be so far apart," he said. "I wish we didn't have to go."

"I hate goodbyes." I started to cry. "Don't you dare come to the bus tomorrow," I said fiercely, then buried my face in his shoulder.

He leant his head against mine. "We'll write, OK?"

"But you don't like writing; you said it takes you ages," I said in a muffled voice.

"Well, I'm no great shakes at it, but I will."

"You could send me postcards in between letters." I wiped my eyes with the back of my hand. "Then I can imagine where you are." He nodded. I sat up and went on. "And drawings. You could send me sketches of what you're working on."

He gave me a squeeze. "You can put them on your wall where you're working," he kissed me on the cheek, "then every time you look up," he kissed me on the forehead, "you can remember that I'm thinking about you." He kissed me on the lips and the kiss was warm through the salty taste of my tears.

When at last we drew apart, we climbed down from the stile and went on together. We walked uphill to the back of Garton's, so that I could take a last look at the farm from Deeper's field. the faint sound of a radio reached us from somewhere in the farm buildings.

"Are you going down?" Philip asked. "I'll come with you if you want."

I shook my head, feeling the familiar jolt of loss. "It's past mending," I said.

The light was slanting low over the blond fields, their gold edged by the dark green of hedges and trees. I looked out over the valley, memorizing the scene, the folds and contours of the land, the buildings I'd played in, the beasts I knew by name, the woods and the river. Strange, I thought, this storing up of memories, this desire to give each thing its due; this is how we make it bearable to let go. From up here, Mum's moon was a flash of brilliant copper as it caught the last of the sun. I squeezed Philip's hand.

"Is that enough?" he said.

"Let's walk slowly," I said, and we set off for home with our arms round each other's waists.

*   *   *

The next day Gran, Tom and Grandad all came with me to the coach station in town. The bus pulled in and Gran started lecturing me about behaving myself and being a good ambassador for the family. Grandad tried to lighten the atmosphere by teasing me about the amount of luggage I was taking, then gave me a bear hug. Gran pressed her cheek briefly against mine; Tom, suddenly all grown up in front of the people in the queue, formally shook my hand.

The bus driver got out and shouted, "Coach for Birmingham! Last call for Birmingham!" He opened the luggage compartment and I piled my stuff, packed in every tatty suitcase we possessed, into the space. I gave the thumbs-up to the family, mouthing to Tom, "I'll ring you. Look after Lolly." Then it was my turn to climb up the steps into the coach, with its little orange curtains and smell of hot upholstery.

I shuffled along the aisle right to the back and put my rucksack down beside me, then knelt up on the seat to wave to the others, my heart starting to beat faster as the coach revved up, the engine vibrating, ready to go. We pulled away and Gran and Grandad both raised a hand, while Tom suddenly lost his composure and waved frantically with both arms, as if he were clearing a plane for take-off. The coach turned out into the street and they were lost to view.

The familiar places drifted by — the department store, the cinema, the waste ground, smaller shops, then houses, petering out eventually into open fields.

I watched the fields of my county slipping away behind me, the river a line of green and silver trees winding its way lazily in the early-morning sun. Over the rounded tops of the trees a heron flapped westwards, its legs trailing and its wings beating the air like wet sheets, as it searched the bank for a good watching post. It was grey all over; it had no white or black markings, and hadn't yet grown its wispy crest.

It fell behind as we sped on. We passed a sign for the next county. I pulled a package out from the pocket of my rucksack and carefully unwrapped Mum's bird book from its tissue paper. I turned to the page after her last entry.

14th September 1976, I wrote. *Young heron at the county boundary, following the river.*

Also available in ISIS Large Print:

After River

Donna Milner

Growing up on a dairy farm in British Columbia in the 1960s, just north of the American border, Natalie Ward knew little of the outside world. But she had her family, a family so close and loving that Natalie believed they were the envy of everybody in the nearby town of Atwood — particularly her eldest brother Boyer, whom Natalie held especially close to her heart.

But Natalie began to question her family's idyllic existence the summer she turned 15.

The arrival of a soft-spoken stranger, an American draft-dodger called River, tests the morals and beliefs of the family and the community to breaking point. The series of events following that summer day leaves relationships shattered and the Ward family changed forever.

ISBN 978-0-7531-8056-3 (hb)
ISBN 978-0-7531-8057-0 (pb)

The Rain Before It Falls

Jonathan Coe

Rosamond lies dying in her remote Shropshire home. But before she does so, she has one last task: to put on tape not just her own story but the story of the young blind girl Imogen, her cousin's granddaughter, who turned up mysteriously at her party all those years ago.

At the centre of the narrative is Imogen's grandmother, Beatrix, whose flight from her husband after the war in search of freedom and excitement left a damaging legacy. Damaging to her own daughter and granddaughter, but also to Rosamond. She became caught up in the ensuing turmoil and found herself the beneficiary of a sudden, intense happiness; a happiness which was just as suddenly snatched away . . .

ISBN 978-0-7531-8098-3 (hb)
ISBN 978-0-7531-8099-0 (pb)